DEATH IN
CASTLE
DARK

DEATH IN CASTLE DARK

Veronica Bond

BERKLEY PRIME CRIME
New York

BERKLEY PRIME CRIME
Published by Berkley
An imprint of Penguin Random House LLC
penguinrandomhouse.com

Copyright © 2021 by Julia Buckley

ISBN: 9780593335871

First Edition: August 2021

Printed in the United States of America
1 3 5 7 9 10 8 6 4 2

Book design by Alison Cnockaert

Even if all the castles of all the world were destroyed, in the minds of men they would be built anew; the wizard called imagination would raise high walls and towers out of ruins.

—From *Castles*, David Day

I had fastened my door, gazed leisurely round, and in some measure effaced the eerie impression made by that wide hall, that dark and spacious staircase, and that long, cold gallery, by the livelier aspect of my little room. I remembered that, after a day of bodily fatigue and mental anxiety, I was now at last in safe haven.

—from *Jane Eyre*, Charlotte Brontë

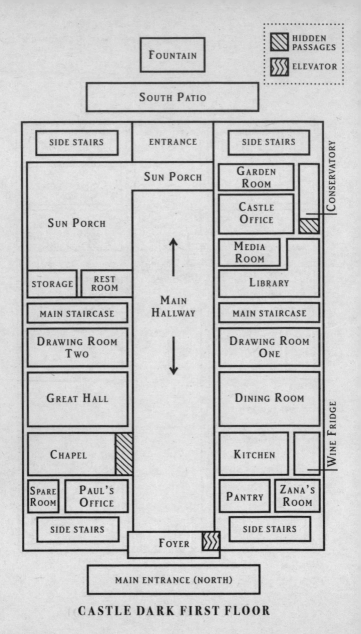

CASTLE DARK FIRST FLOOR

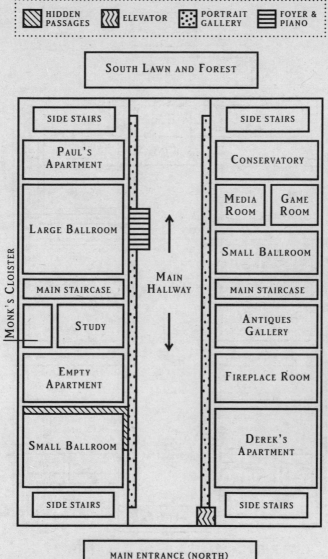

KEY

HIDDEN PASSAGES · ELEVATOR · PORTRAIT GALLERY · FOYER & PIANO

SOUTH LAWN AND FOREST

MONK'S CLOISTER

SIDE STAIRS

PAUL'S APARTMENT

LARGE BALLROOM

MAIN STAIRCASE

STUDY

EMPTY APARTMENT

SMALL BALLROOM

SIDE STAIRS

MAIN HALLWAY

SIDE STAIRS

CONSERVATORY

MEDIA ROOM · GAME ROOM

SMALL BALLROOM

MAIN STAIRCASE

ANTIQUES GALLERY

FIREPLACE ROOM

DEREK'S APARTMENT

SIDE STAIRS

MAIN ENTRANCE (NORTH)

CASTLE DARK SECOND FLOOR

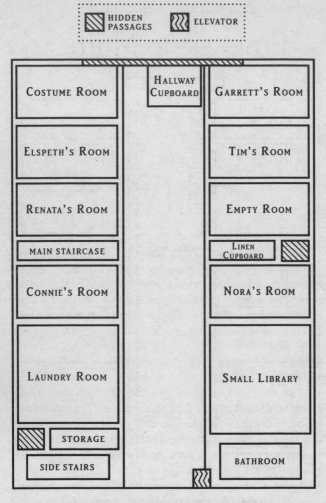

CASTLE DARK THIRD FLOOR (THE DORMS)

Prologue to Murder

THE DINING TABLE shimmered with candlelight reflected in antique glassware; silver clinked gently while people ate their prime rib and chatted quietly in the enormous room. Then the man at the head of the table stood to make a toast, and the twenty diners went silent. "Thank you all for coming to this dinner honoring my late uncle Harold, or Harry, as we lovingly called him. He would have so enjoyed this evening and this visit from all of you."

"Not *all* of you," said the beautiful blond woman to his left, glaring at the faces around the table. "He hated some of you, and you know who you are." As if to punctuate her statement, a giant black dog sidled into the room with a menacing expression, a stone on his collar glinting in the candlelight.

"Quiet, Constance," said the man. "Tonight we're honoring Harry, not digging up old grudges. Just because you didn't get along with him doesn't mean you can assume it of everyone else."

"She got along with him a bit *too* well!" I shouted, planting my hands on either side of my plate so that everyone could see my long red (press-on) nails.

Our host looked at me, then glared at Constance, his dark eyes intense in his handsome face. "Apparently news of your affair has gone beyond our private conversations," he said with a grim smile. Then he looked at me. "And what a surprise that *you* would be pointing fingers, Nora. We all know that if Connie were out of the picture, you would get a much heftier inheritance."

"That's not true," I shouted. "And I can prove it. I had Hastings make copies of Harold's will. You'll all find one underneath your seats."

The guests dutifully found the sheets of rolled parchment beneath their polished heirloom chairs and began to read the contents. Connie laughed, an unpleasant sound. "I think it's time to come clean, Derek. We have witnesses now. The one with the best motive for killing Harold is *you*—the man who just wants to *honor* the dead man."

"You're deflecting, Connie. No one needs to look farther than you for a significant motive. Shall we tell everyone what it is?"

Another man stood up, his hands trembling with anger, his blond hair gleaming like a halo under the chandelier. "I know you hated my father, Derek, and I'll prove that you killed him."

They stood facing each other; Derek smirked as though he knew a secret. "Don't be a fool, Timothy."

"You're the fool and the murderer. And I'm going to make sure everyone knows it. I invited a police detective to sit in on our dinner tonight. Did you spot our visitor? Detective, go ahead and stand up."

With a whooshing sound, ten chairs went back, and ten people stood up.

"Well, hello, Inspector," I said drily.

1

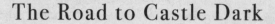

The Road to Castle Dark

WE CALL THEM all Inspector," Derek Corby had told me during my interview. "Most mystery parties assign the guests as suspects who have to learn their backstories and then stumble their way through conveying that information to everyone. That's how we're different: our visitors are detectives—all the same detective, actually— and they get badges and notebooks when they enter. Then they can jot down notes as they dine, as they mingle in the drawing room, as they walk the grounds with the suspects. And this is why we can charge so much for the Castle Dark experience, and why people are more than willing to pay it, by the way: we hire real actors, we cater elegant dinners, and we give people the experience of total immersion. They are living in this castle, moving from room to room, touching the objects, sitting on the furniture. And when they leave, they feel clever, because they took notes and made observations and came up with theories. Our customers routinely rate us at five stars, and almost ninety percent of them return for new story lines."

Derek had been the first surprise about Castle Dark. I had expected, for some reason, a bearded old man who looked vaguely like a sea captain. Derek was young, perhaps thirty-five, dark-haired, clean-shaven, and well-dressed. He had a thick swoop of coffee-colored hair that gave him a slightly Byronic appearance and a charming smile that he employed on a regular basis. I might even have developed a crush on him except that I sensed he already had a great deal of esteem for himself.

"It sounds very interesting," I'd said. I wasn't convinced, and the interview itself had happened in a nondescript office in a Chicago strip mall. Derek assured me that I had already earned a chance at a second interview. "Then you'll see the castle itself, and you'll get a sense of how fun it is to be in the cast. And while I know the pay I'm offering isn't exactly princely, our actors have told me that it's a real bargain to get a room in the castle and to eat catered meals. Room and board—that would certainly help a struggling actor, wouldn't it?"

It would. And so far, it had been his best selling point. The idea of joining the cast of a murder-mystery party at some "castle" that his great-grandfather had built in a wooded area in Wood Glen, Illinois, sounded a little bit creepy and rather trite, as well. And the name—Castle Dark—sounded like some dreadful video game that my little brothers would play.

Derek studied my expression and seemed to read my mind. "I know you're a good actor, Nora. Sheena Preston sent me a tape of your audition for *Evita*. You were terrific. Your acting, your singing. The fact that you accompanied yourself on the piano—it's obvious that you're a natural talent. Frankly, after seeing that recording, I was shocked that she cast the person she did."

It still rankled; I swallowed the lump in my throat. "I was surprised, as well. I thought I had the part."

"Still, Sheena was impressed with you, and she knew I had an opening." Someone named Carly who had previously played the role of the secretary had left abruptly to get married, he had told me with a dour expression. "It's a great role. Yes, everyone has to be a bit melodramatic, but there is a lot of fun to be had with melodrama, and our set is fantastic." He punctuated this idea by thumping his hand on his desk. "Our props are amazing." *Thump.* "The whole experience will be worth your while."

"It's a neat offer, Derek," I said, prepared to turn him down.

He held up a hand. "Take a day. Look at our website. Read the reviews. Check out the virtual tour. And then come see me at the castle; if your answer is no, it's no. But you can't decide until you see what's on offer, right? I haven't showed you the place that you'd be staying, free of charge."

The free apartment was a temptation. Some months I could pay my rent with no problem, and other months I fell short. I hated the uncertainty of it, and to live free—who was I to look that gift horse in the mouth?

On the other hand, I needed to be close to Chicago so that I could keep going to auditions, and Wood Glen was out in the boonies. I didn't want to live that far away from my friends and my family. But Derek Corby's handsome face wore a very persuasive expression.

"So you'll come and see me at the castle?" he asked.

"Yes, all right," I said.

"Wonderful. This is Monday, so let's say Wednesday for tea? I'll give you a map."

ON WEDNESDAY I drove out of Chicago in my elderly Saab, hopped onto the toll road south, then took an exit that led quickly into farmland and some wooded subdivisions.

After that came more scenic vistas of just grass and sky, and the air became intoxicating with the scent of sweet summer grasses (and a hint of manure). Finally I saw a sign that read: NOW ENTERING WOOD GLEN. Not much later I saw a giant billboard dominated by a picture of a castle. The top of the billboard read: THE MOST MYSTERIOUS FUN YOU'LL EVER HAVE! And along the bottom was just the web address CastleDark.com.

Derek had told me that the billboard was surprisingly effective; many people drove past and then looked for the site on their phones.

I followed Derek's map, worrying that I wouldn't find the "subtle opening" that would take me down a wooded dirt road and then up the long driveway to the castle itself. But Derek surprised me: I saw a red balloon staked into the ground in front of a stand of pines, and a sign that read: WELCOME, NORA.

"That's a cute touch," I murmured, slowing down, then turning onto a road carpeted by fragrant pine needles. I assumed that "castle" was a euphemistic way of referring to some big banquet-hall type of place. The website sported some impressive interior pictures, but not that many outdoor shots of Castle Dark, which had made me suspicious.

Still, when I reached another gap in the trees marked by a sign that read: ENTRANCE TO CASTLE DARK. I felt a little flutter of anticipation. The driveway was long and curving, flanked by magnificent summer bushes with flowering blooms—I thought the rich pearly pink blossoms might be gardenias—and the sweet scent lifted my spirits.

"It's like going to Manderley," I said to myself, and when I steered around a slight bend, there was an opening in the wall of foliage, and before me was a real, bona fide castle with turrets and gray stone and mullioned windows. It was enchanting and surprisingly large. How in the world did Derek pay for the upkeep of this place?

I followed a sign that pointed to a parking area, then got out and stretched. The air was fresh here, and a cool breeze wafted over me as I contemplated a gray-stone-and-brick wall. For just an instant I had a feeling that I had traveled back in time and across the sea, where castles were more plentiful and dotted country landscapes just like this one. . . . But of course that was the effect the builders had been going for. I walked up the pebbled parking area, then turned left and stepped onto a brick walkway that led to the main entrance and its massive wooden door. I lifted the gold knocker and let it fall; a moment later the door opened and a blond woman peered out at me. She was pretty and young, probably in her mid to late twenties, and she wore an eager expression. "Oh, are you Nora? God, you're perfect for Carly's role. All that dark hair. Very dramatic. Elspeth will have a field day doing your makeup."

"Um—"

She laughed and reached out with both of her hands to pump one of mine in welcome. "I'm Connie. I'm in the cast. I play Derek's cheating wife. Derek says if you take the part I need to walk you through your lines and the basics of our mystery and of course the castle itself."

"Okay, great."

She grinned. "I suppose I should invite you in."

"I am pretty curious, now that I've seen the outside. It's a *real* castle."

Connie opened her blue eyes wide. "Right? I thought the same thing—that it would be some tacky old casino-looking junk heap in the woods. You're going to be impressed, Nora, really."

I followed her into a large room with dark paneling. Stairways on either side of us curved up to a second-floor gallery, which had obligatory portraits hung at regular intervals against the distant cream-colored walls. "Are those actual ancestors or just props?"

She shrugged. "I don't know. We only reference one of them in our act—the lady in the red dress. She's supposed to be Great-Great-Aunt Elizabeth, the dead man's ancestor and there's a plotline involving her and some lost rubies. Oh, and speaking of rubies, here's Hamlet. Come here, boy!"

I jumped as a massive dog materialized in the dim hallway and came galloping toward us—he looked to be part black Lab and part King Kong, and I shrank back from him. Connie, on the other hand, started some hilarious giggling as Hamlet reached us and tried to lick her face. "Cut it out, you beast," she cried, ineffectively pushing him away. She began to scratch his ears, which he seemed to think was a good compromise; he regarded me with a placid expression and eventually closed his eyes to enjoy the massage.

"He's huge."

"But gentle as a lamb." She kissed Hamlet's giant snout.

"What do you mean, speaking of rubies?"

"Hmm?" Connie said. "Oh, because Hamlet is a member of the cast." She pulled out his jowls in a comical way and said, "Meet your colleague."

I laughed.

"Seriously, though, Ham is trained to come in when the conversation turns to suspects and who hated whom. Eventually the visiting detectives are supposed to find the ruby on his collar and connect it to Liz up there." She pointed at the portrait of the woman in red.

I bent to look at Hamlet's collar, and he thrust his giant nose into my face to give it a sniff. I laughed. "You're just a big softie, aren't you?" He licked my ear, and I studied the stone on his collar—it glowed red. I looked up at Connie. "This can't be real, can it?"

She made a scoffing sound. "God, no. Derek got it at a Wood Glen antiques mall; it's just some old bauble. He gets tons of our props there. You have to go with me someday!"

she said excitedly. "Relics is amazing, and you can sort through all kinds of glorious junk."

I looked up at her; she seemed to be entirely guileless and unusually friendly. I didn't know yet what I thought of Castle Dark, but I thought I might love Connie. I stood up, giving Hamlet one last pat on his very hard head. "That sounds fun. I don't know if I'm taking the job yet, though."

She touched my arm in a confidential, affectionate gesture. "You've *got* to take it. You might not realize it now, but it's a dream job. We get fairly good pay, free room, free food, tons of free time, and access to a *castle*. And look at the view!" She made a sweeping gesture toward a window near the door I had entered, and I followed her gaze: a large clearing of well-tended, outrageously green grass that seemed to sweep around the entire building, and then lovely and mysterious woods as far as the eye could see.

Connie sighed. "There's a brook, too. I walk down there sometimes and just toss in little pebbles and listen to the sound of the water. It's better than meditation."

I turned to her, suspicious. "Does he pay you extra for the hard sell?"

She laughed. "Oh, God, I know I'm coming on strong. It's just that I'm the only person my age who lives here. The only young woman, I guess. The guys are no fun, and Bethany doesn't live at the castle. She lives in town with her husband. Carly—the girl you'd be replacing—was okay, but she spent all her time texting her boyfriend. So I guess I'm a little lonely." Her eyes once again were sincere and irresistible. "I'm here on my own behalf. Derek didn't ask me to show you around; I asked if I *could*."

"Ah."

She played with one of Hamlet's silky ears. "My ex-boyfriend said that my enthusiasm was *relentless*."

"He sounds horrible."

She brightened. "He was!"

A door slammed somewhere above us, and she got serious. "Okay, enough of my gossiping. Let's get this tour going. Hamlet, you can come with us."

So we went, we three, through the entrance hall and then a series of rooms, each one more striking than the last—the great hall, the library, the drawing room, the small ballroom, the dining room, the kitchen, and the pantry—and finally down an unexpected hallway that led to the chapel.

"There's a *chapel*," I said. "It's beautiful." It was a modestly sized room, soothing and silent, dominated by stained glass windows populated with various Catholic saints. There were only twelve wood pews and an elevated stone platform with a stone altar.

"Do they say Mass in here?" I asked.

"No. People who want to go to church drive into town. Derek has made this a quiet meditation room. There's nothing . . . consecrated in here. The altar is old, though, and the stained glass was imported from Europe. Isn't it lovely?"

"It is. Do you care if I take a picture?"

"No, go for it," said Connie, plopping down in a pew and gazing upward.

I snapped an image and sent it to my family chat room, which included my parents, my little brothers, who were about to be seniors in high school, and my older sister, Gen, who lived in New York. My phone buzzed almost instantly; it was a response from my brother Luke:

Did you go to the past?

Luke and Jay were incapable of being serious about anything. My father always said, with a scowl, that they were a part of the "ironic generation," but I feared that Gen and I fit that description, as well.

In the hall outside the chapel, Connie pointed at one of

the ornate panels on the wall. "Touch that curlicue there," she said.

I did, and the panel opened with a snapping sound. "Wow." I peered behind it; there was just enough space for someone to hide in and then a curving passage. "That is super creepy."

"Yeah. Derek writes it into our story line sometimes. He loves this castle and all its hidden surprises. I guess that lets out near the ballroom on the second floor. There are these weird skinny stairs. I've never had the courage to go all the way through; I've read too many Edgar Allan Poe stories and I'm afraid someone would lock me in there forever."

"That's horrifying!"

Now Connie smothered a yawn. "There are a few of those hidey-holes. I'll show you them all sometime. Well, we've touched the main rooms, but I haven't showed you the creepy cellar or the upstairs bedrooms. Those are pretty luxurious, and then there's a third floor with smaller apartments, where servants used to stay. Now it's where the actors live. Appropriate, right?"

"So, sort of like dorms?" I asked.

"Don't sound so disappointed. They're much nicer than dorms. Come on."

She led me up another grand staircase and marched me down a red-carpeted hall. "That's Derek's apartment—isn't it massive? We're always trying to guess if he smuggles someone in at night. I've been here more than a year and there's been no sign of a love interest, but Tim—that's another castmate—he thinks Derek is seeing someone."

"Huh," I said.

She pointed southward. "Down that hall and to the left is Paul's apartment. That's Derek's brother. He's here only once in a while; he works out of town, but they're co-owners of this place."

"Neat."

"And there are more cool rooms down that way: a ball-room and a sort of greenhouse and a media room. But . . . let's climb one more flight and get to the cast rooms."

"Is there an elevator by any chance?"

She nodded. "Yeah, near the entrance. I'll show you later. I like the stairs because they keep me in shape. And I can pretend I'm a queen."

She led me to a door bearing a sign that read: PRIVATE QUARTERS—NO VISITORS ALLOWED. She opened the door and we climbed some normal-looking stairs to a third floor, which had a convent-like feel.

"Such a long hall," I said.

"Yeah. Like I said, not all of the actors live here. Right now it's me, Tim, Garrett, Elspeth, who is our makeup ge-nius and an occasional character, and Renata, who plays the dead man's wife. And you, if you take the role, right? Did you plan to live here?"

"Uh—if I take the job, yes." The place felt surreal to me and not at all like somewhere I could call home.

Connie was walking and pointing. "Here's a laundry room, so you don't even have to leave this floor. And you don't need quarters, either."

"Nice."

"Then across there is the small library."

"*Small* library?" I peered into a pleasant room with a luxurious looking carpet centered on a polished wood floor and books filling wood shelves on every wall. In the center was a long wooden table. "Ahh," I whispered.

Connie was still marching, past two doors that she did not identify. "All the rooms have a little crown on them. See? Derek is so clever with little touches like that. Each crown is a different color. So let's start at the south end of the hall here." She got to the end of the long hall with me following obediently. "That's the costume room, across from Garrett's room; he's White Crown. You can see we're right by the stairway—you can take this downstairs if you're ever in the costume room and you get hungry." She scratched her nose with one hand while patting Hamlet's head with the other. "Then here's Tim's room next to Garrett's, in Gold Crown. I'll introduce you to Tim later; I think he's out cycling, anyway." She tried his doorknob for some reason and found it locked. She shrugged and smiled at me.

"Elspeth is right there in Purple Crown, next to the costume room, which is convenient because she runs it. Then Renata next to her, in Red Crown." She gestured vaguely as we began walking back to the door we'd come through. She indicated a door to her left. "That room next to Tim's is empty." She pointed to her right. "This is me, in Blue Crown. And kitty-corner across would be you, in Green Crown."

My jaw dropped. "The room right next to the library?"

Connie laughed. "I'm guessing you like books. Wait. You haven't seen anything yet."

She stopped in front of a gray wooden door with a green crown placard, turned the knob, and pushed it open. I stared. This was hardly the domain of a servant. I stepped inside and said, "Wow." A large bed sat on an elevated platform; behind it, floor-to-ceiling windows let in a world of light, and through them, I could see the grounds and the woods. To my left were a small bathroom and a tall dresser, along with what seemed to be a walk-in closet. To my right was a stone gas fireplace, and next to it was a secretary desk. A tiny enclosure had a sink, a small refrigerator, and a baker's rack; and then there was a low dresser with a tall mirror above it. A large colorful rag rug sat on the stone floor in front of the fireplace; another one sat next to the bed. "This room is extraordinary!"

Connie grinned, watching me. I moved forward, drawn by the amazing view, and a doe strolled out of the woods, leading two fawns. They bent to munch on something in the grass, then looked up when they heard some minuscule sound. "He paid the deer," I whispered. "He paid them to walk out on cue."

"Ha!" Connie said. "Those guys are around constantly. A whole giant herd of them sometimes. We also get foxes."

"A herd of deer." The only wild animal I'd ever seen, aside from squirrels and birds, was maybe a raccoon or the occasional possum in a Chicago alley.

Suddenly overwhelmed, I sat on the bed. It was comfortable. Hamlet, who had been following us for most of the tour, padded into the room and climbed up to the elevated platform, then flopped on the rug as though it was a familiar sleeping spot.

Connie ran a hand through her plentiful blond hair, fluffing it. "The only rule is that we have to clean our own rooms; Derek's cleaning service focuses mainly on the first floor, and they do the second floor every third week. As you can imagine, it's quite expensive."

"Yes, I *can* imagine." I looked around, feeling as though I had shrunk myself and entered some amazing dollhouse. "It would be a privilege to clean this space."

"*Your* space," she said, "if you want it."

My phone buzzed. It was a text from Gen.

Where in the world *are* you? That chapel is simply gorgeous.

I imagined Gen visiting me here: me leading her casually around a castle.

I turned to Connie. "You say the job itself is fun? It's a challenge for an actor? Not just some goofy haunted-house nonsense?"

She shook her head. "It's sophisticated, Nora. And an improviser's dream."

I already knew then that I would say yes. But I still wondered if Connie was some sort of attractive lure, friendly and open but essentially false.

My sister, Gen, said that she could always tell if she was simpatico with someone by asking them one simple question: who's your favorite comedian? It worked, she said, because if they picked someone sexist or racist, she knew they wouldn't get along. If they picked someone who wasn't actually funny, then she knew they didn't have a sense of humor. But if they picked someone great, she knew they had the basis for a friendship.

"Hey, Connie," I said, "who's your favorite comedian?"

She shrugged at me, not at all nonplussed by the question. "Oh, gosh, there are so many good ones. But all-time? Like the best ever? I'd probably say Carol Burnett. My mom and I watched all the old reruns of her show when I was a kid. She's just so funny." She sighed. "But more recent, I guess I'd go with funny actresses like Tina Fey or Melissa McCarthy."

"*Spy* is one of my favorite movies," I said.

"Yeah, that one is hilarious."

"And whenever my sister and I are arguing, one of us eventually sends the other one a GIF of Carol Burnett as Scarlett O'Hara wearing that giant curtain rod in her dress."

Connie laughed and slapped her knee. "Classic," she said.

When Derek appeared, searching for me, Connie and I were sitting on either side of Hamlet, petting his silky fur and chatting like long-lost sisters.

2

Cast of Characters

Now, a little more than two weeks later on a sultry Saturday night, here I was at my debut dinner, confronting the various Inspectors who wanted to solve our mystery. "Inspector," I said to the closest visitor, a girl of about thirteen, "perhaps you'd like to come into the drawing room and see some of Mr. Thompson's greatest treasures. As his secretary, I was expected to catalogue them all and make sure that none of them went missing." I cast a suspicious glance at the other actors, who in turn demonstrated various levels of defensiveness.

The little Inspector (and several other Inspectors) followed me into the next room, a richly carpeted space dotted with upholstered red divans and brown leather armchairs, as well as discreetly placed antique lamps that filled the room with gold light. I led my visitors to a giant fireplace, on the mantel on which sat a family picture of our actors (including Derek's own uncle Jim, who had gamely posed as the victim).

"Here's poor Harold, Inspector, in case you want to get

a good glimpse of him. And here's his wife, and the two children, all of whom you met tonight. Then of course there's Derek, your host and Harold's nephew. You might wonder why it's Derek holding court in the castle. Well, the will told all, didn't it? The bulk of the estate will go to Harry's nephew if his son and his wife don't resolve their differences."

I made eye contact with all the lingering Inspectors: the girl, her parents, another man who seemed unrelated to them. "As you can see, Derek has it all. But it's a bit more complicated than that. Anyway, I was going to show you Harry's treasures," I said, handing the photo to the girl.

She turned it over and said, "A clue! I found a clue!" In a moment all ten Inspectors were gathered around her as she unfolded the piece of paper behind the frame. "It's another will!" she cried.

This shocked everyone. Renata glided into the room, her red satin gown looking genuinely expensive in the lamplight. "I'll take that. Thank you, Inspector," she said, and the girl handed her the new will.

She looked around dramatically. "This is dated later than the previous will—and it's notarized by Jacob Snell, a lawyer here in town."

A small *ahhh* from the crowd. Derek made his handsome, forceful way through the Inspectors and said, "This is a plant. I'll have this verified by an independent counsel, Renata!"

Renata studied his face, her eyes bright. "And why do you assume the will goes against you, Derek? Do you perhaps know what is in this will? Perhaps it's the other one we should have carefully examined!"

They faced each other dramatically, then moved aside to continue their argument in a corner. I shrugged. "As I was saying, Inspector, Mr. Thompson—Harry, I called him—catalogued all of his most prized possessions." I pointed to a clock on the mantel. "This beautiful antique timepiece belonged to his great-great-grandfather. Its value is inestimable. Don't touch it, please," I said as one of the Inspectors leaned forward. One of them said, "There's some kind of code on the clock!" They rushed in to jot down the strange hieroglyphics carved into the side.

I shrugged, moving down the mantel. "And this saber is an authentic cavalry officer's sword from the American Revolution—a British sword, though, because Harry's great-great-great-great-grandfather fought for the other side during the revolution. If you look closely, you'll see it's inscribed with his name."

One of the Inspectors pointed. "There's blood on it!"

"What!" I cried.

Other Inspectors leaned in. "Yes, it's blood!"

The girl held up a hand. "But that doesn't matter, because Harold Thompson wasn't stabbed to death. He was shot."

They thought about this; then the girl's mother said, "Yes, but he did have that mysterious wound on his finger. Maybe it was a defensive wound!"

The Inspectors made a semicircle around the sword and examined it.

Connie came swanning up, looking gorgeous in a blue sequined dress. She had a way of seeming to glare at everyone at once. "You're barking up the wrong tree, Inspector. Oh, and speaking of barking, here's Hamlet again. I'm not surprised he was Harold's favorite hunting hound."

A few Inspectors tuned in to what she was saying, and then their eyes went to the dog. One of them dove onto the carpet. "Look at his collar! Another clue!" He pointed to the faux ruby, then consulted his notes. "Isn't it true that the rubies of the woman in the portrait went missing long ago? Her name was"—he consulted his notes—"Great-Great-Aunt Elizabeth!"

A woman knelt down next to him to study the collar. Hamlet panted and looked pleased. He had an easy gig.

"But if this is a real ruby, what does it mean? And what could it possibly have to do with Harold's death?"

They looked uncertainly at one another, and then Elspeth appeared in the doorway wearing a fortune-teller's robes and some spectacular eye makeup. Connie was right: Elspeth was a genius with makeup. Tim appeared beside her, looking jubilant. "Hello, everyone. This nice lady is traveling door to door, offering to tell fortunes. I thought that this would be a perfect time for some of us to hear our destinies, especially those of us who are going to end up in jail," he said, glaring directly at Derek.

Now Harold's daughter walked in. She was played by Bethany, the woman Connie had said lived in town. Her blond wig made her look like Connie's sister. "I want my fortune told," she said, flouncing past everyone and going to the front of the group. "This is my house, and I'm going first."

Derek muttered something under his breath, but the fortune-teller went to Bethany and began murmuring to her. The Inspectors leaned in, trying to hear.

Our last cast member appeared in the door; he was Garrett Perth, who played the gardener. In Derek's mystery, Garrett was in love with Bethany, despite their age difference.

People turned to look at Garrett as he entered, but turned back to Bethany when she screamed and fainted.

Renata, her mother in this story, bent to revive her, and Bethany fluttered her eyes. "What did she tell you, darling?" Renata asked.

"She said that I was marrying a murderer," Bethany gasped.

"Marrying?" Renata asked blankly.

"She's in love with Garrett," said the youngest Inspector. "She's wearing a ring with his initials on it." She was a sharp one.

"I didn't kill anyone," Garrett yelled. "But the night Mr. Thompson died, I saw *her* leaving with a bag that made clanking sounds, like a bunch of valuables was in it." He pointed at me and put his hand defensively on a gilded knife at his belt; it glinted with a faux emerald because evidence would reveal the gardener was Harold's bastard son, and he'd been given the expensive dagger by his father.

Heads swung in my direction and I put up a hand, flourishing my red nails. "I did nothing wrong. As I said, Harry looked to me to protect his valuables. He was concerned that *someone* might steal them."

Now the Inspectors didn't know where to look, so I added, "The same someone who tried to smuggle the ruby out by putting it on Hamlet's collar. The same person who was able to create an authentic-looking will that made it look as though Derek was the guilty one, but you might notice that this person got exactly what he or she wanted out of the will. I'll leave you to mull that over, Inspector. I'll be enjoying some dessert—I believe the chef has put out torte."

The Inspectors looked almost as excited about the torte as they did about the new information. We left them to their calculations, encouraging them to walk all around the castle. There weren't that many clues left to find, but people loved the ambience. The doors to personal rooms on the second floor were locked, but others were labeled with character names, and props had been put inside.

I went to the kitchen and took one of the plates of pre-sliced cake. While some Inspectors roamed, others asked us questions. I was actually eating the torte because it was good (Zana, the chef, had promised to teach me how to make it), and I was alone in the kitchen. Tim appeared and sat down next to me, holding his own plate. He concentrated on getting some dessert onto his fork, his blond head bent so that I couldn't see his face. His hair was almost the same shade as Connie's. "God, this is good," he said. "The chef will make us fat, Nora." He grinned at me, and I grinned back.

Then two Inspectors appeared, their notebooks closed. One of them was the thirteen-year-old girl, who showed surprising compassion when she looked at Tim and said, "Mr. Thompson, I'm placing you under arrest for the murder of your father, Harold Thompson."

Tim put his fork down, scraped back his chair, and stood up. He looked at the little Inspector and then the taller Inspector, then smiled and said, "You win!

"OF COURSE, TIM won't always be the killer," Derek explained to me as I sat with the cast in the kitchen, eating popcorn and drinking water. I smirked at Connie, who had told me Derek was outrageously generous one moment and almost ridiculously frugal the next. She warned me that I would need my cell phone flashlight to get upstairs at night because Derek worried about his astronomical electric bill.

"Will he be the killer at our next event?" I asked.

Derek grinned. "Nope. *You* will."

I must have looked surprised, because he patted my hand. "I have three alternating scripts with the same basic characters. That way we can run this way for a while but customers can't come in and simply know the answer, assuming one of their friends told them. It's written in our literature. See?"

He reached behind him to a stack of publicity postcards on the sideboard and handed me one, pointing to the line that read: *No two solutions are the same!*

"Not strictly true," he said. "But it has kept the cheaters at bay so far."

"But eventually, if you have die-hard fans, they will figure it out."

"Yes. But I keep track of repeat customers. They wait a few months before returning—we're expensive, don't forget—and by then we have a whole new cast of characters. You'll only be Nora Thompson for another month or so. I'm already working on the next story line. Then you'll be Nora someone else."

"Why don't we have character names?"

He nodded, seemingly appreciative. "I started out that way two years ago. But one of my actors kept slipping and calling his colleagues by their real names. It was a tic he couldn't overcome, but he was terrific in every other way—the visitors loved him."

"You fired him?"

His mouth opened; I had shocked him. "Fired? No, of course not. He left—got a pretty great role in a movie. He lives in LA now."

"Wow!"

"But I learned my lesson. Stick with the names we know and just adapt to different character types. Otherwise we risk looking unprofessional, forgetting names when I switch out the scripts every six weeks."

I nodded. "That makes sense."

Derek looked around the table. "Well, I know you've already been introduced to everyone here, and now you've done a performance with them. But maybe we could go around and say a few words about ourselves so Nora will get a better sense of us. You start, Nora."

Curious faces looked at me, and they seemed benevolent.

"Okay—well, I'm from Chicago. My parents still live there with my teenage twin brothers, and I have an older sister in New York. She works in fashion, and she would love Elspeth's costume room."

The room, at the end of the dormitory hallway, was a glittering kaleidoscope of costume racks, masks, hats, boas, wigs, and tutus. Like Derek, Connie had said, Elspeth haunted the antiques shops for vintage clothing and occasionally found cheap accoutrements on Amazon. One whole wall of her space was a makeup table with a long utilitarian mirror, and the cast had sat there companionably earlier in the evening, waiting for a turn with Elspeth, who transformed them into other people. Elspeth herself looked like a cross between a hippie and an eccentric heiress; she had long gold brown hair on which she invariably wore some sort of headdress, often a tiara. There was one gray stripe in her hair, but her face was youngish; she was forty at most.

"And where did you train?" Derek asked me.

"I had a double major at Michigan State—drama and English. My senior year I starred in a production of *A Streetcar Named Desire*, and that got me an audition for a play at the Goodman." Some appreciative sounds from the group. "I didn't get the part, but I did get into the cast, a bit part, and I've been doing the Chicago theater scene ever since, with varying degrees of success."

"We're lucky to have you," Derek said. "Connie, your turn."

Connie smiled her winsome smile. "I'm Constance Lancaster. I know that name makes me sound like I'm from Boston or London or somewhere, but I'm from South Bend, Indiana. I didn't major in drama the way Nora did, but I was in all my school plays. I was doing office work when I saw Derek's ad about a year ago, and I guess my audition went well, because here I am."

"And your family?" Derek prompted.

"Oh, yeah—well, my mom is a kindergarten teacher and my dad sells farm equipment. I have three big brothers." She gave us all a thumbs-up.

We looked expectantly at Tim, who sat beside Connie. He smiled, revealing dimples I hadn't noticed before. "I'm

Tim. I got as far as off Broadway before I realized I missed the Midwest. I came here, got onto a cast at a dinner theater, then was recruited by Derek. In the script we had back then, I had to play his son, even though we're essentially the same age," he said, and we laughed. "Anyway, my dad died, but my mom lives nearby and I get to see her a lot. I'm an only child, I love cycling, and I have a girlfriend named Amy."

"Thanks, Tim. Elspeth?" Derek said, like a suave game-show host.

Elspeth smoothed her long hair. "I'm Elspeth. I'm from Cincinnati originally. I majored in theater production and design, with a focus on costuming. I've done costumes for about forty productions, and they were all fun. But having my own costume room in an actual castle—it's kind of a dream come true." She looked up and saw that we were waiting for more. "Oh, uh—divorced, no kids, two parents and a sister in Ohio."

We looked at Garrett, who said in a quiet voice that he was a retired drama teacher and that he had greatly enjoyed being a part of the Castle Dark team for the last two years. "Really the best of both worlds," he said. "So much free time and scenery to explore, but some challenging acting and a regular paycheck. An actor's dream." He nodded, looking at his own folded hands. "I've been dating some-one in town, so I divide my time between here and her place. I still think of the castle as home, though. I get to be an actor on the main floor, but up in my tower room, I feel rather like an author in a garret. Or more of an artist, I sup-pose. I like to sketch up there. And of course I have that amazing view of the grounds."

I nodded at this, remembering the wonder-filled drive I had made on the day of my second interview, now two weeks in the past.

Next came Renata, who with her noble bearing looked like a queen in her scarlet robes. She held up her handsome head. "I am Renata Hesse. My parents were German immigrants; they, too, were interested in drama, but it took the form of a puppet show that they put on at a children's theater in our town in Minnesota. It was quite popular and lucrative, as well. I followed in their footsteps, in my way. I studied Shakespeare and Shakespearean drama. I've been lucky enough to play several of Shakespeare's women, and one of his men, in a gender-blind *Macbeth*."

"Ooooh," I said, and everyone clapped a bit.

"My parents have died," Renata said. "I have one sister, Una. Like Elspeth I am divorced, no children. I suppose I am married to the stage."

More clapping. Something about Renata made even the simplest words feel like a performance.

Finally there was Bethany, who had short red hair, freckles, and a sweet smile. "I can't top Renata's story. I'm from Bloomington, and I went to ISU because I'm lazy and I didn't want to leave town." We laughed, and she said, "I married my husband, Tyler, last year, and we're enjoying living in Wood Glen. He's an EMT, and I work here, playing a spoiled daughter of a rich man. Tyler and I auditioned at the castle together—we were both drama majors—but right now his job takes most of his time. People say we're both super dramatic, though. We still feel like newlyweds, and we're utterly devoted to each other." She smiled at Garrett, who sat across from her, and he nodded in his quiet way. He was sketching something with pen on his paper napkin—some sort of beautiful tree. He had said he liked sketching, and I could see that Garrett was even a talented doodler.

Her introduction completed, Bethany took some popcorn and looked back at Derek; we all swung our attention to him, and he nodded. "Okay, fair enough. You all know I'm Derek Corby. Until four years ago I was the vice president of a bank in Chicago. My brother, Paul, is also in finance, and my sister, Erin, is a nurse. When our uncle Calder died, he left the three of us this building in his will, but he had run out of money at the end, and the castle ended up in foreclosure. Erin had no interest in maintaining the place, and she sold her share to us. Paul and I put together our resources so that we could buy it back at a tiny fraction of what it was worth, and then we devised a plan: we would make it a working castle. As you know, we hold weddings and parties here, along with the regular murder-mystery nights and weekends. Paul routinely negotiates through an agent to have movies made here—so far there has been one feature film and one series filmed on our lot, but we're looking to increase that number. Meanwhile, it's the movie people who have helped the most in paying our bills—electricity, water, gas, and general castle upkeep. It takes a crazy amount of money, frankly, but Paul and I have grown to love this building, and we couldn't bear to lose it. And all of you are essentially our family."

We clapped again, and I raised my hand. "Derek, may I ask—how did this castle *get* here?"

He laughed. "Oh, yes—it's beautiful but entirely unlikely. And Calder himself inherited it. It was actually constructed by his great-grandfather, who had seen a similar castle when he was in Europe during the First World War. His name was Philip Corby. Philip had come home from the war and gotten himself a job at a steel corporation, and he rose through the ranks quickly. Steel was booming, and he made shrewd decisions that got him promoted; eventually he was a CEO, and he made crazy money before CEOs were really making crazy money. He had also inherited some money from his father, and he made a very lucky investment that paid off. And suddenly, at the age of twenty-nine, he was a megamillionaire with money still flowing in."

"A tough problem to have," Tim said, smiling at the table.

"I'd be willing to try it out," Garrett said, and we laughed.

Derek grinned. "Philip never forgot about that castle he saw. He kept wanting to visit it, but then he had another idea: he would reconstruct it and live in it."

"This land was probably cheap then," Bethany said.

"Bingo. He got the land for a song, and he imported some of the stone from France or England—we're not exactly sure where his original castle is located—so that it would look like the European original. It took seven years to build it." Derek shook his head. "It's entirely pointless. This is not a country, or an era, that requires castles. Yet here we are. It's kind of like living in a museum within a museum."

"It's amazing," I said. "Even the dorms upstairs are just gorgeous."

"We love it. Paul still has his job in Indianapolis, but eventually he plans to quit and move out here, help me run the place full-time. As it is, he returns every few weeks to catch up with his paperwork. We divide the office tasks between us."

"I look forward to meeting him," I said.

Derek pointed at my face and turned to Elspeth. "Whatever you did with her makeup, El, keep doing it. She looks perfect—just the way I pictured the secretary: prim but sultry and sexy."

This made me blush, but no one seemed to notice. Connie smiled at me and said, "Nora, you'll soon find that Derek is always thinking about the story—either he's writing one in his head or thinking about how he'll direct it or what he needs to produce it. He's the whole Hollywood package."

For a moment there was a curious expression on Derek's face, but it morphed into a smile so quickly, I couldn't identify what it had been.

We said our good nights soon afterward, and Connie and I used our cell phone lights to ascend two unlit gargantuan staircases. "It's still surreal," I told her outside my bedroom door. "I can't believe I live here or that we spent the evening telling lies to people who paid to hear them."

Connie's giggle helped to alleviate the gloom "You get used to it. And it's fun." There was a pause, and she added, "It's almost everything I wanted." Her words, and her voice, made me feel suddenly sad.

We lingered outside of our doors in the long, ink-black hall. "My brother joked about me going back in time, but look at this." I pointed into the gloom. "I half expect Henry VIII to come stomping toward us, wearing his Tudor nightshirt."

"Yeah, that feeling fades eventually," Connie said. "Then it just kind of feels like home."

She turned to unlock her door, then sent me a little smile. "Good night, Nora. Welcome to Castle Dark."

3

A Murder at the Murder

ON SUNDAY MORNING I went down for breakfast, which was laid out on the sideboard as though we lived in Downton Abbey. I helped myself to eggs, bacon, toast, and a cup of tea and sat down at the table, where Derek had left a pile of scripts that were labeled *Scenario II*. We had been instructed to study these and rehearse them with one another so that we were ready for the next performance, which was scheduled for Monday night. I read through the script while I ate and saw that I was indeed the perpetrator; I had grown quite possessive of Harry's collections and felt that I valued their history more than he did. But I was a hypocrite, because I also wanted to sell them— a betrayal that I would try to pin on Derek.

"What a conniver I am," I murmured.

Zana came in with some more scrambled eggs, which she added to the chafing dish. She was a small woman with dark hair and dark-rimmed glasses.

"This is delicious," I said. "And are you still going to show me how to make the torte today?"

"Sure," she said. She didn't smile much with her mouth, but her eyes were very friendly. "I'll have breakfast cleaned up around eleven if you want to peek in then."

"I would love it. Meanwhile, I'm going to take a hike. Tim recommended some trails to me."

"Oh, yeah, it's beautiful around here, and you barely see another human soul."

"I kind of like it that way," I said. "I'm a classic introvert."

"You and me both," she said, and this time I got a full smile.

I DESCENDED THE stone steps in front of Castle Dark and spied the gardener. I had noticed him a few times over the last week as he toiled away, looking fit. Today he wore a navy blue tank top and a pair of jeans. I tried not to look directly at him as I moved toward the flower bed he was weeding. The only information I could get out of Connie was that his name was "maybe John."

"That's it? It might be John?" I complained.

"I don't know! He's just some gardener."

It was true; he was *some* gardener.

"Hey," he said to me as I walked past.

I stopped. "Hello. Are you in charge of this whole place? It seems like a lot of work for one person."

He stood up and wiped his hands on his jeans. "I'm John," he said, offering his hand.

I shook it. "I'm Nora. I'm one of the actors." I used my head to point back at the castle.

"Ah. You look like an actress. Like you could be in the movies."

"Well, thanks."

He lifted a water bottle from the ground and took a few healthy swigs. It was going to be a warm day, and it was already a bit muggy. He set the bottle down and said, "And no, I'm not the only one on staff, but I work when I can, so the others might be around at different times."

"We all have odd hours," I said. "This is like a place outside of time, anyway."

"Agreed," said John. He considered me with intriguing hazel eyes. His brown hair looked as though it could have used a trim, and he needed a shave; the stubble on his cheeks gave him a slightly primitive aura, but not a sinister one.

On a wild impulse, I said, "I was just going to hike a bit through the forest. I don't suppose you'd like to go with me and give me the gardener's tour."

His expression said that he would, in fact, like very much to go with me into the woods, and something fluttered inside my chest. But then a sense of duty clamped down on him, and I watched him become disappointed by his own decision. "That sounds fun. Unfortunately I have to finish weeding these beds and then hop on the riding mower so that the lawn is finished by one, when Derek will be inspecting."

"That's cool. I don't want to get you in trouble."

"Maybe another time," he said. "Have you found the creek yet?"

This perked me up. "No, but I'd love to see it. I heard about it from Connie, and she made it sound quite alluring."

"Good. Later on, then," he said. He bent down and plucked a purple petunia from the flower bed and handed it to me. "Nice to meet you, Nora."

I had played in romantic scenes with a variety of male leads and never found the task intimidating. That little gesture, though—that tiny purple flower plucked from the earth, dirt still clinging to its stem—somehow found a vulnerable spot inside me.

I nodded, suddenly self-conscious, and made my way down the path and onto the wide clearing that led to the woods, still holding the little purple flower. I didn't look back until I was in the shelter of the trees, but by then the gardener named John had disappeared.

I WENT BACK to the kitchen after my hike and drank a full glass of water, contemplating the shining copper pots that hung from chains extending from a wooden ceiling beam. Zana watched me in her quiet way. I finished drinking and said, "Ah!" like someone on a soft drink commercial, and she laughed.

Leaning on the counter beside her, I said, "Do you like working here?"

"I really do. Derek is nice, and he lets me do my own thing. I can get as creative as I want with the menus, as long as I have stuff ready on time and take note of any dietary restrictions of the guests."

"Your food is great."

She nodded her thanks, then looked ready to confide. "If you want to know the best part of the job, it's the library."

"Really?"

"Derek lets me take whatever I want to read, and I can sit and read it in there if I like."

"What sorts of books does he have in that big room? I thought it was full of props, even though I've visited the small library upstairs and found real books in there."

"Oh, he didn't have much at first. But he started building up a collection, with different genres and stuff. For a while he was dating this librarian from Wood Glen. She worked at the big main library, and after the book sale was over last year, they still had like two thousand donated books left over. She let Derek take them all."

"*Really.*"

"Yeah. It's endless reading material now."

"I will be visiting there after rehearsal today!"

"You'll probably find me there." She stood up straight and said, "So I can't make a torte right now because I don't have all the ingredients, but I'll walk you through it. The biggest secret is these pans."

"They look like big, flat pancake pans."

"And that's about how flat the cakes turn out—but there are eight of them, and you pile them up with frosting in between, and . . . well, you saw the result."

"It was like something from the most elegant bakery."

"I used to work in one," she said quietly, stowing the pans under the counter.

"Wow! You are full of surprises."

She pointed at a giant red tome sitting on a green wire standing shelf. "The recipe is in this book; once Derek replenishes my pantry, I'll put the torte back in rotation, and I'll let you know when I'm making it."

"Great! Thanks, Zana. And now I think I have a few hours of rehearsals in front of me."

"Have fun," she said. "I'm headed to the library." The prospect clearly pleased her, because she offered me a full smile, and it changed her face. She looked youthful and pretty.

WE DID IN fact rehearse for much of the afternoon. Elspeth practiced her fortune-teller predictions, but then she played the role of the Inspector, trying to catch us out with her questions. Her interrogations were extremely helpful.

I floundered at one point and Derek flew over to me. "You have to be absolutely ready with your answers and your evidence, Nora. Tonight you are the guilty one, and everyone has to help to make that trail clear while appearing to make it cloudy. But you have to be the *only* one with both motive and opportunity. We can't have some guest offering a viable alternative scenario; you all have to be ready to shoot those down. So why aren't I guilty?"

Tim said, "Because you were seen in town with some mysterious woman at the time of death."

"Good. And why isn't Connie guilty?"

"Because she actually loved Harold and wanted to leave you for him, as expressed in her diary that the Inspectors will find lying in the hallway," I said.

"Great!" Derek said, smiling at me.

We went through them all: Harold's son, his daughter, his wife, his gardener, even the fortune-teller. None of them could have killed him because of at least one piece of ex-onerating evidence. Only I had no alibi, and my own mo-tive was going to be made clear through several clues and a crucial dialogue with Derek at the dinner table.

"Okay, everyone," Derek said, "take a break. Zana made cold sandwiches; they're in the kitchen with some chips and soft drinks. Then you're on your own until six, when we'll do a run-through. See you then." He waved and strode out of the room.

"Derek always looks busy," I said to Connie.

"He always *is* busy," she said.

I grabbed a sandwich, a bag of chips, and a Diet Coke from the kitchen, then made my way to the back of the castle, where Connie had shown me the very modern el-evator. I climbed in and rode it to the third floor and fol-lowed the already familiar path to my room. It definitely felt like *my* room, my space, now. My family, sans Gen, had descended on the castle ten days earlier and helped me move in, after which they received the tour. My brothers, Jay and Luke, had made me promise to invite them for an overnight stay so that they could get "a serious game of Murder Ball going." Murder Ball was just their name for hide-and-seek, except that when someone found someone else, they fired a Nerf ball at them, and they were "dead." My little brothers were relentlessly bloodthirsty.

"We could go nuts in this place," Luke had said, running

his hand along a stairway banister that only a glare from my mother had kept him from riding down to the main floor.

"Yeah, seriously," Jay agreed. "I'll bet it's full of ghosts."

I did not appreciate that sentiment. "It has no ghosts, because it's not an old building. It has no history, no skeletons in the closet. It's a made-to-order faux castle."

"Well, it feels real and super spooky," Jay insisted.

Right now, with the sun streaming in my window, I felt only a benevolent vibe in my room. But at night, when I walked the halls of the dark castle with just my cell phone to ward off the clouds of darkness around me, I had to agree with my brother: Castle Dark was terrifying.

There was a little table in front of my window with a flower arrangement on top; I set the flowers on the floor and put my lunch on the table so that I could look out at the view while I ate. I arranged my Coke, sandwich, and chips and remembered that Connie said she had binoculars I could borrow. We were starting a bird-watching challenge.

I walked across to her door and tapped on it. "Connie?"

She wasn't in the room, but her door had opened slightly when I knocked. "Con?" I saw the binoculars on her desk and figured she wouldn't mind if I borrowed them. I strode in and grabbed the "field glasses," as Connie called them, and saw that she had several brochures on her desk, as well—several pieces of promotional literature about the castle and the mystery night. And on her wall, just above the desk, she had tacked an article from the features section of the *Chicago Tribune*. It had a huge picture of Derek laughing, the castle in the background behind him. The headline read:

YOUNG ENTREPRENEUR BANKS ON
LOVE OF MYSTERY

"Well, aren't you loyal?" I murmured.

I went back to my room and settled down at my lunch table, using the binoculars to scan for birds while I chewed my sandwich. Connie had given me a list of birds to try for, with pictures of them. So far I had easily found a robin, a cardinal, a brown sparrow, several wrens, and a blue jay. I scanned the tree nearest my window, then panned down to look for any birds that might be pecking at the feeder that Renata filled each day.

"It's another contradiction about Derek," Connie had told me once. "He complains that he can barely feed us, but he spends tons on bird food and salt licks for the deer and even treats for the chipmunks that hang out on the back patio."

I focused the binoculars and scanned to the left, then found myself looking at Derek in close-up. He was talking to John, the gardener. He was not exactly yelling, but he was doing a lot of gesticulating, and John was nodding. Did Derek think John had done a bad job on the lawn? It looked pristine to me. Derek finally turned away and stalked off with a slightly disgusted look on his face.

The gardener didn't look particularly distressed. He stood, hands on hips, and stared down at the grass with a contemplative expression.

AT THE MAKEUP table Monday night, Elspeth put my hair in a loose arrangement on top of my head, letting two long dark strands hang down. "Derek says we have to draw attention to the ruby earrings. Tonight the rubies are being stolen by you, along with the collectibles. You're just a terrible thief."

"Apparently, since I'm going to get caught," I said, grinning.

She was still studying my reflection. "But he wants all your other makeup the same. I was really happy with your eyes. They're so striking—that black hair and those sea green eyes. I barely had to use eye shadow at all to bring out the green."

My gaze wandered down the long table to admire the costumes and makeup of the others: Renata, glowing like royalty; Connie, her sweet face contrasted with a rather severe dress that suggested her paradoxical nature; Bethany, with a blond wig to cover the red hair and foundation to disguise her freckles; Tim, hiding his dimples to become solemn as the angry son of the dead man; Garrett, innocuous and unobtrusive in his gardening clothes. Elspeth looked perfect once again as the Fortune-teller who would help to reveal secrets.

It was fun, I realized. *I was having fun.*

Elspeth caught my gaze in the mirror and said, "Not a bad gig, huh?"

"Not at all," I said, grinning.

THERE WE WERE again, dining at the long table, playing the roles of the wealthy in some indeterminate era, surrounded by the castoffs of genuinely wealthy people. We ate Zana's food and argued about a fictional dead man. Derek and Tim scowled, Connie sneered, Bethany pouted, Renata preened, and Garrett brooded, playing absently with the knife from his gardening belt so that the Inspectors could see the "emerald" on the hilt. I did my best to project a feeling of superiority with occasional traces of fear. One Inspector at least had picked up on it and was watching me, taking notes. I ran my fingers over my ruby earrings, making it look like a nervous gesture, posturing for his benefit.

After dinner Derek suggested that the Inspectors should wait in the parlor while the dinner table was cleared. They could read the pamphlets about the history of the castle while they waited. This gave us all a little downtime to find a corner somewhere and practice our lines. I darted down the hall and into the library, practicing various gestures and expressions while looking into a small mirror on the wall.

A young man peered in. "Have you seen Bethany?" he asked. He held up a jacket. "She forgot this, and it's kind of cold tonight." How sweet. I realized this must be Bethany's husband.

"I think most people are in the parlor or down some hallway practicing lines."

He nodded. "Okay, thanks." He disappeared out the door, and I glanced at my watch. Perhaps just one last run-through . . .

Minutes later I returned to the great hall, where the Inspectors waited to begin their game. It was Renata this time who suggested that an Inspector should follow her to hear more about Harry and his great-aunt and her missing rubies. She led him (and all the rest of them) to the chapel, pointing out the stained glass windows and the simple altar. "But it was outside this chapel that my poor husband was found. Perhaps he had gone to say a prayer," she said, her voice breaking slightly, her hands trembling with admirable emotion. Then the tour moved on, this time with Tim as the leader, saying, "What my mother failed to mention was that Father was cheating on her! But we'll save that as conversation for our after-dinner drinks. Let me take you to the portrait gallery and tell you about Great-Great-Aunt Elizabeth and her lost rubies."

Dutiful, we traipsed into the hall outside the chapel. My eyes rested briefly on the hidden passage; had the door moved? But of course it hadn't. The opening was flush with the wall. I shook my head and followed the group to the stairs. One of the Inspectors tripped on the carpet on the grand staircase and fell down. There was a communal "Oh!" and I joined the crowd that rushed to his side. He was an elderly gentleman, and he was more embarrassed than hurt. He took his time getting back up, however, and used the moment of attention to tell a story about a different time he had fallen down and how he had met his wife because of it. He pointed at another Inspector, a white-haired woman who stood next to him and laughingly verified his story. We chatted for a while (Derek's philosophy was "Let the Inspectors set the tone!"), allowing some casual time with a group that seemed jovial and eager to chat. When we started moving, I focused on my character; soon I would need to fend off accusations about rubies. I touched my earrings again, only to find that one was missing. Oh, no! In my mind I was going over the speech I would make when we got back to the drawing room, but the earrings were the centerpiece of my monologue. When we reached the portrait gallery, Tim encouraged the Inspectors to walk around and take notes. I decided I had some time to retrace my steps and find the lost ruby. As I passed Tim, I whispered, "Lost an earring—be right back!"

I moved through the milling crowd, actors and Inspectors alike, who were chatting and dropping clues or catching them.

It was too hard to see anything on the floor with so many people walking around. I figured I'd go all the way back to the dining room and start from there, but when I reached it, I found nothing under the dining table or on the floor. A lonely Inspector was looking for clues on the deserted table. I said, "I'm just looking for my ruby earring. I mean, my *earring*." There, that should have helped this wayward Inspector, who was clearly not getting the point of the game.

I made my way to the chapel; I moved swiftly, fearful that I would miss my cue upstairs. Nothing in the hall, nothing outside the chapel. Surely it would glint in the hallway light? I had gone inside the chapel earlier, following the Inspectors, so I went there now, and I spied the earring immediately, at the end of the final pew. With a sigh of relief, I strode the length of the pew and bent to retrieve it.

Then I saw a hand.

For a surreal moment my brain could not process what was there, but should not have been there. A hand, connected to an arm, in the aisle near the wall. Questions swirled in my head in a matter of milliseconds. Had Derek changed the script? Was someone playing the part of Harold? As far as I knew Derek had never provided a victim before.

Slowly, I leaned forward and peered around the edge of the pew.

Garrett lay there, his eyes fixed sightlessly on the ceiling, his hands flung out to his sides in what seemed like submission or despair. Not even Elspeth could have created special effects this good—especially because a rivulet of blood was running down the narrow aisle.

I scooted away and struggled to stand up, tripping over myself in the process; I didn't realize I was screaming until Derek and Tim appeared in the doorway, their faces white with shock.

4

In the Dark

THE REST I remember only in nightmarish flashes: the jumble of faces peering into the chapel, the ambulance attendants with their macabre stretcher, the dark blood that stained the tile next to the final pew, the cold stone of the wall that I slumped against as I answered questions in a voice not recognizable as my own. And then, for some reason, the gardener speaking with Derek in one corner, his face grim and somehow official. Derek raked his hand through his hair again and again, and Connie appeared beside him to pat his arm in an attempt at comfort.

Then the gardener walked toward me where I stood, using the wall for support.

"You're in shock," he said. "Let's get you out of here." He took my hand and led me out of the chapel, past some uniformed police officers and down the long shadowy hallway. All of our Inspectors had vanished.

"We didn't finish the mystery," I murmured. "We didn't reach the resolution."

"There's a different mystery that needs solving now," he said. "Let's go in here."

He led me into the room that Derek called drawing room two, which held the obligatory fireplace, bookcases, sumptuous wooden desk, and leather furniture. He pointed at a couch and I sat in it, thinking nothing.

He sat beside me and pulled out a notebook and pen. He jotted something and said, "Can you tell me your full name?"

I frowned. "What? Why do you need that?"

"For my notes."

"Why are you taking notes?" I asked. I'm sure I looked utterly blank.

"I'm sorry. I thought you heard back there." He took out a badge. "I'm Detective John Dashiell from the Wood Glen Police Department. This is a murder investigation."

"You were gardening. I thought you were the gardener."

He nodded, his face solemn and patient. "Yes. There was a reason for that; I can't go into it now."

"Okay. I see." I didn't see.

"Your full name, please?" His voice was gentle, but there was some impatience there.

"Nora Blake."

"And you've been here for how long?"

"About two weeks. A bit less."

"And you're one of the actors."

"Yes. Tonight I was the murderer." The last two words, juxtaposed with the image in my mind of poor Garrett's blood, made me gasp. "Not—not like that."

"I understand, Miss Blake."

He made some notes, and I glanced around the room. The lamplight seemed menacing, as did the shadowy corners. Someone could have been hiding there. . . .

"Miss Blake?"

"I'm sorry?"

"I asked if you could take me through the events that led up to your discovery of Mr. Perth's body."

"Oh, God. Garrett. I can't believe it. It's weird—he was playing a gardener." I looked up and met John's hazel eyes. They looked dark brown in the weird lamplight. "And you were playing a gardener."

"Yes. Can you tell me what happened?"

I sighed. "I was wearing these earrings." I gestured to the faux rubies in my ears. "They're supposed to be a clue that would lead the guests to realize I was—the killer. We went to the chapel, and people milled around looking for clues. Then we moved down the hall and up the north stairway to the portrait gallery." I pointed vaguely upward. "They were supposed to study the portraits and take notes. One of the older gentlemen fell, and it ended up being a kind of long distraction; then I realized up there that one of the earrings was missing. I figured I had a few minutes, so I decided to retrace my steps, looking for it in the hall and the chapel. I told Tim where I was going."

He pointed at my ear with his pen. "You found the earring."

"Yes, at the end of my search, in the chapel. Right before I saw Garrett." The last word came out as a whisper, and I cleared my throat. "I just saw his hand, at first. I thought it was some weird prop, something Derek had added into the story. He has lots of props."

"Sure."

"Then I thought the story line had changed, and someone was playing the role of the dead man—my employer in this script. And then—" I remembered with horror, and John Dashiell reached out to pat my hand. His hand was warm.

"Let's think back to your walk from the portrait gallery to the chapel. Who did you see?"

I stared at him. Whom had I seen? "On the way back? I don't think I saw anyone. Everyone was supposed to be up in the gallery, you know. So—I mean—I know someone must have stayed back at the chapel when we all moved toward the gallery, but in all honesty I can't recall. Tim led us up to the next level, telling us the history of some of the people in the portraits. So I know he was at the head of the group. Other than that—I'm not sure. I was behind some Inspectors, and I was trying to figure out how I could unobtrusively drop some clues pointing to my own guilt. Focused on my performance, you know. So I wasn't—keeping track."

"Right. Listen, I'm going to write down my phone number. If at any point in the evening you remember something, text me, okay? That will be the easiest way of making contact in this big place."

"Okay. I'm sorry I can't seem to remember more about who was up in the portrait gallery."

"Understandable. But Tim you saw?"

"Yes, he was there. And everyone else had to be, really, because we had all moved on, and they all had parts to play. And I would have seen someone when I returned to the chapel unless—"

He leaned forward. "Yes?"

"Well, unless for some reason they were in the hidden passage."

He leaned forward. "What hidden passage? Is that part of the game?"

"No, at least not this script. But the passage is part of the castle. Connie showed it to me. I don't know how many of the actors know about it. But when we came out of the chapel—"

"Yes?" His dark eyes grew darker.

"I thought the door moved. But it was an optical illusion, because when I looked again, it was flush with the wall."

"Can you show me the entrance?"

"Yes, of course. I'm sorry I didn't mention it sooner, but I . . . I'm having some trouble concentrating."

"It's understandable, Miss Blake."

"Nora. You can just call me Nora like you did when you were a gardener," I said, rubbing my suddenly tired eyes.

"Nora, can you take me back to the hidden passage?"

"Yes." A fear assailed me. "Do I have to go—"

"No, you won't need to look in the chapel."

"Okay. Thank you." I looked down at my hands and saw that they were shaking. "I wouldn't have thought I'd react this way—I'm normally a calm person."

"You saw a murder, Nora. No one is calm when that happens. You're doing very well; I appreciate your help."

"Okay, thanks." I stood up. "I'll take you there. I'm surprised Derek didn't show you."

He stood up, too; he was quite tall. "He was distracted by some other things." His expression was inscrutable.

"Yes, of course."

I led him out of the room, and we walked in silence back to the chapel. My mind was racing, and he seemed to be deep in thought, as well. Who could have done this? And why? Could one of the Inspectors be a criminal? An enemy of Garrett's? Surely it wasn't one of our actors?

I thought of shy, quiet Garrett, the former drama teacher who liked going to town to visit his girlfriend. . . .

I spun around to speak to John the gardener, now a policeman. "He had a girlfriend. Someone needs to notify her."

He nodded. "I believe Derek is doing that duty. Is this the spot?" His eyes raked the wall across from the chapel.

"Yes, just up here. Wait. Where was that— Oh, here it is." I touched the curlicue in the wood that held the mechanism, and the panel opened with a click.

Detective Dashiell donned a glove and pulled gingerly on the doorframe, then peered inside. A uniformed officer appeared at the end of the hall, and Dashiell held up a hand, signaling him. "Get the crew," he called.

Within minutes the hallway was cordoned off, and the hidden passage was illuminated; people in protective clothing went in and out, looking like a blend of surgeon and astronaut. I made my way to the dining room, where I huddled with Connie and Zana. Tim joined us eventually, then Elspeth and Renata, and finally Bethany, who had been on the phone with her husband. She was wearing a jacket, so obviously he had found her. . . .

We were numb and frightened; Tim looked particularly dejected. "I can't believe this," he said. "Why Garrett? He was such a sweet person and a good friend. This makes no sense."

Bethany wiped away a tear. "I only wish I'd gotten to know him better," she said. "We really only started talking in the last few weeks. I was planning to invite him for dinner sometime and introduce him to Tyler." Her eyes widened as she realized this could never happen.

Renata looked thoughtful. "He always made a point of making other people feel appreciated." Her eyes, too, glistened with tears.

Elspeth stared at her folded hands. "He was always very complimentary about my makeup skills."

Zana stood, went to the counter, and retrieved a pan of brownies. "I was supposed to serve these when the mystery was solved," she said. "But they interviewed those players, took their info, and sent them home. So help yourselves." She started slicing the brownies and putting them on cake plates; those she passed around. "Food is comfort," she said. "That's what my mama always said."

It *was* comforting somehow, eating together and drinking glasses of water in Derek's frugal kitchen. Connie poked at the crumbs on her plate. "Who could have done it?" she asked.

I studied the faces around the table; each one looked shocked and supremely innocent, and I realized that these were *actors*. If any one of them had committed murder, they could certainly make us believe that they had not. My hands began to tremble again, and Connie put an arm around me. "Poor Nora. It must have been terrible, finding him like that."

I nodded, looking at my plate, but when I looked up, I caught some varying expressions on the faces of my companions, from sympathy to speculation to downright suspicion. Shocked, I said, "I didn't even know Garrett. He seemed like a very nice person."

Now everyone's eyes held sympathy and compassion. Had I merely imagined the suspicion?

Derek wandered in, looking weary. "Oh, good, I'm glad you're all here. I have some updates." He sighed and sat down. "Zana, is there any coffee?"

Zana sprang up, returned with a pot, and poured him a cup.

He thanked her and smiled a sad smile. "It will keep me awake, but I'll be up all night, anyway, with police traipsing all over the castle."

We nodded, waiting.

He took a bracing sip of coffee, then said, "Garrett has been brought to the St. Elizabeth Hospital morgue. His girlfriend, Sora, will go to see him there; she has also agreed to notify his family. Apparently he has a brother somewhere and some nieces and nephews. Sora took it hard, but she's been really great, under the circumstances. This isn't the first partner she's lost, which is sad."

We nodded in silence.

Derek drank some more coffee. "I have arranged for someone to come and clean the chapel when the police are all finished. It's a beautiful part of the castle, and eventually I want people to feel comfortable in there again. I have a friend in town, a Catholic priest. I got to know him because we both enjoy antiques. Father Jim has agreed to come and say a prayer for Garrett and a blessing over the chapel. That will bring us all some peace, I think."

I was surprised that Derek had summoned the presence of mind to make these arrangements; then again, he was in charge of this giant building and the events that went on within it. He would have to be focused on the future.

"Were the visitors okay about not finishing? Did they know what happened?" Tim asked.

Derek nodded. "They were told that a man was dead and the police were investigating. They were all given rain checks, and they were quite polite about it. I hate to say it, but I think it actually made the whole thing more thrilling for them, knowing that a real murder happened at Castle Dark."

This brought a new silence around the table. Derek's dark head drooped as he stared at the brownie Zana had put in front of him. He toyed with the handle of his coffee cup, then looked up suddenly, his dark eyes meeting mine. "Nora, are you all right? I didn't really get a chance to talk to you in all the chaos—"

All eyes were back on me. "I'm fine. Thank you. It was a shock, but I've had some time to get over it. Zana's brownie helped a lot. You're right, Zana. Food is comfort."

She smiled and nodded.

Elspeth leaned forward. "Derek, this might sound rude, but in terms of the mystery parties and our jobs . . ."

"Your jobs are safe." Derek pushed away his coffee. "Obviously we'll have to shut down for a couple of weeks, maybe more; we'll see what the police say. But we'll be working carefully on PR, making sure that while Garrett's death is something we will mourn, we will still be opening the castle to the public in the future. We might offer online events that would require us filming you all in some mini mysteries that people can pay to solve. For the time being, you can all just lie low, answer whatever questions the police have. Dash has asked that no one leave Wood Glen for the foreseeable future."

"Dash?" Connie said. "Who is that?"

Derek made eye contact on one side of the table, then the other. "Dash is Detective John Dashiell. He has been on the grounds for the last few weeks, gardening."

Renata's voice was crisp with the suspicion that I also suddenly felt. "A police detective was doing your gardening . . . why? He needed extra money? He was moonlighting in the middle of the day?"

"No." Derek sighed. "The fact is, Detective Dashiell had been working undercover regarding another matter. A matter unrelated to poor Garrett's death. That is why I was able to quickly summon him to our aid."

Bethany's green eyes were wide. "A matter unrelated to Garrett's death—but having to do with something here at the castle? I feel like we should have been privy to that information, Derek."

She folded her arms, her eyes flashing, and something Connie had said came back to me: *Bethany is a good actress, but she's so* over-the-top *in real life. I know we're all dramatic, but Bethany takes exaggeration to new heights.* It was true. Everything about Bethany was a bit exaggerated—her expressions, her gestures, her reactions. It was a source of good-natured humor among the cast.

Our gazes swung back to Derek. His mouth was a firm line. "You did not in fact need to be privy to anything, Bethany. It's a private matter that doesn't involve you. Let me remind you that the castle is my property and my home."

Bethany didn't look convinced; I sensed that she was itching to grab the cell phone that sat near her on the table, perhaps to text her new husband.

Tim stretched suddenly, stifling a yawn. "Derek, do you think we're finished down here? I feel like heading up to my room."

Derek nodded. "Yeah, I think they're finished with our group for the time being. You can all retire to your rooms if you wish." I was struck by his formal phrasing. It sounded like something we would have said to the Inspectors.

Tim went to the sink with his plate and cup; he rinsed them out and put them on the drain board. We all followed suit, and Zana said, "Thanks, guys. I appreciate it."

Everyone wandered out, bound for their rooms, but I waited for Connie, who was lingering at Derek's side. "Do you need anything?" she asked. "Are you holding up okay?"

He looked at her for a minute, his dark eyes intense. Derek could have been the model for a cover of some Gothic romance: *Wuthering Heights* or *Rebecca*. How fitting that he lived in a castle. He touched Connie's hand. "That's sweet of you. But I'm okay."

A man appeared in the doorway; for a surreal moment I thought it was Derek, somehow casting himself across the room without seeming to move. Then my eyes adjusted to the new face and I realized that he merely resembled Derek, but he was a bit stockier, and his hair was shorter.

"Paul," Derek said, "I thought you'd be here hours ago. You know Connie. And this is Nora Blake, our new cast member."

Paul Corby took a few steps and thrust out a hand. I shook it and said, "Nice to meet you."

He smiled grimly. "Under terrible circumstances, but yes, it is nice to meet you, too, Nora."

Derek pointed at the counter. "Zana made brownies if you want some. Where were you?"

Paul's eyes slid sideways, away from his brother's gaze. "I've been around, running errands. Sorry you've had to deal with all this."

Connie backed away slightly and said, "I guess we'll say good night."

Derek smiled at her. "Good night. Thanks for your support, Con. Nora, try to rest and recover. Things will look better tomorrow."

I nodded and followed Connie out of the kitchen. We were headed toward the main staircase, which would take us up, up into the dark castle, and something in me rebelled.

"Connie? I need some fresh air."

She turned to study my face, then patted my shoulder. "Of course you do. Let's go look at the stars."

She went back to the dining room doorway and leaned in, murmuring something about how they shouldn't lock us out.

"Let's go out the back way by the fountain," Connie said.

I followed her to the north entrance, where a police officer heard our request for air with slightly narrowed eyes before she finally let us pass.

We went down the staircase and crunched through some landscaping stones until we reached the fountain and then the soft grass beyond it. It was difficult to see in the velvety blackness, although the muted light from the castle allowed us some shadowy vision. Connie grabbed my wrist; I wasn't sure if she was showing me support or seeking it as we moved through the darkness, making no sound besides the slight rustling of grass.

Eventually we stopped. I took a deep breath of the clean, chilled air, and then I looked up. How different the sky was here far from the city! The stars were everywhere, scattered across the night in a glittering, luminous display.

"They really do twinkle," Connie noted. "Why do they make me want to cry?"

"That's stress," I murmured. "We're all under stress. But it's easier to breathe out here."

"It is," she agreed.

We were silent then, thinking our own thoughts. I allowed myself to relax, to focus on nothing but the silver shine above me. It was indescribable, the power of that night sky, a canvas for the poetry of the stars.

Despite the refreshing vision above me, I turned, almost against my will, to look at Castle Dark, its windows like gold eyes winking in the darkness. It stood silhouetted against the navy blue sky, a jagged black shape that crouched like a bird of prey in the middle of the forest-rimmed field. What had brought me here? Why had violence visited the once peaceful castle, which now would be associated with blood and fear?

Connie's voice said, "You're not looking up." She put a friendly arm around me.

"This was starting to feel like home."

"I know. It will again. We have to get over the shock." I nodded.

"Let's go in, Nora. The next time we look at the stars, we'll make sure we're in happy moods. We don't want to associate that beautiful sky with sadness."

"Right." I followed her as she headed toward the north door; something ran across the path in front of us, and Connie let out a yelp.

"What was that?" she cried.

"I don't know. It was bigger than a rabbit. A fox, maybe? A raccoon? I didn't get a good look at it."

"It's kind of creepy, thinking of night creatures crawling around out here."

As we climbed the stairs, I couldn't help but think of other night creatures roaming freely in the castle despite posing a nocturnal threat. We had learned through terrible experience that predators were found not only outdoors.

I WAS GLAD to have Connie's companionship as we returned to the darkened hall. "I don't want to take the elevator in the dark," I whispered.

She nodded. "But that main staircase is even creepier to me than the side one. Let's take the servants' stairs."

There had never been servants in Castle Dark, just paid employees, but Derek's great-grandfather had preserved the idea of class separation in his architecture. Connie and I turned right instead of left, our cell phones creating thin beams of light as we headed for the narrow side staircase that would let us out at the end of our hallway instead of in the middle.

Connie opened the stairway door. "Why is it always cold in here?" she said. "It's summer!"

I shivered, but not only from the cold. The building had been frightening enough when it was just a simulation of some ancient castle in which knights might actually have battled enemies. Now that castle of antiquity felt terribly real, and the very walls around us seemed sinister and strange.

Connie seemed to feel the same way, because she nudged closer to me as we began to ascend the stairs. "Our lights make weird shadows on the wall," she whispered.

Something cold touched my leg, and I let out a fearful yelp before I realized it was Hamlet joining us for our journey up the stairs and pressing his cold nose against my skin for a quick sniff. "You almost gave me a heart attack!" I said to the hound moving placidly at my side.

Connie giggled and reached over to pat Hamlet's giant head. "He's been sleeping in my room the last few nights. I'm not sure why; his bed is in Derek's room. Frankly I like having the extra protection."

I liked the idea of Hamlet nearby, too, and I petted his back, suddenly as grateful for his bulk as I had been fearful of it moments earlier. Connie and I reached the top of one staircase and swung around to ascend the second one, which led to our third-floor dorms.

Connie's voice seemed weird and different in the dark.

"It must have been strange to find him like that," she said. "Garrett, I mean."

"It was horrible. I don't want to think about it."

"You'll feel better tomorrow," her voice said. Derek had uttered something to that effect, and Connie spoke in the same soothing tone.

"That's assuming I get any sleep."

We reached the top of the stairs, huffing slightly with the effort. Connie aimed her light down our dark hallway. Because we had taken the north stairway, we were far from our rooms. A couple of doorways had thin bands of light beneath them, suggesting that our fellow actors were awake and unwinding in their rooms.

Garrett's room was the first on the left, the costume room directly across on the right. I grabbed Connie's arm. "Garrett's door is open a little," I said. "See? Didn't he always keep it shut?"

"Maybe the police were in there," she said.

"I'm not sure if the police are even aware that Garrett lives here. Are they? Do they know that any of us live here?"

"That guy Dashiell must know. He's practically been living here himself," Connie said.

"Yeah, what's that about? Why was he here?"

"Got me," Connie said. "Let's just take a peek, make sure everything is okay." Before I could protest, she lunged forward and pushed on the open door, then flipped on the light in Garrett's room. "Oh, no," she said with a gasp.

I followed her in and saw that Garrett's room, though simple and streamlined as a monk's cell, had still held enough possessions that someone had been able to strew them all over the bed and the floor. A scattering of paper money, photographs, clothing, and books lay everywhere, as though a tornado had come in one of the windows from which Garrett had enjoyed his view.

"Someone tossed this room. That's what they say in my crime shows," Connie said. She started to walk forward, and I pulled her back.

"That window is open," I said, pointing to the head of Garrett's bed, where one of the mullioned panes was pulled to the side, letting in night air. "Maybe all this mess just got blown around by the wind?"

Connie shook her head. "No way. Some of this stuff is heavy." She bent over as if to grasp one of the books on the bed.

"We can't touch anything. The police need to see this."

"Oh, right," she said, pushing her cloud of blond hair off her shoulders. "I'm creeped out. Let's get out of here."

I agreed, and we returned swiftly to Connie's room at the other end of the hall.

In my phone contacts, I found Dashiell's number. I texted him.

We found Garrett's room open on the third floor.
It's been ransacked.

"Who's that?" Connie asked, pointing at the phone.

"The detective. He told me to text him if I remembered anything."

"Remembered? What would you remember?"

"Anything from the chapel. Finding Garrett."

"Oh, I see." She sighed, then showed me a photograph in her hand. "This was under the corner of Garrett's blanket. I don't think the police care about some random photo. Look how sweet! A picture of him and his girlfriend. The poor woman—Derek said she's lost another boyfriend, or a husband, before this. I figured she'd want the photo."

I didn't think Connie should have taken anything, but she was already here with the photo in her hand.

Moments later a bright light illuminated the hallway; we heard a noise and peered out of Connie's door to see several policemen come barreling down the hall, led by Detective John Dashiell. Hamlet ran alongside them, his jowls swaying and dripping, looking far too much like the hound of the Baskervilles.

5

Brightness in the Shadows

WE SAT ON three chairs in my room: Connie, John Dashiell, and I. Hamlet lay in between us, exhausted by his police work. Dashiell was beginning to look tired; I wondered how early he'd gotten up to "garden" outside the castle. His brown hair was starting to fall down onto his forehead and into one eye, making him look like an outlaw.

His eyes met mine. "And how was it that you discovered Garrett's door was open? Connie says the hall was dark."

I nodded. "But we use our cell phone flashlights. Otherwise we wouldn't have been able to see our hands in front of our faces."

"I see. And is it that unusual for someone's door to be slightly ajar? No one comes up here, right?"

Connie rubbed her arm with an absent expression. "I've been here close to a year, and I've never seen a door left open. Why does it matter, though? You saw what someone did inside his room."

"Yes." Dashiell looked at her. "But Garrett could have

done that himself, couldn't he? Before he came down. He also could have left his door open."

Connie frowned. "That doesn't make sense. Garrett was super neat. Also it's clear somebody was looking for something."

Dashiell said, "Hmm."

Something seemed to occur to Connie, and she leaned forward. "I just remembered something Garrett said to me once. It was a month or so ago—we were having a birthday party for Elspeth. Everybody was there. I was standing next to Garrett at one point, drinking punch. He put his mouth by my ear and said, 'Do you trust him?' I said, 'Trust who?' but then something happened—I think someone came in with a cake and we all sang. It just—kind of got lost. And he never said anything like that again."

Dashiell studied her face. "He said *him*. Which men were present?"

"Well—everyone." She shrugged. "Elspeth was turning forty, so it was a big party. People brought their spouses and stuff. So Derek and Paul and Tim, and Zana and Bethany brought their husbands, and Renata had some man there. She said he was just a friend. I don't remember his name."

"Thank you," said Dashiell. "Please share any anecdotes you remember whether they seem important or not. Anything to do with Garrett."

"Okay," she said.

"His window was open," I said. "I'm sure you saw that, but it seems odd."

"Why?" His dark eyes studied me.

"I don't know. It had no screen in it; all of my windows have screens. I suppose Garrett took it out for some reason, but then why would he leave it open? The room would fill with flying bugs."

"Hmm," Dashiell said, writing something down.

My conscience made me say, "And we should confess,

we took one thing out of the room." I looked pointedly at Connie.

Dashiell bristled. "I'm sorry?"

Connie shrugged. "I took a picture of him with his girlfriend. Sora, I think her name is. I want to give it to her."

The detective stared at her. "You can certainly do so after we're finished with it. May I see the photograph, please?" His eyes were cold, as was his tone.

Chastened and clearly disappointed in me, Connie went across to her room.

Dashiell rubbed his eyes.

"You must be exhausted, Detective."

"Just John is fine," he said. "Or Dash." He smiled at me briefly and was transformed into the attractive gardener I had chatted with on the lawn. "I'm sorry I had to mislead you."

"Yeah, about that—"

Connie burst back into the room and handed the photo to Dashiell. It was an innocuous snapshot, taken from a distance, of Garrett and his girlfriend in front of a waterfall; they wore hiking clothes: jeans, T-shirts, sturdy shoes. Their seemingly smiling faces suggested an easy companionship.

Dashiell studied it, flipped it over to inspect the back—I assumed for distinguishing marks—and then took a picture of it with his phone. He then returned it to Connie. "Fine. I'll add it to my notes; you can pass it on to his girlfriend."

Connie brightened. "Thanks! I'm sorry I took it without asking. I just—I would want to have it. If I had lost someone . . ." Her innocent look was back, along with the sadness that I had glimpsed on the day I met her.

Dashiell nodded, then stood up. "Thank you, ladies, for your cooperation. I am fairly confident this is the last time we will bother you tonight."

"Some might suggest that I'm the one who bothered you," I said, holding up my phone to remind him of my text.

He tucked his notebook in his pocket, then smiled at me. "No bother at all, Nora."

Hamlet dragged himself to his feet to escort Dashiell to the door. Dashiell half bowed to us and said, "Ladies." Then he turned and disappeared down the hall.

Connie turned to me, her jaw dropping. "He is *into* you!" she said.

"Oh, stop."

"You stop! Did you see that look he gave you? I got kind of excited by it, and it wasn't even *aimed* at me."

I was glad I hadn't imagined the warmth in his expression. "He's just being polite."

"Yeah, right," she said, narrowing her eyes at me. Hamlet chose that moment to thrust his giant snout into her hand, and she giggled. "Ew, his nose is so wet. If he's up here, that means Derek already let him out. He wants to go to sleep, so I guess I'll wait until tomorrow to discuss the gardener who is suddenly investigating a murder."

"I grant you, that is weird."

"We agree on that, then," she said, already in the hall with Hamlet at her heels. "Good night, Nora."

"Good night. Be sure to lock your door."

She turned, her eyes wide with surprise. "What? Oh, God, you're right. Someone in this castle killed Garrett. Someone is a murderer."

"Don't think about it. Just lock your door and know that Hamlet is guarding you."

"Yeah. Thanks, Nora. I'm glad you're here." She shut her door, and I heard the lock click into place.

I closed and locked my own door and turned to look at my room, formal and elegant as a movie set. I had straightened it up that morning before I went for my walk, and I had noticed that Dashiell's eyes had flitted around the space before he started asking questions.

I was relieved now that I had made my bed.

6

Castle Contraband

THE SUN WOKE me the next morning, shining warm on my face and filling the room with dappled light. I lay for a while, trying to determine how I felt. The horror of yesterday had receded, replaced by sadness for Garrett, his girlfriend, and his family. I pitied Derek, too—hopefully his business would recover after this terrible event. I recalled how passionate he had been at my interview: how lovingly he had spoken of Castle Dark, how handsome and vibrant he had looked when he enumerated the joys of living there.

My thoughts turned to the previous evening: Garrett's ransacked room, the police tape everywhere, the long questioning sessions.

I got up and padded to the bathroom; I glanced at the mirror and was surprised to see a furtive smile on my face. What had I been thinking about just then? The clock in the washroom said almost eight; I decided to shower and take a walk, and in the process I'd try to "take the temperature" of the crowd, as my high school drama teacher had once said.

Since we wouldn't be practicing or performing, I went for a casual look. I braided my shower-damp hair and slipped into a white blouse and a pair of jean shorts. I pulled on some white canvas gym shoes and made my way into the hall. There was no sign of Connie or anyone else.

Alone, I descended the giant staircases and made my way into the dining room, where I found Elspeth and Tim eating pancakes. "That looks good," I said.

"Nora looks better, too," Elspeth said to Tim. "We were just saying that a sunny Tuesday morning has helped to dispel some of our gloom." She wore some muted pink lipstick, and in place of a tiara, she had woven some Ophelia-like faux flowers into her long hair.

I went to the sideboard and helped myself to two pancakes and some bacon. Then I slathered on some syrup, grabbed a pat of butter, and joined them at the table.

"Coffee?" Elspeth asked, lifting the carafe.

"Please." She poured me a cup, and I watched the fragrant steam rise. "Thanks, Elspeth. It's still hard to believe, isn't it? Like we're inside of one of our own scripts."

Elspeth traced a pattern on the tablecloth, her expression thoughtful. "I still remember doing his makeup yesterday. He didn't seem tense at all, just friendly and smiling as always. He said he was impressed by my artistry."

"Garrett was a class act," Tim said. "I was actually in a couple of his drama classes at West Vale High School back home."

"What?" Elspeth said, sitting up straight. "You never told us that."

Tim's face reddened. "No. I never told Garrett, either."

We stared at him, and he said, "It was clear, when I got the job, that he didn't know me. I should have just said up front, 'Hey, you probably don't remember me, but I'm Tim Jenson. I took your classes at Vale.' But it was awkward, him not remembering, so I didn't say anything. And then the longer I waited, the weirder it would have seemed to bring it up. So I never did." He looked down at the class ring he wore on his right hand, with a square blue stone. "Apparently he never noticed this, either."

I swirled my pancakes in some syrup, avoiding eye contact. "I guess it makes sense that you didn't tell."

Elspeth said, "Yeah. It's a shame, though. I think he would have liked knowing you were a former student."

"I know," Tim said. He raked a hand through his thick blond hair and looked earnest. "I guess I always thought I'd bring it up sometime soon."

I made a show of enthusiasm about my food so that I wouldn't have to comment. Why would Tim mention his connection now, the day after Garrett's death? If he had kept it secret for two years, what was the point of bringing it up at all? Then again, what did it matter? Tim was the one person who clearly had not killed Garrett.

"Is there any sort of plan for today, or are we on our own?" I asked.

"Derek said we can do our own thing, but that we can't leave town," Tim said.

"I assume that last part came from the police," Elspeth added, playing with one of the flowers in her hair.

"Are they still here?" I asked, surprised.

Tim scowled. "Some of them. Others left with promises to return. I hope they're finished soon."

Elspeth nodded. "Of all the places to have cordoned off as a crime scene, our sweet little chapel!"

I finished wolfing my food and took a few more sips of coffee. Then I stood up, gathered my dishes, and carried them to the rinse bowl next to the sideboard. "I think I'll take a walk," I said. "Get rid of some of this tension."

"Already a little hot out," Elspeth said.

"Better to go in the morning, then." I lifted a hand in farewell. "See you later."

They both waved back, looking suddenly rather listless.

I went out of the entrance nearest the kitchen, an unobtrusive door flanked by flower beds.

Something glinted in the grass to the left of the walkway; I moved closer and saw a jagged shard of glass, perhaps four inches long. I picked it up and scanned for any other pieces. I saw no more glass, but did find a piece of what looked like hammered silver, flat and pretty, but also jagged and broken. "Yikes," I said. I had nothing to put them in, so I turned and set them on the windowsill. I could grab them when I returned.

I moved back to the sidewalk and ran into Renata, who rounded a wall of the south wing, walking briskly. "Oh—be careful," I said. "There's some broken glass around here."

"Glass?" she said. "Where?"

I pointed to the area. "It was there. I think I got it all."

She glanced where I was pointing, then shrugged. "A broken window, perhaps? I think there was a brief storm last night."

"Maybe." I took note of her neat bun, her T-shirt and shorts, her sturdy shoes. "Have you been hiking?"

"Yes." She stretched her arms behind her back. "I like to get in a mile or so before breakfast. Get the blood flowing."

"Yeah, I had the same idea. Something about the view makes me want to always be in it."

Renata moved a bit closer, seemingly willing to talk. "You have an ingenuous look about you, like a girl in a fairy tale. Gretel about to get lost in the woods, or Red Riding Hood off to meet the wolf." She smiled at the final image, and I laughed.

"No, the fairy-tale girl would be Connie, who looks like a perpetual ingenue. My dark hair often gets me cast as a villainous woman."

Renata's face grew serious. "I don't see anything of the villain in you."

"I'm glad," I said, grinning. "Have you eaten? There are delicious pancakes in the dining room."

She gave me another small smile, then bowed at me. "I will seek them out. Thank you, Nora." She swept past me, smelling of roses, and dug out her key to let herself back into the building. Derek kept the doors locked at all times. *For everyone's security,* he said. He had issued us all numbered keys.

I moved down the walkway and headed across a clearing toward a cluster of woods I had not yet investigated. Something in my peripheral vision caught my attention, and I turned to see a girl coming toward me, holding a wicker basket. She was a teenager, perhaps the age of my brothers or even a bit younger. She had reddish hair and dark-rimmed glasses; she wore an orange romper and brown sandals. The basket seemed to be full of motion. I squinted and saw that her little hamper was filled with—animals. By the time she reached me I could tell that they were kittens.

In a surreal taking-stock moment, I thought, *The illusion of Castle Dark continues. A girl with a basket of kittens has wandered across the lawn as though cued by a director.*

"Hey," said the girl.

"Hey. What have you got there?"

She held it up. "Three left. I'm hoping to unload them here so I don't have to consign them to life in a cage at the Humane Society. Want one?"

She swung the basket up toward me and one of the kittens, perched halfway on the edge of the basket, almost fell out onto the ground.

"Oh—careful!" I said. I lifted the kitten in question, a solid-gray animal with a sweet and inquisitive expression, and snuggled it against my chest, where it began to purr. "Hey, little guy," I said to its fluffy face.

"Actually, that's a girl. All three of them are. I had some

boys, but people took those. That's patriarchy for you," she said with a shrug.

I laughed. "I would love a kitten," I said. "I really, really would. But I don't know if they're allowed in my apartment."

She pointed at the giant castle behind us. "You live there? Old Derek wouldn't mind; he's a softie."

"You know Derek?"

"Yeah, sure. He's part of our Wood Glen Community Theater. He directs some of the productions, and he acts in them, too. He directed me in *School of Rock*. I'm hoping he'll cast me in *A Christmas Carol* this winter."

"Oh, a fellow thespian," I said, extending my hand. "I'm Nora."

She shook it with her free one. "I'm Jade." She studied my face; the remaining kittens were looking dangerously interested in jumping out.

"You're about to lose them," I said.

"I'll just set them down. They can't go far before I catch them. As you can see, they have very short legs."

I laughed. The kittens were adorable: all three were grays, but only the one in my arms was solid gray. One had a white bib and white paws, and the other had a white ear and white chops, along with a white tip on her tail. "I've always loved cats," I murmured. "We still have two family cats at home. My little brothers named them Woody and Buzz."

"See, males again," she said with a contemptuous curl of her lip. "The females get neglected. Maybe because their recovery time is longer after a spaying." She pointed at the two who were climbing out of the basket. "These ladies are already spayed, by the way. So no expense to you."

"Where did you get them?"

She shrugged. "My dumb neighbor didn't spay his cat, and she got pregnant. He didn't want the kittens, so I took them after they were weaned. The vet at our shelter spayed them for free because she knows me. My mom kept one of the boys, and my acting coach took two more. I figured I'd see if some other actors wanted one."

The two escapees had suddenly lost their sense of adventure, and sat very close together in the grass, their heads turning rapidly with each new sound. The one on my chest had gone to sleep.

"I'll take them," my voice said.

We stared at each other in surprise. I could hear my sister saying, *You are such a creature of* impulse*! It's going to get you in trouble.*

Jade blinked at me. "You'll take all of them?"

"Yes, all three. They are obviously already bonded."

She threw a dramatic fist in the air. "Well, all right! Women supporting women."

"The feminism is strong with this one," I said in my best Yoda voice.

"You bet," she said. "I'm president of the Feminist Lens club at my school. We've recruited lots of male members to support our cause."

"That's great."

"Yeah. Well, this gives me more time in my morning, so I'm going to go bug my mom at work and mooch lots of food." She knelt down and tucked the two kittens back in the basket.

"Your mom works around food?"

She squinted up at me, tucking a red strand behind her ear. "She owns the Balfour Bakery. I'm Jade Balfour, heiress to the donuts."

A laugh burst out of me. "You crack me up," I said.

She stood up and handed me the basket, grinning. "Tell Zana I said hi. She used to work at the bakery till Derek stole her."

She spoke of Derek with the easy familiarity of an adult. I had seen that before with young actors—the world of the

stage was egalitarian, and it ended up shaping the way that
they lived in the real world, as well.

"I've been enjoying Zana's food very much," I said,
carefully putting the kitten I was holding back with her
sisters.

"Yeah, she's great. Her daughter is in my homeroom.
We hang out together a lot."

"Oh?" I had forgotten that Zana was married, much less
that she had a daughter in high school. Zana looked about
thirty to me.

"Yeah. Her name is Eriza. Because Zana's husband is
named Eric, and they combined their names to make hers."

"Oh, that is lovely."

"Yeah. Anyway, I'm going to bolt. Take good care of the
girls. I might come and visit them."

"You'd be more than welcome."

"I need to visit Hamlet again soon, anyway. Be sure to
ask Derek about how he got Hamlet. It's a funny story."

That was interesting. "I will!"

"Nice to meet you, Nora."

"You, too, Jade." I waved as she made her way back toward the main path. She bent to pick something off the
ground and I realized it was a bicycle. I gaped at her as she
rode away. How had she gotten three kittens here in an
open basket while riding a *bicycle*?

The kittens had nestled together; perhaps the fresh air
had made them tired. "I am very glad I rescued you before
you had to ride home that way," I said.

The fully gray one looked up at me with her wise eyes;
her sisters tucked against her, their eyes closed. "I forgot to
ask her if you had names," I said. "Never mind. I want to
name you, anyway. Now, how to get you inside?"

I wasn't sure how Derek would feel about the actors having pets in their rooms, and my sister's ghostly voice was
being proved correct as I considered the various obstacles

of suddenly owning three cats. With instinctively surrepti-
tious movements, I walked around to the back of the castle.
That distance in itself was a fair morning jaunt. Connie had
shown me the "back lawn" on my third day. The gray-brick
patio contained a stone fountain, presided over by a naiad
carved from white marble. I crept past the trickling water
and exchanged a glance with the nymph before I went to
the back entrance, an unobtrusive door in the gray edifice.
My key would not open this door, but Connie had confided
something in me on that day: *Derek says he understands
people get locked out sometimes. So he hides a key at the
back entrance. This is top secret, Nora! No one is to know
but castle staff.*

She had showed me the loose brickwork at the bottom
of the back wall and how one of the bricks had a false bottom in which resided the back door key. I found the key
now, unlocked the slightly rusty lock, and put the key back
in place. I grabbed my basket of sleeping kittens (even the
gray had finally succumbed) and eased my way into the
back hall. I flipped the dead bolt behind me, then moved
through the shadowy hallway and up some steps to another
door, which led to a large foyer, a match to the foyer that
stood opposite the front door, which was flanked, in a mirror image of the north entrance, by two stairways that led
to the portrait gallery. From this vantage point, it was possible to glimpse the long carpeted hallway that connected
the front entrance to the rear one. I heard someone's footsteps descending from the third floor and voices talking
loudly; I assumed the speakers were members of the police.
I darted to my right, through a doorway into what Derek
called the sunroom, which was essentially a wide porch
that curved around with a view of both the east and south
lawns. The room was indeed full of morning sun. I realized
I could traverse this veranda all the way to its other entrance, in the middle of the main hall, after which I could

dart up the middle stairs to my room. Pleased with this plan, I walked past several chaise longues, where suddenly a figure unfolded itself from one of them and loomed before me, making me shout in surprise.

"Hello, Nora." It was Detective Dashiell, holding one of Zana's coffee cups.

"Oh, hi. I didn't think anyone was in here." I slung the basket to my left side, away from him, and he noted the movement.

"Obviously. And you have a guilty look on your face. What's in the basket?" His face was neither friendly nor unfriendly; I couldn't gauge his mood.

"Do you suspect me of something illegal, Detective Dashiell? Do you think this is a basket full of drugs?"

"Dash. Or John."

"Same question, Dash." I was glaring a little. My hair had fallen into my face and I brushed it aside with my free hand, impatient.

"I suspect nothing; I am merely curious. I thought this room was a quiet place to have my morning coffee, and instead a woman has burst upon the scene with a mysterious parcel, looking rather desperate."

"Desperate" was the word. What if the kittens woke up and started mewing? Would it echo through the whole castle, betraying my actions? "Okay, fine. I am guilty. I don't even know if this is allowed." I slung the basket forward, almost as careless as Jade had been, and revealed my pile of gray kittens.

Whatever he had expected, it wasn't that. First he looked utterly blank, then surprised, then almost joyful. "Well, what do you know?" he said. He bent in half to study them more closely and said, "How did you end up with a basket of cats?"

I sighed. "I went out for a walk. There was a girl out

there holding the basket, saying she wanted to see if anyone in the castle wanted a kitten. I felt like she was being a little . . . reckless with them. So I took them."

"Impulsive," he said, his eyes meeting mine.

"Yes, yes. I always have been. Now I don't even know what Derek would say. So if it's not against the law or anything, I am hoping to hide them in my room until I have a plan."

"Would you like a police escort?" he asked, taking a final gulp of his coffee and putting the cup aside on one of Derek's antique tables.

"That's not necessary," I said. My face grew hot. "I'm sure you have things to do."

"Yes. And one of them is to ask you a couple of questions about your arrival in this room."

"What?"

"Let's walk." He gestured toward the door, and I strode to it with him close behind. We went back to the main hallway, and I moved to the foot of the stairs.

He pointed down the hall. "My crew has blocked off the hall down there," he said, gesturing toward the front entrance, "which means that somehow you came in from outdoors and got here without them knowing. How did you do that?"

I felt ridiculously guilty despite my innocence. "Um—I came in the back."

"I was given to understand that no one has a key to that door except Derek."

Guilt again. I was not supposed to reveal the location of the hidden key. Connie had practically made me take a blood oath. "Um—"

"Nora?"

The kittens were beginning to wiggle. "I have to get upstairs," I said. "Let's keep walking."

"Fine."

He marched alongside me, and we began to ascend the first staircase. I said, "When Connie gave me the tour of this place, she said that Derek had a fail-safe for any staff who might inadvertently be locked out."

"Ah. And what is that method?"

"Under Derek's instructions, she made me swear not to tell. You would have to ask Derek. But let's just say that I used that fail-safe to get in with my kittens, in hopes of being undetected. Instead I got nailed by the fuzz."

His lip twitched, and we turned to climb the third staircase. Finally he said, "That's pretty old-fashioned slang. Nowadays they call us the heat. Among other things."

"Duly noted, Detective."

We were quiet for a while. I peered at the kittens, two of whom were watching us with sage expressions.

My eyes returned to my companion and I saw that he remained in cop mode. He said, "Did you happen to see anyone else use that entrance?"

I shrugged. "No one at the south entrance, no. I came out of the east entrance, and there I just saw Renata taking a morning walk like me."

"But she had no kittens?" There was a glimmer of humor in his eyes now.

"No. She was free of encumbrances. I told her to be careful—" We reached the top of the stairs and began to walk down the dormitory hallway.

"Careful of what?"

"I had noticed some broken glass on the ground. I meant to bring it in and throw it away, but then I got sidetracked and had to come up with this devious—and exhausting—plan," I said, winded from our climb. "Anyway, I left it on the windowsill." I pointed eastward, down the hall. "Huh."

"What?"

"It's just—my room looks out onto the woods, but directly under my window is the south lawn. Somewhere down there is the fountain and the back door."

"Yes."

"But Garrett's room down there—" I pointed. "It's at the end of our hall, and his windows actually face two different lawns—the south and the east. You saw it. He mentioned his amazing view once."

"Okay. Why is that significant?"

I handed him the basket and dug in my pocket for my key. "I don't know if it's significant. I'm just thinking out loud. But remember that his window was open? And I found broken glass on the east lawn. What if it's right under Garrett's window? I found some metal, too, or something like silver. Just a piece."

"So you think it's a piece of the window?" he asked, scratching the ears of an appreciative kitten. Her purr was still a kitten purr, shaky and uneven.

"The window seemed intact. And the glass that fell was too thin to be window glass. What if someone threw something out of the window? Something that shattered?"

He was interested in this. He pointed the basket at me. "If someone wanted to get rid of something in the room, why not just take it with them? They were gone before you got there, right?"

"Hang on." I opened my door, took the basket from him, and went into my room. I walked swiftly to the elevated platform and set the basket on the bed. The kittens peered over the side, curious.

Returning to Dashiell, I said, "The thing is—it was very dark. We turned on a light in Garrett's dorm, but we didn't walk around. We were nervous, and we went back to Connie's room to call you." I pointed at my west wall. "I have that little bathroom and that little kitchenette. I guess Garrett does, too, although I didn't really study the layout of his space. Someone could have been there." I shivered and rubbed my arms. "They could have left while we were in Connie's room."

He thought about this, staring at his shoes. "Assuming they were downstairs with the rest of you while Derek briefed you, they had very little time to get to Garrett's room and do their ransacking."

"They had about ten minutes. Connie and I were talking to Derek, asking if he was okay. Connie was doing most of the talking; I was just standing there."

He looked up at me. "You were in shock. How are you doing today?" He had a way of focusing on a person when he talked that was both gratifying and discomfiting. He had tamed his hair, and he had shaved, as well, although I noted a spot that he had missed, right near his ear.

"Better," I said. "Thank you." I looked back at my bed, where the kittens had found their way out of the basket and walked around on the comforter as though they were exploring the surface of the moon. "Those three will be a nice distraction."

He looked at his watch. "Your secret is safe with me. I'm going to go investigate your theory. You say you put the glass shard on the windowsill?"

"Yes. To the left of the door."

"Thanks, Nora." His smile was a little bit crooked. "Enjoy your contraband."

He walked swiftly down the hall, pausing at Garrett's room to study something on the door. Even from a distance he looked tall.

I went back into my room. The three cats sat in a peaceful cluster in the center of the bed. The sky had turned darker; rain was coming. The gray cats, juxtaposed with the metallic sky, brought sudden inspiration.

"Oh, my goodness! You are my little Brontës!"

I knelt in front of the bed and gently scratched their tiny

heads. I touched the nose of the solid gray one, who was fluffier than her sisters. "You're Emily, of course. You're gray as the Yorkshire sky, and your shaggy fur captures the wildness of the moors." Then I looked at the one with the clean white bib and four tidy white paws. "You're Charlotte. Jane Eyre was always such a neat, quiet person." I turned to the third kitten, with her white ear and white chops that gave her a rather comical air. "And that leaves Anne. You're my little Annie."

They seemed pleased with the names, but even more pleased with my bed. Emily stretched out to her full length (which wasn't very long), and I watched her little belly go up and down as she relaxed into slumber. The other two stayed where they were, heads together, eyes closed.

"Okay, promise not to pee," I whispered. "I'll see about getting some equipment."

CONNIE OPENED HER door wearing a tangerine blouse that made her look like a sunbeam. She raised her brows. "You look urgent. What happened?"

"I need to tap into your well of creativity. We're not supposed to leave town, but there are some things I desperately need. And also, no one can know that I need them."

"Intrigued," Connie said, smiling.

"Can you keep a secret?"

Her face looked uncertain. "Does this have to do with—?"

"No! God, no. This is my own personal secret."

"Okay, what?" She leaned in, her blue eyes sparkling. "I know. You slept with that cop!"

"*Connie*. No." I took her hand and led her across the hall, into my room, and up to my bed. The Brontës were still asleep, their little bodies sprawled in a luxury of exhaustion.

Connie was about to squeal, so I said, "Shh."

She covered her mouth, then uncovered it and whispered, "They're so sweet!"

"I didn't go out looking for them. Jade Balfour came by with all of them in a basket."

"Oh, Jade. She's priceless. I was in a play with her in the local community theater. We have to get you involved in that."

"Yeah, well, she was holding them and sort of swinging them around, and it made me nervous. I just said I'd take all of them."

She bent low to study the tiny forms. "I love them."

"I smuggled them up here. I'm worried because I don't know what Derek would say, and I don't have anything for them! No food, no litter, no toys. But there are police at the door, and we're not supposed to stray too far."

Connie smiled. "No problem. You came to the right person. We can fix this without even leaving the third floor."

"What? How?"

"Come with me," she said.

She left the room and I followed her, carefully closing my door behind us. She went down the hall, almost as far as Garrett's room, which sat right across from Elspeth's costume room.

Next door to the costume room was Elspeth's actual room; Connie knocked on the door, and Elspeth opened it a crack. "Yes?" she asked.

"Hey, El. Is Oliver around?" When Elspeth's eyes flitted to me, Connie said, "We have a reason for asking."

"Well, come in, then," Elspeth said. She flung back her door, and I saw a room similar to mine, but draped in a way only an imaginative costumer could create, with midnight blue curtains and a blue-green patchwork quilt on the bed. Suncatchers hung in all her windows, and even in the grayness, the room glittered with refracted light. A giant armchair sat in front of her windows, and in this was a very large marmalade-colored cat. His face was majestic and pleased with life, and he eyed me with a mild distrust.

"This is Oliver," Elspeth said in an indulgent tone. "We've been together ten years, haven't we, Ollie?"

"He's gorgeous!" I said. "Can I pet him?"

"Sure. He would love it."

I walked forward and knelt in front of the big cat. His face was still wary, but when I started scratching his ears, he relaxed into the pleasure of it, squinting at me in a friendly manner. His purr, when it started, was as loud as a motorcycle. We all laughed, but Oliver ignored us.

"Does Derek know?" I asked.

Elspeth shrugged. "I've never mentioned him. I don't know if Derek has figured it out. At first I felt bad, cooping up Ollie in here. But actually he's got a nice amount of roaming space. I can keep the door open to the costume room, and suddenly it's like two full apartments. And then see that closet over there?"

I looked where she was pointing, at a closet next to her bathroom door. "That's one of the many secret passages. It goes along this back wall, across the hall to a little storage room right in front of Garrett's room. So between my room, the costume room, and the hidden passage, Ollie has a lot to do. He's caught mice in there."

"Ew," I said.

Connie knelt down and played with Oliver's long tail. "The reason I needed to introduce him to Nora is that she has unexpectedly ended up with her own secret. And she needs supplies. Litter, food, maybe some toys."

Elspeth's eyes lit up. "Show me!" she demanded.

We left her room, closing in the half-sleeping Oliver, and ran giggling down the hall to my room, where we showed Elspeth the kittens. "Oh, my *Lord*!" she cried. "I forgot how small they can be. Ollie was just three pounds when I got him. How did they end up here?"

I told her the story, and she nodded her approval. "They'll be happy as clams, especially with one another to play with. If need be, we can arrange playdates with Ollie." She sighed. "Oh, this is an antidote to the sadness."

"Agreed," I said.

"What will you name them?" Connie asked.

"I already have! They're all female, and gray, and I saw them against that cloudy sky and said, 'You're the Brontë sisters!'" I pointed at each cat. "Charlotte, Emily, and Anne."

"That's perfect!" Connie said.

"They're darling," Elspeth told me. To my surprise, she spent a moment unwinding the white cloth flowers from her hair; they were little blooms, all affixed to one slender string. "Here's the first thing they can play with," she said. "It will look like butterflies flying through the air when you wave it around. They'll go nuts." She tossed it on the bed.

"Elspeth, that is so sweet of you. Thank you!" I said.

She smiled at the tiny sleeping felines. "I'd like to be their toy supplier. It will give me a reason to visit." She clapped her hands and said, "Now, to get you set up with a litter box!"

BY NOON THE cats were getting familiar with the space. They had a little cardboard box full of litter (to which I had introduced them all several times), a "toy box" with about five kitten toys that Elspeth said Ollie no longer played with, and bowls of food and water. "You can get them Kitten Chow soon enough, but it's not going to hurt them to eat the adult food for a while," she said.

I thanked her extravagantly and she insisted that "Aunt Elspeth" would always be ready to help. We laughed, and then Connie wandered in, holding a crown.

"I like this one, Elspeth."

"What's happening?" I asked.

Connie shrugged. "Derek is toying with a new script idea, focused on a royal family and their servants."

Elspeth petted Connie's hair, her expression indulgent and motherly. "He's got Connie pegged as his princess, which makes sense. She looks like a Disney cartoon."

Connie smirked. "Anyway, he asked Elspeth to come up with some sort of headdress that suits me and that looks— what did he say?—modern but traditional."

"No, he said classic with a modern twist."

"Oh, right," Connie said.

Elspeth clapped her hands. "Okay, let's go to the costume room and play."

Connie looked at me. "Do you want to come, Nora?"

I shook my head. "In all honesty, I'm starving. I'm going to hunt around for some lunch."

They waved and moved down the hall, Connie chattering happily in Elspeth's ear.

It was a dreamlike moment: Connie's blond hair glinted in the dim hallway light, and the gold crown glimmered in her hand. Tall Elspeth looked like a lady-in-waiting for some historical royal, and the wood panels in the middle of the walls looked antique enough to be from just about any era. Just for an instant, I once again had the sensation that I was being drawn into some elaborate illusion, that everyone around me was playing a part, that I was somehow being duped, deceived, lured into a web of intrigue in a remote castle where I would not be able to run for help. . . .

Connie and Elspeth disappeared into the costume room, and I shook my head. I'd read too many book jackets, performed in too many plays. Real life wasn't full of intrigue, at least not all the time.

I just needed a bite to eat. I thought of something my brother Luke had said once, as he worked at my parents' kitchen counter, creating, with lunch meats and cheeses, what he had assured me was a masterpiece. He had contemplated me with the eyes of a philosopher. *There is no ill that a really good sandwich can't cure, Nora.*

So far I had never proven his theory wrong.

7

Hamlet's Castle

I FOUND ZANA IN the kitchen chatting with Bethany, who looked casual in a pink tank top and a pair of white shorts. A pair of sunglasses sat on top of her pouf of red hair.

Even in the gray light the kitchen was a beautiful place. It was dominated by a giant white stone fireplace, flanked by walls tiled with white and ocean blue. A huge farmer's table sat in the center of the room, and white marble-look counters dominated two other walls. Zana was unpacking a bag that sat on the table. Bethany lifted her hand in a friendly wave.

"Hi, Nora," she said. "I just dropped off a few groceries Zana needed. I guess you guys are sort of on lockdown, huh?"

"I'm surprised they let you leave the castle."

"They did a fair amount of interrogating. But I showed them my driver's license, and they saw how close we live, so they just said not to leave Wood Glen." She gave an elaborate shrug. "And then I came back here with a bag of groceries. I don't suppose that looks suspicious, although poor Tyler is waiting in the car, and the cops were giving him the evil eye when I came in."

Zana nodded, her face sympathetic. "You should go. Don't make that boy sit out there all alone."

Bethany ran a hand through her pretty hair and then sent a beseeching look to Zana—probably a well-rehearsed expression. "You're right. Can I bring him a sandwich, Zana?"

"Sure. We've got plenty. Let me pack you a bag." She went to one of the giant counters and began to tuck things inside a small tote for Bethany and her husband.

I studied Bethany. "Where's Tyler waiting?"

Her gaze moved to me. "What?"

"I mean, which entrance did you come in? I only ask because I know they're being super strict about people entering. I got the third degree myself when I came back from my walk. Did you come in the back by the fountain?"

Bethany's eyes slid away. "No, we didn't. He parked in the driveway near the east door. I used my key there."

"Does Tyler know about the back entrance key?"

This question seemed to upset Bethany; even Zana looked at me over her shoulder, her mouth an O of surprise.

"I'm just curious because the police asked me about that entrance today, and I didn't feel I had the right to give them the information. I told them they had to ask Derek."

"So?" Bethany asked. Her voice was a bit frostier than usual.

"So I'm just wondering how many people actually know about that key. That is—how secure is the castle, really? Could a stranger have come in and hurt Garrett last night?"

Bethany folded her arms. "My husband does know about the key in the brick, if that's what you're asking. But Tyler wouldn't tell a soul, so no need to worry about that." She lifted her chin in a defiant gesture. "They could have used Tyler here that night. He's really good at martial arts, and he could have taken on whoever it was. He accidentally broke one of our chairs once when he was showing me a karate move. He doesn't even know his own strength." The final comment pleased her immensely.

I studied her pretty face. "But he was here. He brought your jacket."

She shrugged. "I mean, he should have been here when some criminal was stalking Garrett. He just dropped off my jacket and left. Remember how cold it was last night? I texted him and asked if he'd stop by. He didn't mind; he likes coming to the castle. He pretends he's a knight. Anyway, the back entrance doesn't matter," she added, putting her hands on her hips and tossing her head in a dramatic way. "It's obviously a stranger who killed Garrett. Any one of the Inspectors could have let him in any number of entrances. We give them free rein of the castle, remember."

This was true, and yet the evening before we had all instinctively assumed otherwise, hadn't we? Our suspicions had been focused on one another.

Zana adjusted her glasses on her nose and looked at me. "What's bothering you, Nora? You seem to be brooding over something." She had finished wrapping a sandwich, and she handed it to Bethany.

I shook my head. "I'm starting to be paranoid, I think."

"Anyway, I've got to be going," Bethany said. "Thanks for the food, Zane. Let me know if you want me to make any other deliveries." She waved at us both and darted out the door.

I turned back to Zana. "Did you go home, too?"

She shook her head. "No, I stayed here last night. I have a little room across the hall for the nights when we have evening events that Derek wants catered. Sometimes it's easier, after I finish cleaning up, to just crash here. My family is used to it."

"I heard you had a daughter."

She stiffened. "Where did you hear that?"

"Jade Balfour."

She relaxed. "Oh, that kid. She and Eriza get up to the craziest things together."

"That's a beautiful name. I think it's very romantic."

Zana shrugged, smiling. She pushed her glasses up on her nose. "We had our moments when we were young."

"When you were young? I didn't even believe that you had a daughter when Jade told me. You look like a kid."

"I got married at twenty-one," she said.

"Well, you look great. And I hope to meet your daughter one day."

Zana nodded. "She's here once in a while. She's helped me with some of the bigger events, she and Jade both."

"Do you mind if I take some of this delicious food?"

"It's for all of you. I'm not the hostess. I'm the paid cook." She said this lightly as a joke.

"Well, great. Thank you. Something about this weather, or the stress, is increasing my appetite. You'd think it would be the other way around."

"No, that sounds about right," Zana said. "Stress affects everyone differently. I've been kind of hungry myself, though."

She handed me a plate with a sandwich and some chips. "Drinks are in the fridge," she said.

"Thanks." I opened the large stainless steel refrigerator and found a diet soda, then went into the dining room and sat at the giant table by myself. While I ate, I thought about the last day or so in the castle and how unlikely it all was. Perhaps one of the reasons I didn't feel a constant sadness about Garrett's death was that it didn't feel real. Sure, I had seen him lying there, but afterward I saw nothing. Perhaps my fragile state of mind was best revealed by the fact that I kept pursuing this idea in my head: Detective Dashiell had led me away. I didn't see the stretcher leave. What if it had been an elaborate hoax? What if Garrett was still in the castle, hiding out in a different room?

Tim appeared in the doorway, wearing a bike helmet.

"Need to unload some stress?" I asked, cracking a potato chip in half.

He nodded. "You look a little stressed-out, too, Nora. Do you mind if I say something?"

Usually when people prefaced a comment with something like that, it was a strong indicator that they were about to say something inappropriate. I shrugged. "Sure, go for it."

"Derek showed me your audition tape. The one you did in the city, but that you essentially used for your audition here. It was amazing, Nora."

My face grew hot. "Well—thanks."

"You are a natural actress, but your singing was beautiful. It was like your soul came out in your music."

His face was so earnest, it was almost childlike. "Tim, that is such a sweet compliment. Thank you."

"The only reason I bring it up is, I wonder if you know that there's a piano in the castle."

I sat up straighter. "Really? Derek never mentioned—"

He nodded. "I doubt he thought of it. No one ever plays it, and Derek thinks of it as a prop. But I think it's tuned. It's a gorgeous thing, a big old Steinway that he got at an estate auction. He told me he paid more to move it than he did for the piano itself."

Now I was almost drooling. To have my hands on a keyboard again! It had been so long. . . . "Where is it?"

"It's in the second-floor lounge—do you know where that is?"

"No—I thought the second floor was kind of off-limits. The owners' bedrooms and stuff."

"Get Derek to give you a tour. It's terrific. Some of my

favorite spots in the castle are up there." He adjusted his helmet strap and sent me a charming smile. "Anyway, you seem like someone who could de-stress through music. Just ask Derek if it's okay."

"I will. Thank you, Tim."

He waved and disappeared through the kitchen.

Zana poked her face in a moment later. "I eaves-dropped," she said. "I didn't know you were a singer! And a pianist! Do you take requests?"

She was serious. I laughed, embarrassed. "I—I never played that way. I just grew up playing the piano, and it's been like second nature to me. When I was preparing to audition for shows, I could be my own accompanist and it helped me to be less nervous. Sometimes they let me play the piano in the audition, too."

"Seriously, will you play for me? This sounds weird, but I've never known a musician. I've always admired it, the ability to just pull a song out of an instrument, especially something as big as that piano he has up there."

"You've seen it?"

"Oh, yes. It's gorgeous."

"I have to find this piano." I stood up and wiped some crumbs off the tablecloth and into my hand. I transferred these to my plate and carried it into the kitchen. Zana followed and took it out of my hands. "Just go. I'll do this. But I'm serious. I want a song."

"Okay, you've got it," I said. "Do you know where Derek is?"

She shook her head. "Not sure. Mostly at this time of day he's either in his office on the first floor or his office in his apartment. I'd check one of those."

"Got it. Thanks."

I left the dining room and turned left in the main hall-way, moving past the drawing room, the conservatory, and the library. At the south end of the hall, across from the sunroom, where I had been caught in the act by Detective Dashiell, there was a small room with big windows on two sides and a floor-to-ceiling white bookshelf on another. The only furniture in the room was a giant wooden desk that faced the door, on which was a placard that read: CASTLE OFFICE. The room was empty.

I went to the large staircase and ascended to the second floor, an unknown territory. I knew which room was Derek's, because Connie had pointed it out. It was at the other end of the hall. Meanwhile I passed intriguing-looking rooms: in one I glimpsed a pool table; in another what looked like a giant birdcage; in still another what must have been a little theater. How had Derek *paid* for all of this?

Halfway down the hall was a marble-floored anteroom to what looked like a little ballroom. There sat the piano. I gasped and moved forward without conscious thought. I reached the instrument and touched its polished surface. It *was* a Steinway, a very old one that had obviously been refinished. The rosewood glowed a brownish red, and the ivory keys, though slightly dusty, made a beautiful sound when I played a chord. "Oh, exquisite," I said.

Then I backed away. I couldn't play it without permission, and suddenly it was imperative that I find Derek.

I went back to the hall, though the piano felt like a magnet that wanted to pull me into the marble foyer. I marched down the red-carpeted runner until I reached the room that was Derek's. My visit here felt like an intrusion—what if he was sitting on his bed or taking a personal call?

But I needn't have worried; Derek's door was open, and when I peered inside, I saw what looked like another office: a plush one with maroon-colored walls and an expensive-looking Persian rug on the floor. Hamlet lay on the carpet, flat as a black crocodile. Derek was studying some papers on his desk; he lifted what looked like a large photograph. I thought I caught a glimpse of a man with reddish hair, and then I knocked.

"Derek?"

His face smiled and looked pleased, but his hands gathered the papers hastily and shoved them into a manila envelope, which he then slid hastily into a drawer. The disconnect between his placid features and his urgent gestures disoriented me for a moment. "Nora! What a nice surprise. What can I do for you?"

"I'm sorry to bother you—"

"Don't be silly! Come in. You've never seen my apartment, have you?"

I had not. Derek led me on an impromptu tour, and I realized that Connie was right—the second-floor residences were not like the "dorms" on the third floor. These were actual apartments, and Derek took me down a hallway that branched off into a small kitchen, two bedrooms, a full bath, and his office/living area, which he had wisely located at the entrance. It was an attractive space that was adorned with the antiques that he loved so well and that looked so perfect in the setting of a castle wing.

"It's beautiful," I said. "You have such an eye for good things." I stood admiring a beaded Victorian lamp, brilliant with color and adorned at its center with a bright blue peacock. "And you have a flair for decorating. Really, Derek."

I smiled into his handsome face, and he gave me a casual one-armed hug. "Thank you. I appreciate that. And may I say that you fit in very nicely here in the castle."

"Thanks. Until yesterday evening, I was really having a lot of fun."

He grew solemn. "You will again. Time heals."

"I don't feel bad for me. Just for Garrett and the people who loved him."

"Yes." We had reached his living area again, and Derek

gestured to a plump cocoa-colored couch. "Have a seat. What was it that brought you here today?"

I sat down, and he sat beside me. Hamlet left his spot on the carpet and strolled over to set his giant head on the couch between us. I laughed and scratched his ears. "Someone told me I should ask how Hamlet came to live here."

Derek pointed at the dog. "Look at him! He wears all black. His name is Hamlet—where does he belong but in a castle?"

"True." I kept watching Derek, and he finally relented.

"Well, there is a story. About three years ago I was dating a woman who loved animals. Her old dog had died, and I thought it would be a great surprise to get her a dog for her birthday."

"Ooh. Always a risk."

Derek hmmphed, then said, "I went to the Animal Care Center in town. They had quite a few puppies, and there was one enclosure that held Hamlet there and a couple of his siblings. Little black Lab puppies or a black Lab mix— we never have quite figured out ol' Ham's parentage."

"And you picked Hamlet."

"Oh, no. Hamlet picked *me*. He literally made eye contact with me, then walked to the glass partition and put his big paws on the divider. I swear he acted like he knew me." He grabbed Hamlet's jaw and shared a look of love with his dog. "I said I'd like to see him, the attendant took him out, and we bonded right away."

"That's wonderful."

"So the plan was I would kind of socialize him for a while and then surprise Linda on the big day. I was still getting the castle ready back then, and I had a lot of work to do; Hamlet helped me with it all. He couldn't have loved it more, even though he was so tiny. He just looked right at home in this place from the start."

"So when her birthday came?"

He shrugged and smoothed the sleeves of his blue cotton shirt. "I gave her a necklace."

I laughed.

"We had started to cool toward each other, anyway," he admitted. "I realized that I couldn't necessarily see Linda as part of my future, but I could definitely see Hamlet there."

I patted Hamlet's head with new affection. "Derek, that is beautiful. Thank you for telling me the story."

"Sure." He leaned forward and looked into my face. "But there's something else that brought you here."

"Why do you—?"

"There's a certain gleam in your eye. You look like a woman on a mission."

I straightened in my seat. "You're intuitive." I paused. "Tim happened to tell me that you have a piano. I don't think you ever mentioned that."

His brows rose and his face grew bright. "That's right, you *play*! I never thought of that Steinway as an actual musical instrument—more like a gorgeous antique, which it is, and a perfect prop for visitors to gawk over. But it works, Nora. It's in tune. I would love to hear you play it!"

I smiled. "I have to admit, since Tim mentioned it to me, I've been dying to get my hands on it."

"Let's go!" Derek said. He jumped up again and took my hand, practically dragging me off the couch in his enthusiasm. "This way," he said as we left his apartment and began jogging down the main hall in the direction that I had come.

We reached the piano, which seemed to glow even more than it had before.

Derek gestured. "Go ahead. What would you like to play?"

I sat down on the green-velvet-padded bench and ran my fingers lightly across the keys. I thought of what Zana had asked me. "Do you have any requests?"

He grinned at me; like Tim, he looked very youthful when he smiled. Perhaps everyone did. "I'll be making a list—you can count on that. I'm trying to think of something for Garrett. Something in his memory." He paused, looking at his feet, then snapped his fingers. "Got it. He loved that song 'You'll Never Walk Alone.' It was from some musical—"

"*Carousel,*" I said.

"But he also liked it because he follows this British football club, Liverpool FC. It's their theme song. It got him really choked up when he heard it."

"I know the song. I did *Carousel* in high school."

"Sing it, Nora. I'd love to hear it."

I bowed my head, already excited at the idea. "Let me find some sheet music for it on my phone." I did a quick search, found the music, and did some sight-reading, letting the melody come back to me. I played some introductory chords to warm up, and Derek ran to the lounge and brought out a chair so that he could be my audience of one. "This is perfect," he said. "Music in the castle! Never mind the royalty idea. I'm going to write this into the next script. You'll be an eccentric Broadway star or an itinerant musician."

I laughed. "Okay, here goes." I played the introduction, and my fingers began to feel the music while my voice ventured into song. The piece began tentatively, quietly, offering hope to the listener and comfort to the unquiet heart. Then the volume increased, the intensity escalated, as the message became one of courage while facing the storm. As I always did, I became lost in the song, sailing into the high notes while keeping control of the overall message.

Innocently or intuitively, Derek had positioned the piano for the most perfect acoustics—in a spot that allowed melody to fill the entire main hallway, where it bounced off the marble walls and created a full, powerful sound.

I closed my eyes after a while, sure of the chords and invested in the tune, until I soared into the final high note and the hushed last word.

My eyes had filled with tears; I opened them to see not only Derek but John Dashiell, who stood at his side. Both men were staring at me with stunned expressions. I wiped the wetness from my cheeks and said, "I got a little carried away."

Derek shook his head. "It was amazing, Nora. Just beautiful. I hope Garrett heard it, wherever he is."

Dashiell said nothing, but his eyes hadn't left my face. I sent him a tentative smile, and he sent a brief smile back. Then he turned to Derek. "Sorry to interrupt, but we've had an incident."

Derek stiffened and looked fearfully at Dashiell. "Is this regarding Garrett—?"

Dashiell shook his head. "No. Something else."

Derek stood. "Nora, thank you so much. Play as often and as much as you want. I'll catch up with you later." The two men walked away, talking in low voices.

I stared at the piano, still emotional from the song and shaken by the expression on Dashiell's face. What had happened? Had someone else been murdered? But he had said it had nothing to do with Garrett. That it was "something else."

It was none of my business. Yet my mind darted here and there, examining possibilities. Did it have something to do with the "private matter" that Derek said Dashiell had been investigating before Garrett's death? Why in the world would he need a police presence at the castle?

Despite my affection for my new residence, I felt mildly resentful that Derek hadn't hinted at my interview that police were on the premises. But of course then I wouldn't have taken the job. . . .

Connie's face suddenly appeared before mine. She sat

down next to me on the piano stool and hugged me. "Elspeth and I heard you upstairs. I didn't know you could sing like that, Nora! We should be singing show tunes together every day!"

I grinned. As usual, Connie's irrepressible excitement was impossible to resist. "We could sing a show tune now if you want."

"I want!" she yelled up at the ceiling. "But how to decide? I guess we should pick a duet. You know what I did in high school? *Annie.* You know that song "I Don't Need Anyone but You?"

"Oh, it's just perfect. Let me find the music. That one's certainly a more up-tempo choice and happier, too."

"But that song you sang, Nora—it was inspiring. Elspeth and I were crying, and we were a floor away."

I swiped around on my phone. "Well, thanks. Here we go. Ooh—let me practice for a minute, Connie."

I set my phone on the music stand and limbered up my fingers on the introduction. "You can peer at my screen and see the lyrics, too," I said. "Which part are you?"

"You be Daddy Warbucks. I was Annie, and I still remember the part."

I turned to look into her blue eyes. "You were Annie? That's so cute."

She shrugged and smiled. "I think it was my favorite part ever."

"Okay, here we go."

We stumbled through the song, harmonizing perfectly in parts, falling apart in others, and enjoying ourselves throughout. At the end we faced each other with folded arms, pretending to be Annie and her new father, and then we burst into laughter. Connie wiped at her eyes. "I think we need some practice."

"I'm happy to practice every day! Look at this *piano,* Constance."

"Constance, huh? Playing a Steinway made you feel all formal."

I sighed, my hands still on the keys. "I should go check on the Brontës."

"Yeah. Make sure they're not tearing up your room with their tiny claws."

"Absolutely. So why can't I move?"

She slung an arm around me. "Because you need to play one more song for Connie. Derek told us all about your great *Evita* audition. That's why I was so excited to see you on the day you came out. We knew in advance that you were super talented."

"You are all doing wonders for my wounded ego."

"So would it hurt too much? Or will you play me that song 'Don't Cry for Me Argentina'?"

"I did grow to love that number, getting ready for my audition. But it hurts, I have to admit, knowing another woman will be singing it onstage every night in just a few weeks."

Connie confronted me with a frank blue gaze. "How many does the theater seat?"

"Hmm? Uh—I don't know. About three hundred?"

She sniffed. "Not that special. Will that woman ever get to sing the song in a *castle*?"

I grinned. "No, she won't. Okay, you've convinced me."

"Good." She got up and walked to the chair Derek had vacated, then closed her eyes. "I'm ready."

After a deep, calming breath, I began to play and sing. Once again, I closed my eyes and felt my way into the music, and once again, I finished with tears on my face.

I opened my eyes and looked at Connie, who was also crying. "Did I mention that I get emotional when I sing?" I joked.

She shook her head. "If you can't feel the song, you can't do it justice. It was perfect."

"Thank you, Connie. This was really nice. Tim said it would be good therapy, and he was absolutely right."

I turned on the stool and saw that I had one more audience member: Hamlet sat like a sphinx in the shadow of a hallway pillar, staring at us with his dark eyes. I wondered if he had been there for the entire concert and whether he had followed Derek and me from the start or if he had been drawn by the sound of music.

He turned and blended into the shadows, and despite Connie's happy chattering beside me on the bench, I felt a sudden chill of loneliness.

8

Subplots

THE BRONTËS WERE not on the bed, nor were they immediately apparent anywhere else. Nervous, I checked my kitchen, bathroom, and closet. I looked under my dresser and desk; I was starting to fear that they had somehow gotten out when I glanced at the long red curtains that flanked my windows. The one on the right was twitching slightly. I moved swiftly to the curtain and pulled it back to find Emily halfway up, stuck on like Velcro with her sharp kitten claws, and Charlotte stuck on in a similar fashion about six inches from the floor. Only little Annie remained on the carpet, but she looked up admiringly at her sisters and meowed some encouragement.

"Now, see, this is what I was afraid my boss would object to if he found out I had kittens—shenanigans like this could get us all kicked out, Emily Brontë." I removed the tiny claws one by one and succeeded in detaching fluffy Emily from the thick drape. I set her on the floor, then removed Charlotte, giving her a similar sermon. I scooped all three of them up and brought them to the bed, where I let them leap around in quest of one of Elspeth's feathery cat toys.

Eventually they stopped jumping, and I sensed that they were tired. I checked to see that they had food in their bowl, that they had in fact found the litter box. I hunted out the basket in which Jade had delivered the kittens and tucked them inside for a rest. To my surprise, the plan worked, and they began to groom one another's ears lazily, a sure precursor to a nap.

Flopping on the bed, I lay back, looked up at the ceiling, and took some deep breaths. It had been an eventful day, and it wasn't even dinnertime. I closed my eyes.

My phone rang beside me, jarring me. The ceiling appeared again, and I fumbled for my cell. The caller ID read: Melanie Blake. My mother. Instantly I felt that something was wrong.

I swiped on the phone. "Mom?"

"Hi, sweetheart! How are things going in your new job?"

"What's going on? I can tell from your tone that you have bad news."

"Not bad, just—unexpected and a little scary."

"What is it?" I had bunched up the comforter in my free hand, and I squeezed it hard.

"Lukey had a stomachache, and we took him to emergency."

"Oh, no. What did they say?"

"He has appendicitis. They're prepping him for surgery."

"Oh, God." My little brother. An image of Luke, two years old and sitting all fat and happy in my lap wearing pajamas with bears on them and eating Teddy Grahams, flashed through my mind. "Is he going to be okay?"

"Now, don't panic, hon. They said it was good that we caught it now and everything should be fine. Luke said to tell you not to panic."

I wiped away a tear but laughed at the same time. "Except he didn't say 'panic,' right?"

"No. He said, 'Tell Nora not to be a spaz.'"

"Well, I am freaking out just a little. When is the surgery?"

"Within the hour. I'll keep you updated."

"How long will it take?"

"Between one and two hours, the doctor said. He'll be fine." Her last words seemed to be a way of managing her own anxiety along with mine.

"Okay, well—please check in with me. Is Jay okay?"

"He's hanging in there. You know how they are. Connected at the hip. He's been pacing and talking a lot, but claiming that he's not worried."

"That's Jay." I took a calming breath. "Did you tell Gen?"

"Yes. She was ready to fly in from New York! I told her to stay put and we'd keep her updated. She can FaceTime with Luke once he's feeling better. So can you."

"Yeah, okay. And Dad's all right?"

"Yes. He's been keeping busy. Filling out some forms right now. I should get back and see if the nurse has any updates."

"Okay—thanks for calling, Mom. Please let me know—"

"The minute we know anything. I promise, sweetie." My mother's voice was comforting, despite what must have been her own worry. This had always been the dynamic: she calmed the rest of us down.

"Good, okay. I'll talk to you soon."

We ended the call. Now I felt nervous, unmoored, aimless. I paced around my room for a while, then checked on the Brontës, who were sleeping in a pile of soft fur and sweet pink-padded paws.

I walked across to Connie's room and knocked on her door, but she wasn't there. Restless, I moved down the hall. I passed Renata's room and found her door open. She sat on a chair near her window, looking out at the view with a sad expression. Her body was admirably still while mine jangled with nerves. I must have made a noise, because she turned and spotted me. "Hello, Nora."

I stopped walking. "Hi. Sorry to bother you. I'm just pacing the hall. Burning up some nervous energy."

She stood and glided to the door. "You are nervous?"

"Oh—sort of. I just found out—my little brother is in surgery."

"Oh, I am sorry." She looked it, too; her brows came together in a compassionate frown. "Come in for a cup of tea."

"No. No, thanks. I think the trick right now is to walk the halls like a castle ghost. Get that energy out."

She nodded. "Perhaps that is a good idea. Wait just a moment." She went back into her room and disappeared from view; I saw that the layout of her room was slightly different from mine. It had no elevated platform, but instead a little hallway to the left of the living area that led to spaces unknown. She returned a moment later, holding something in her hand. "Did I tell you that I was once in *Macbeth*?" she asked.

"Oh, yes. A gender-blind production."

She nodded. "Yes, that, too. I was Macduff in that one, if you can believe it. That was a college production. But I'm referring to a later production, in a Chicago theater. I played Lady Macbeth."

"Oh, wow! What a great part."

"Yes." She brushed some of her silky hair behind her shoulder. I realized this was the first time I had seen her with it down, but even so she retained her aura of formality. "I was quite nervous on opening night, as you can imagine. It's a challenging role. I feared I would forget my lines, or miss a cue, or burst into tears."

"I know that feeling."

"My castmate, the woman who played Lady MacDuff, gave me a beautiful pep talk and managed to calm me down. I cannot explain how soothing it was—it almost felt as though she had hypnotized the fear right out of me. And that first performance was perhaps my best."

"That's wonderful."

"But here is why I tell that story. She gave me a talisman. She said it had been hers, but that it was meant to be passed on when people needed it. I wore it on my gown that night and every night."

She held up a glittering brooch in the shape of a crown—probably just a piece of costume jewelry, but lovely nonetheless. It glinted in the light of her overhead lamp. "I pass it on to you now, Nora. It will comfort you, and you can wear it for your next performance here in the castle."

"Renata—that is too generous. This is tied to your memories. It has personal meaning—"

"But as my friend Kate said when she gave it to me—it was meant to be passed on. That's the beauty of it. It blesses the recipient and absolves the giver."

She pressed it into my palm and I looked down at a glittering diadem, about two inches tall and filled with what looked like cubic zirconia stones of crystal and ruby. "It's beautiful. Thank you. It is such a thoughtful gesture."

She smiled at me. "I am certain your brother will be fine. This exchange of goodwill has helped to ensure it, or so goes the legend of the talisman, correct? That it protects from harm."

"I don't know any legend, but thank you. I really appreciate it. I feel like I should give you something."

I was briefly distracted by some trees that bowed in the wind outside her window, in the bright space behind her. When I looked back at her, she was smiling, but her eyes were rather sad. "You already gave me a gift, Nora. I heard you sing today. You cannot know what that song meant to me."

"Oh! Well, I'm glad."

She nodded, a gesture both quiet and wise. "Enjoy your walk."

"Thank you, Renata."

I turned and continued down the hall. I heard her door close softly behind me; I took care to tuck the brooch deep into my pocket so that I wouldn't lose it in some shadowy castle hallway.

At dinnertime we got a group text from Derek:

Pizza in the kitchen, a serve-yourself affair that you can take back to your room if you wish. There will be a short meeting in the great hall at eight; Detective Dashiell will be briefing us on a few things.

Normally I would have found this very intriguing, but my worry over Luke eclipsed my curiosity about whatever Detective Dashiell was going to reveal.

Connie had reappeared in her room by dinner, and we walked down together, chatting quietly while we put pizza on our plates and grabbed soft drinks from the big refrigerator.

"I don't feel like taking this up all those stairs," Connie told me. "Let's just eat in the dining room and we can clean up our crumbs. I don't think Zana is even here right now."

"Didn't Derek include her in that text about the meeting?"

Connie shrugged. "But he has to know she has a life outside this place. She's got a husband and a child. She can't just be here all the time."

"And yet she has a bedroom here, right?"

Connie led the way into the dining room and flopped

into a chair at the big table. "I guess. I don't know exactly what the arrangements are."

I poked at my pizza. "My brother is in the hospital. In surgery."

She dove forward to take my hand. "Oh, *no*! What for? One of the twins who came here?"

"Yes, Luke. The one with the longer hair."

"Why does he need—"

"Appendicitis."

"Well." She studied my face. "That will be okay, Nora. It's a standard operation. My dad had it, and he was laughing and joking the same day."

"I know. I know. I just hate being so far away."

Her eyes squinted with commiseration. "I get that."

We grew quiet as Tim and Elspeth showed up with their own plates and then, to my surprise, Paul and Detective Dashiell.

Paul sat beside me, and Dashiell sat down next to Connie, a seat almost directly across from me. "Good evening, everyone," he said, but he was looking at me.

We all murmured a greeting, and I glanced at my phone. No texts.

It must have looked rude, because Connie rushed to explain. "Nora's expecting an important call," she said.

"Nora," Paul said, "Derek told me that you are the one I heard singing. That was fantastic! Your voice filled the castle."

"Oh—thank you," I said. "Tim suggested it as a way of de-stressing."

Tim waved to me from down the table. "And did it work?"

"It did, for quite a while. Then new stressors appeared." I sent him a halfhearted smile.

"What stress—," Dashiell began, but Zana appeared in the doorway with Jade Balfour and a dark-haired girl that I assumed was Zana's daughter.

"Hey, everyone," Zana said. "I think you all know Jade, right? And my daughter, Eriza?"

We all nodded and waved, even though I had not in fact met Eriza. She was a petite girl with short hair and large eyes; she looked a bit like an anime cartoon.

Zana put an arm around each girl. "These two are dropping me off for the meeting; do you care if I grab them some pizza?"

"Not at all," Elspeth said, sliding one of the pizzas to the edge of the table. "It looks like Derek ordered for an army."

Zana thanked us and lifted the box Elspeth pointed out, presumably to take it in the kitchen and pack some for the teens. She was about to say something when Renata and Bethany entered, talking in low voices. They looked up, and both of their faces registered surprise.

"Wow—a full house," Bethany said. "I thought it was grab and go."

"We didn't want to take two flights of stairs with our food when we could just eat it here," Connie said. "I'll help clean up, Zana."

Zana waved that away, still clutching the pizza box. "No problem. It's good for you all to be together right now. Talk out some of your anxieties."

Connie looked at me, which made all heads turn toward in my direction. I stared down at my plate. Bethany said, "You know what's weird? When Tyler was driving me here tonight, the castle looked amazing. I've never seen it look more beautiful—all stark and dignified against that glorious sunset. Did you all see it?"

"We've been cooped up in here," Tim said, looking moody.

"I saw it," Zana said. "And you're right. The girls commented on it."

"I said it looked like a Disney cartoon," Jade said, meeting the eyes of the adults with her unusual teen confidence.

I realized that her description was the highest honor she thought she could bestow, and Eriza nodded, looking impressed, as though Jade had uttered poetry.

"Anyway, I like to think it's because of Garrett. Some kind of cosmic tribute to him," Bethany said with a dreamy expression.

I stole a glance at Detective Dashiell, who obviously thought that was utter nonsense but was pretending to be thinking about it, like everyone else at the table. He caught me looking at him, and my smile suggested that I could read his mind.

His brows went up, and my phone buzzed. I jumped, tense and wired, and then swiped on the screen. I put the phone to my ear with a slightly trembling hand and said, "Hello?"

"Hey, Spaz." It was Luke's voice, quieter but still utterly disdainful. Relief flowed through my veins.

"Luke? Oh, God. Hang on. Let me go in the hall."

I rose hastily from the table and went into the cool hallway to speak to my brother in private. Derek was just arriving, and he waved at me as he went into the kitchen. Then I was alone.

"Luke? Are you okay?"

"Yeah, considering they sucked one of my organs out of my body."

"But, I mean—your prognosis—"

"Yes, I'm fine. Mom told me to call you so you didn't cry all night and stuff."

"Well, that was good of you," I said, my older-sister-wryness back in place, "because I know you must have so much to do right now."

"I do have an adult coloring book and a stuffed animal fox for some reason and a balloon that says 'Get well.' Those are supposed to help me pass the time. I was hoping I could play video games, but Mom said no."

"Good. You need to relax, not kill things in some virtual world."

"That is relaxing," he protested.

"Is Jay there?"

"Yeah. And he keeps trying to make me laugh on purpose. He's actually trying to murder me or make my wound gush open."

"Do you want me to talk to him?"

"Nah." His voice was indulgent, amused. "It's pretty funny."

"You two," I said. "When will they let you go home?"

"Tomorrow afternoon, they said. I have young, springy skin that is already adapting to the cavity within."

"Are you on drugs?"

"Yeah, some kind of painkiller. It's pretty nice."

"Did you talk to Gen?"

"No, I have to call her next." He sounded suddenly tired.

"Do you want me to call her?"

"Would you, Nor? I think I might take a nap, even though I'm afraid Jay might steal my drugs or harvest my other organs," he said softly.

"Tell Mom to make Jay leave."

"No, he's okay."

"You're tired. Luke? I love you."

"I know. I love you, too," he said, half embarrassed.

"Go to sleep. I'm glad you're fine and I'll talk to you tomorrow."

"Bye, Nora."

I ended the call, then pressed speed dial for my sister, Gen. "Nora?" her voice said, urgent as mine had been. "Is Luke okay?"

"Yeah, I just talked to him. He was going to call you except he started falling asleep during our chat. He sounds good, though."

"Was he being sarcastic?"

"Incredibly."

"I guess he'll survive, then." There was a pause, and I pictured her pretty face, her chin-length reddish blond hair swinging silkily as she moved around her room.

"Were you as scared as I was?" I asked softly.

"God, yes. And feeling so cut off up here."

"Yeah. You in New York, and me in this weird castle in the woods that feels like it's in the Renaissance."

She laughed. "I really want to visit that castle. I'm thinking I might take some time off in fall, come to stay for a while, if your boss will let me. Maybe I'll buy a ticket to be one of the detectives."

"That would be fun. Listen, Gen—there's something you should know."

"Yeah?"

"One of our actors was murdered yesterday."

"What?"

"Yeah. The police are here, and we're shut down until they find out what happened."

"That's terrible! Are you okay? Do Mom and Dad know?"

"I'm okay. And no, I didn't tell them. I don't want them to freak out. And I'm hoping they won't see something on the news. . . ."

"Nora, do you feel safe there? Do you need to quit?" My older sister's voice took on the no-nonsense quality that it tended to have when she was bossing me.

"I don't think I need to quit. I really like the job so far. The police will figure out what happened, and we'll move on. Most of us are thinking that someone came in from outside; Derek will have to improve his security. I mean, there must have been someone out there with a grudge. You don't just stab or shoot someone randomly."

"That's horrifying, though."

"I know. Anyway, I have to go. I was in the middle of dinner."

"Yeah? Like a sit-down dinner with candelabras and stuff?" She sounded a bit starstruck.

"No, like pizza in the dining room. But it is a great setting for eating pizza or anything else."

"Take care. Find a buddy to walk around with, and lock your door."

"I will. Love you, Gen."

We said our goodbyes and I returned to the dining room, where Connie was asking the group if anyone was going to see Garrett's girlfriend. "I have a picture of the two of them that I'd like to return to her. This great shot in front of a waterfall."

No one responded, so Connie shrugged. "I guess I'll give it to her at the funeral." She looked at Derek. "Do we know when that will be?"

Derek shook his head. "No, I haven't received word yet. I'll certainly let everyone know."

Paul exchanged a glance with Detective Dashiell and then with Derek. "Everyone seems to be here," he said. "Maybe we should start the meeting now?"

Dashiell stood; he carried his plate into the kitchen and disappeared. Paul followed him. Derek shoved the last of his pizza into his mouth, ate it swiftly, and stood, as well, wiping his mouth with a napkin. "If you'll all meet us in the great hall in five, that would be great."

He left, and we stared at one another. "Why another room?" Tim asked. "We're all gathered here already. Is there going to be a slideshow?"

We laughed, but our laughter had a nervous tinge to it, and when we assembled in the great hall, we saw that there was a large screen set up.

I sat down on a couch, shocked, and Connie sat next to

me. "What is this?" she whispered. Bethany sat on my other side, looking similarly surprised.

Derek stepped forward. "Paul and I asked Detective Dashiell to let us fill you in on as much as we possibly could so that you felt you were in the loop. Obviously there are some things that the police cannot tell us because it might compromise their investigation, but there are some things that we might be able to help them with. Dash?"

Dashiell stepped forward. "First of all, let me reintroduce myself to all of you, my name is Detective John Dashiell of the Wood Glen Police Department. As you were told by Derek, I was already on the premises when the murder occurred; I was privy to those early moments that are normally lost while people wait for the police to arrive. This has been helpful to my investigation."

He looked around at the people assembled: Paul, Derek, and Zana on one couch; Bethany, Connie, and me on another; Tim, Elspeth, and Renata on chairs near the door. "There are some things that I would like to make clear. First, Garrett carried a prop knife on his gardening belt that was meant to be brandished in an argument that he has over Bethany. The knife is missing; if any of you see it, please do not touch it, but report it to me or any police officer on the premises immediately. I believe I also gave you all my phone number so that you can text me with information. The knife looked like this." He pointed up at the screen, where a picture of a knife like Garrett's glimmered obscenely.

Elspeth raised her hand. "Are you telling us that was the murder weapon?"

Dashiell gave her a bland look. "I am telling you we are looking for it."

This did not satisfy her or anyone else in the room.

"Second," Dashiell said, "we have evidence suggesting that Garrett spent some time in the hidden passage across from the chapel before he went into the chapel and eventually died." A diagram of the chapel hallway appeared on the screen, and Dashiell pointed out what the police believed to have been Garrett's path on the night of the murder. "Therefore, the initial theory that whoever killed Garrett had done so in the chaos of the group traveling from one floor to the next has now been discounted. Garrett may have been assaulted as early as twenty minutes before Nora found him in the chapel."

"Which means that any one of us could have done it," said Connie in a flat voice.

I stole a glance at Tim; he had been the only innocent party, and now apparently he had no alibi.

Bethany looked scandalized. "Are you saying that poor Garrett staggered around for almost a quarter of an hour before he died, without getting help from anyone?"

"Conceivably," Dashiell said.

"Why?" I said. Why would he not have looked for help? Someone could have come to his aid, saved him. . . .

Dashiell's eyes met mine. "It is possible that he was hiding."

One of the women moaned aloud. I understood what she was feeling; the words were so sinister that they were not easy to contemplate.

Dashiell cleared his throat. "At this point what we need from you is to go back over the night of the performance. Think about how things were supposed to go, and then consider anything that seemed amiss. What little things were out of place? What people were not at their stations? What did you think to be odd or off-kilter? I'd like you all to make some notes tonight—we need this information now, while it's still relatively fresh in your minds—so that we can use all of your testimony as pieces of a larger puzzle."

A woman in uniform appeared at the door. Dashiell pointed. "Derek is going to give you all a pad and pen;

when you've jotted down your notes you can give them to Officer Crandall, who will be waiting at the door."

Zana raised her hand. "Are you saying we have to make these notes now? Before we leave?"

"The ideas will never be more fresh in your mind. This is the time," he said. "Do this for your former colleague and friend."

Derek began passing out notepads. The diagram of the chapel hallway remained on the screen.

Dashiell pointed again. "I believe you all know how to access this chamber, which leads both to the chapel hallway and the ballroom on the second floor. I will be most curious to know if anyone in this room saw someone go into this passage, whether it was Garrett or someone else, or if you saw anyone in the ballroom. Consider things that you might have seen and dismissed.

"Finally," he said, and he had our immediate attention because his tone made it clear he had saved something significant for last, "you should know that Derek has given his permission for us to search the castle, which includes all of your rooms. There are police officers in them now, and we would ask that you not return to your rooms until you get the all clear. Thank you."

There was an explosion of responses varying from surprised to outraged; Dashiell managed to ignore these. He moved to the back of the room, and Derek moved to the front. He held up his hands to call for silence.

"Okay, calm down, everyone. I shouldn't have to remind you that our friend and colleague was murdered in this building only yesterday. The police can search whatever they wish, and if we are innocent, we have nothing to fear." He looked around at us, a calming but slightly reproving presence, and the objections faded away. Derek nodded. "A couple more things. First, Father Jim will be here at ten tomorrow morning to say some words of remembrance about Garrett and to bless our chapel. I'd like you all to come."

The room was silent; no one had questions about this.

Derek nodded. "Second, the police have told me that you can now start moving around a bit more freely, but of course you are not to leave Wood Glen, and if you're going out, you should inform the officer who will be posted at the door."

Derek and Paul exchanged a glance. I was struck anew by how similar the brothers looked. Because of our unfortunate conversation topic and the dimness of the library, it meant that they both appeared rather sinister. Derek sighed and said, "In addition, Detective Dashiell has evaluated our fail-safe method of getting in the south entrance. We will no longer be keeping a key in the current hiding place, and we will be changing the locks. If you somehow find yourself locked out, you will need to text someone inside the building."

Renata folded her arms. "So does this mean we are looking at an outside intruder?"

Detective Dashiell spoke from a chair behind us. "We have ruled nothing out. Obviously it's not impossible to imagine that someone could have come in that way, assuming that word of the key got out to noncastle personnel."

"What about the visitors?" Bethany said. "There were ten of them. What if one of them had a secret grudge against Garrett?"

"We're looking into all possibilities," Dashiell answered.

Derek put his palm against his forehead, looking a lot more like Hamlet than his dog did, but I couldn't fault him for the melodrama, since every actor in the room had taken a theatrical pose: Bethany slumped on the couch beside me as though she'd been drugged; Connie sat wide-eyed, a perfect ingenue; Renata still had that queenlike bearing and

looked incomplete without a crown; Tim had adopted a
rather bellicose pose, leaning forward and widening his
shoulders as if to fight off whatever threat existed; Elspeth
nervously braided the gray stripe in her brown hair, making
me think of a long-ago director who had said, *Don't be
distracting with your hands, but do be* interesting *with
them.*

Poor Zana just looked nervous. Paul appeared the most
calm of anyone in the room, although he did keep exchang-
ing those mysterious glances with Derek.

Derek said, "Thanks, everyone. If you can make your
notes now, we can set you free for the evening."

We dutifully hunched over our notebooks and began to
write. I detailed my memories of that evening, the ones I
had already reported to Dashiell right after the murder.
Still, I tried to provide as much detail as I could recall.
When I finished, I looked around and saw that others
seemed to be finished as well.

Derek appeared in front of us once more, offering a
grateful smile. "You can go eat more pizza if you want, but
don't go back to your rooms until Detective Dashiell says
you can." A thought occurred to me and made me anxious.

People stood and began milling around; I went straight
to Dashiell and put a hand on his arm. "Listen," I said in a
low voice. "Is my, uh—*contraband*—going to be in danger
of getting out into the hall?"

His brows rose, and he smiled. "I did happen to warn
Officer Ramirez that there might be other occupants in the
Green Crown Room."

"Thanks." I leaned in and whispered, "Also in the Purple Crown Room. But I only just found that out."

He stared at me for a moment; he seemed to be sup-
pressing an eye roll. "I'll call upstairs," he said, and walked
into the hall, his cell phone against his ear.

"Are you making arrangements to meet later?" asked

Connie, who had appeared next to me and now leered into my face with an exaggerated expression.

"No, I am informing him that I hope his goons won't let out our precious feline friends."

"Oh!" Connie said, upset at the thought. "Well, I hope he's taking care of it." Then she tipped her chin toward the exit. "Come on. They didn't say we couldn't walk around down here."

That was true. I followed her out of the great hall and we hesitated in the doorway. We instinctively avoided going to our right, which would have taken us to the chapel hallway, so we went left. Even on the main floor, the halls were rather dim, and Connie clutched my arm as we walked along.

"Who held your hand before I got here?" I joked.

She shook her head. "I was scared and lonely," she said in a mock-pitiful voice. "But I took turns making people spend time with me. The older women mothered me, and Bethany put up with me. Tim and Derek were good about taking me on outings and stuff." Her face looked suddenly wistful.

I contemplated the hallway as we traversed it. "I'm not interested in either of the drawing rooms. And I don't suppose the sunroom will hold much interest in the nighttime, aside from a long view of an invisible forest and the silhouettes of plants that look like people in the dark."

"Stop trying to scare me," Connie complained.

"I'm not. I'm trying to *avoid* scaring you. What about the library? I've never done more than glance in the big one. Maybe we can sign out some books. I can read Brontë to the Brontës."

Connie giggled. "That is so cute."

We walked across the hall and down a few doors until we reached the library entrance. The room was dim, lit by a lamp in the far corner. We began moving forward, but then Connie put out an arm to stop me. She pointed, and I saw that in a far corner of the room, at a table with an old-fashioned gold library lamp, Zana sat with a stack of books. She lifted one, fanned through the pages, held it upside down, and shook it, then set it aside. She did the same with the next book and the next, as though searching for something within the pages. It was an odd sight, and coming so soon after our grim meeting, a vaguely disturbing one.

Without talking, Connie and I backed out of the room and returned to the hall, moving past Derek's castle office and a first-floor bathroom to the final room on the hallway, what Derek called the meditation room. It was just a comfortable space with plush couches and pillows and a stereo system into which people could plug their iPhones and select any playlist.

Now Connie flipped on a light and we both plopped onto the nearest couch. "What was that?" she asked me. "Was she ransacking the library?"

I shook my head. "She was just—looking in the books. Maybe she left a bookmark in there or something. She told me she takes books out all the time and that the library is the best part of working at the castle."

Connie thought about this, her lips pursed. "I don't know. It looked weird. Like she was casing the joint."

"Come on! It's Zana. She's sweet and nice and your friend. Maybe she used a twenty-dollar bill as a bookmark, and now she needs it back."

Smirking, Connie patted my hand. "Whatever you need to believe, Nora."

We chatted and laughed in the meditation room for twenty minutes or so, and then a uniformed man appeared at the door. He knocked to get our attention. "Everyone is free to return to their rooms," he said, and then he walked away.

"Well, he was talkative," I observed.

Connie yawned. "Ugh, I'll be glad to get upstairs. I just want to crash on my bed and watch TV or read a book maybe."

"And I need to check on my fuzzy children."

We stood up and left the room, wandering back toward the main stairway. "I'll come by to kiss them good night," Connie said. "It will be nice to have someone to kiss good night."

"You talk a lot about romance. We need to get you a dating app, girl."

She yawned again. "We really do. Before I grow old and moldy in this castle, like some sad princess in a fairy tale."

"At least you're a princess and not a troll or a witch or something."

"It would be interesting to be cast as a witch. I think I could have a lot of fun with that."

"You probably could. But we both know—they'd cast you as the princess and me as the witch, because of my dark hair. I've played my fair share of evil characters."

She thought about this as we started up the stairways, our phone lights on. "Did you enjoy it, playing evil characters?"

"Yeah, for the most part, if they weren't one-dimensional, but had some complexity that I could examine in my performance."

"Evil's not that complex, is it?" Connie asked.

We reached the second floor, and a part of me yearned for the piano. We started climbing toward the third floor. "I think it can be. For example, what if the person doing an evil thing doesn't think it's evil? What if they don't think they're evil, either?"

"Like whoever killed Garrett?"

"Maybe. I really can't fathom that at all, how someone could push a knife into another person. But I would assume that if someone did it, then they found ways to justify it."

"Or they felt a lot of hate or anger," Connie said. "Would any other emotion explain it?"

"I don't know. I guess it's good that we don't understand it, though, right?"

We reached our floor and started walking toward our rooms. Connie stopped in front of hers and said, "Because if we understood it, we wouldn't be the sweet, innocent young maidens that we are, right, Nora?"

In the dim hall, her expression looked strange—ironic and almost spiteful.

Surprised, I lifted my phone higher and saw that it had been a trick of the light. Connie's face was as sweet and friendly as always.

"Right," I said. "Good night, Connie."

"Night," she said, and disappeared into her room.

9

Branches in the Wind

THE BRONTËS, I was relieved to find, were all accounted for and playing happily on my bathroom rug. It was a shag carpet with long pieces of yarn, and the kittens would grab hold of a piece and then flop over sideways, kicking out with their tiny feet. I watched this pastime with delight for quite some time, then replenished the food in their bowl, which brought them tumbling over for an evening meal. Grinning, I went to an easy chair that my parents had donated to my new room. *Because you can't just sit on your bed!* my mother had insisted.

She was right. I tucked into the chair and picked up my phone. I had long been in the habit of scrolling through posted auditions and casting calls on a Chicago theater site. I did so now, scanning the possibilities, even as a part of my brain acknowledged that I had just taken a job. But what if that great part was out there and it was waiting for me?

I set the phone down and let my gaze drift over to the kittens. I couldn't imagine telling Derek, who had been under so much stress in the past couple of days, that I was leaving him in the lurch. And what would I tell Connie, my brand-new friend?

A sigh escaped me, and I leaned my head back in the chair. In any case, the police had told us to stay in Wood Glen; who knew how long that stricture would last?

I needed a distraction; with a sudden burst of brilliance, I realized that I had the perfect diversion right next door. I jumped up and left my room, leaving the door unlocked but closed so that all Brontës were safe inside. My bare feet led me one door to the north, where the small library sat, silent and largely uninvestigated by me. I went through the open door (Derek wanted it to be welcoming to all comers, Connie had said) and felt for a wall switch. Soon the room was bathed in warm white light, and the books beckoned.

On closer examination I saw that they had been loosely divided into categories, with sticky notes indicating the genres. I wondered which of the actors had gotten bored on a rainy day and decided to organize the shelves. Floating toward the mystery/suspense section, I rummaged around until I found a book with a delightfully Gothic-looking cover, written by someone named Victoria Holt, and decided it was perfect for my present circumstances. I tucked it under my arm.

Before I left, I was drawn to the only window in the library, which had a view of the west lawn. I wondered if I'd see deer again or if anything at all would be visible in the dark. I pressed my face close to the glass, but nothing was visible aside from the distant undulations of treetops and some scudding gray clouds against a navy sky. All signs pointed to a peaceful night.

I moved to the doorway, switched off the light, and padded back to my room. *My, but that library carpet was soft!* I greeted the kittens (who had the grumpy look of tired babies), tossed the book on my bed, and plopped into my easy chair, where I sent good-night texts to my family. In another impulsive decision, I decided to treat myself to a bath in the shiny white bathtub I'd been admiring but had not yet used, opting for convenient showers. I went into the bathroom and rummaged around in the little closet beside the door. Ten minutes later I was soaking in delicious bubbles created from a bottle that read: *Lavande de Haute-Provence. Lavender something-something.* Connie had said that Derek fluctuated between ridiculously frugal and strangely indulgent.

"I bless you for this indulgence, Derek," I said to the blue-tiled wall.

My eyes closed, and I must have slept. When the room appeared once again, two of the kittens were still playing with the carpet, and one lay fast asleep in the center of the rug. "Oh, my," I said. "Is it bedtime, my sweethearts?"

I stepped out of the tub, dried off, and contemplated myself in the mirror. My face was solemn, but contented. I brushed my teeth and washed my face, then put on a night-gown and floated into the next room, feeling fragrant and utterly relaxed. I turned off all the lights except for the one next to my bed, then tucked myself under the covers and started reading the book I'd selected from the small library of a castle. I grinned at the very idea—it was like a detail from a little girl's imagination.

The Brontës soon decided to join me in the bed, and they climbed up the side of the quilt, creating slight ripping sounds that made me wince. They all found their way to the top of the mattress and sat purring beside me. I showed them the book cover. "Look at this old Gothic classic! See that castle on the front? Apparently it is located in"—I consulted the book jacket—"the wild cliffs of Cornwall. Ooh, that sounds good, right, my Brontës? My gray goddesses?"

They squinted their eyes at me, purring and making dough on my blanket.

I studied the cover. "Why does the heroine always run

from the castle? Doesn't she ever stay and fight? Why not send the young lady to her job as governess armed with mace or pepper spray or something? Unless it's some ghost or monster that's chasing her, right?"

The Brontës didn't answer, but they seemed ready to hear a story. They bundled together; Emily had already closed her eyes. "Did you know that I already love you?" I asked them.

Charlotte licked one of her tidy white paws; Annie smiled up at me with her comical white chops.

"Okay, this is called *Mistress of Mellyn*. Should I read it out loud to you?"

They seemed to be waiting for just that, so I began the story in a soft voice. It started out like any good Gothic tale—a girl who was poor and had to take a job as a governess. *Clearly influenced by* Jane Eyre, I thought. The more I read to the Brontës, the less I was conscious of the kittens and the more I was drawn into Holt's story. How slowly, how insidiously the tension mounted! I had not even realized I was nervous until a branch outside my window clacked against the glass in a gust of wind, and I jumped an inch off the mattress.

The Brontës, now asleep, didn't move a whisker. I settled back down to my novel, but eventually, lulled by the warm sleeping felines and the cozy room contrasted with the eerie sound of the wind, I grew tired, as well. "Until tomorrow," I told the book. I set it on the nightstand and turned out the light.

I WOKE IN darkness and realized I wanted to use the washroom. "Too much water before bed," I whispered to the still sleeping cats. I gently moved them aside so that I could step down, find my slippers, and pad across the floor. Upon returning to the elevated platform, I glanced briefly through my window to see if the gale was still gusting. The tree on the other side of the casement was indeed still bowing and bending in the wind, occasionally tapping the glass as if to get my attention.

At first I thought the noise I heard was in fact the *click click* of branches, but eventually I realized that it was coming from behind me.

From the hallway.

I glanced at the clock on my bedside table, which had glow-in-the-dark hands that revealed it was two in the morning. Nervous but curious, I grabbed my phone and moved toward my locked door. I put my ear up against the cool wood. A sound of a door opening, then closing again. Connie's door. What would make her want to go out in the middle of the night? Could something be wrong?

Another thought struck me. Could she be meeting someone? Did Connie have a *lover* in the castle?

Now I was the one being overly romantic. Still, I was curious enough to peer into the hall. Her door was closed, but sure enough, she was moving down the hallway in the direction of the costume room. "Connie!" I called softly. "What the heck are you doing up at this time?"

Her figure looked strange, sort of bunchy, as though she wore a winter coat. Laughing, I flicked on my phone light, ready to expose her in the glare. I stepped into the hall, closing my unlocked door softly so that the kittens wouldn't escape. "Hey, goofball," I said, shining the light down the hall.

The form was walking away, slowly, and I realized the head was strangely wide and elongated, as though the person was wearing a hood. I decided it wasn't Connie, but perhaps Elspeth, with one of her odd headdresses. Maybe she and Connie had watched a late movie together.

"Elspeth," I said, but even as her name left my lips I realized that it wasn't Elspeth I was seeing: in a surreal epiphany I saw that the weird garment was a cassock.

Someone wearing a monk's robe was walking down the castle hallway.

A chill rose from my feet to my face. I backed away slightly. I would return to my room; this was not a mystery I cared to solve.

But in that instant the figure turned, and the cowled hood fell back just enough for me to see that there was no face at all, only bones. My mind did not register the nightmarish image at first; I simply stared at the white skull, which seemed to look at me with its sightless sockets. The bones glowed weirdly in the tiny beam of light.

"No," I whispered, and then the thing reached out with its robed arms and lurched forward. It was moving toward me, first slowly, then more rapidly.

"No!" I cried.

I ran. Not to my room, which was too close to the horror, but past it, down the hall to the servants' stairs at the end of the hallway. I wrenched open the door and flew down the steps. I lost my slippers along the way, but I barely noticed.

A monk, a skeleton, a face that was no face. I ran, too frightened to even scream. I passed the second-floor door without thinking. I was soaring down the steps, powered by adrenaline and fear; my feet barely touched the cold stone. At the first floor, I threw the door open and ran out, emerging just outside the chapel hallway.

Was this where he would be returning to say his ghostly prayers? Would he follow me even here to touch me with his bony hands, to kill me as he had killed Garrett in the same spot?

Footsteps sounded behind the door at my back. He was coming with that slow, dragging gait that made me picture the monster once again.

Then a scream did burst out of me, something separate from thought or the voice I knew as mine. A loud, horrified, wailing scream that propelled me forward and out the front door, barefoot and blind with terror. I almost tumbled right down the steps, but I made it to the front pathway and the soft grass beyond it. I could only think, *Run, Run, Run*, and I did so, my legs pumping, my mouth wide and wailing, and then somehow it was on me, its bony clutch on my arm, and my scream must have been deafening.

"No, let me go!" I cried.

Through the pounding in my ears, I heard a calm voice, a man's voice. "Nora. *Nora*. It's me. Tell me what's wrong. What are you doing out here?"

I wiped the sweat from my eyes and squinted them at the figure in the dark. It was Detective Dashiell.

"Dash!" I cried, and I launched myself at him, clinging to him like a terrified monkey, my thoughts still far from rational.

"Nora. What happened? It's cold out here, and you—you don't even have shoes on."

"It's chasing me. Oh, God, it will be here soon! Get out your gun!"

"What is chasing you?" His arms wrapped around me protectively.

"A monk. It was wearing monk's robes. Up in the hallway by my room. I thought it was Connie, but it was a monk, and then it turned and it had no face, just—bones. . . ."

My teeth started chattering, and my arms trembled.

"Let's get you inside!"

"No!" My voice was hoarse now. "It will be there. It will get us."

"Not 'it,' Nora. 'He.' Or 'she.' Someone is playing dress-up, trying to scare you. Let's go find out who it is."

"No."

"Okay, you wait here on the steps, and I'll—"

"No! Don't you dare leave me."

"Then come inside. No one is going to hurt us, I promise you."

His tone comforted me, calmed me. The darkness around us lost some of its terror, and for the first time a rational thought made it through. "You think—someone was wearing a costume?"

He peered down at me. "Do you not have a whole room full of them up there?"

"It was terrifying," I said.

"I believe you. Not even with all your talent could you be acting that kind of fear."

"I am *still* afraid."

"I'll be right here. Let's go back inside."

I followed him up the stairs. My feet hurt; I wondered what I had run through in my headlong burst across the yard.

Limping, I followed him into the main hall, still dark and silent. "No one else heard me screaming?" I asked in a whisper.

He was scanning the darkness. "Derek gave me a room next to the chapel. I heard you loud and clear."

"Did you see—?"

"Nothing, I'm afraid." We were nearing the dreaded chapel now.

"I won't go in," I said. Detective Dashiell produced a flashlight and shone it down the narrow chapel hallway. "Ah," he said.

"What?"

"Give me one second." He darted down the hallway before I could protest, but he was back in less than a minute. "Is this it, Nora?"

He held up a robe with a built-in skeletal face. I turned my head away.

"Someone disrobed and left it right there on the floor. They probably hopped into that secret passage and then made their escape through the ballroom."

"I—I just can't—I'm so—" My teeth were still chattering.

"Come here." He led me to a tiny room next to the chapel, which contained only a bed and a table with a lamp on it. He flicked on the lamp. "You're limping. Sit here." He set the garment carefully on the table, taking care not to touch the mask.

I sat. My body was suddenly so deprived of energy, I felt I had been vacuumed out. I almost tipped over on the mattress.

"Let me see your feet."

I stuck them out, too stunned by events to feel embarrassment or anything at all.

"There are thorns in your skin. God, Nora, you just ran right through brambles and never felt a thing?"

"I was so scared. If you had seen that thing walking in the dark hall—I thought it was Connie. Then I thought it was Elspeth—it only became clear slowly, like in a horror movie or a nightmare."

"It must have been terrifying. But how did they know you would be in the hall?"

I shrugged. "They didn't. I just happened to be up and going to the bathroom. Then I looked out at the branches blowing in the wind, and I heard a sound, as if maybe Connie was leaving her room. So I thought I'd tease her. They couldn't have known I was even awake."

He thought about this while he ministered to my feet. "There. I think I got them all. Does anything hurt when I press here?"

"No, it's fine now. Thank you."

"Take some deep breaths."

I did so several times. Some calm returned to me. "I'm sorry I made a scene," I said.

He looked up at me, frowning slightly. "Do not apologize for the fact that someone terrorized you."

"Okay."

"Nora. I know you don't want to think back to that moment, but was there anything about this figure that might have distinguished it? Something that can help me link it to someone in this castle?"

I pointed at the costume on the table. "Maybe there are fingerprints on that."

"We'll be checking that first thing."

"Other than that, I really couldn't tell. It was just so shapeless, so amorphous."

"Okay. You don't have to think about it again. You're okay, Nora. Everything's all right."

For the first time, I focused. I saw his worried face and his slightly mussed brown hair. He was wearing just a T-shirt and a pair of cotton pants. *His pajamas.* In a rush of embarrassment, I realized that I was wearing a nightgown and sitting on the bed in which he had presumably recently been sleeping.

"Are you going to search rooms?" I asked.

He shook his head, still kneeling and holding my left foot in his hand. "Whoever it was will look innocent now. They'll have a story ready, I'm sure. But this person has taken action tonight, exposed him- or herself; they want something. I just have to figure out what." He brooded, his face intelligent and handsome.

A burst of my vanity returned in the form of embarrassment. "I must smell like sweat."

He blinked at me, surprised. "You smell like a flower. I thought it was the garden when we were outside, but— it's you."

"I took a bath just before . . ."

"Nora?"

"Yes."

"Who's Luke?"

I stared at him. "Luke? What—he's my brother. He had surgery today. I was so worried. . . ." It seemed like a thousand years ago, talking to Luke on the phone.

John Dashiell looked relieved. He patted the sole of my foot and said, "What a stressful day for you. Let's get you back to bed. Sleep will do wonders."

"I don't want to go up there. And I won't be able to sleep."

He stood up and reached for my hand. "Of course you will. Come on, we'll go up in the elevator to spare all the pounding on your feet."

We began to walk toward the south entrance, where the elevator was tucked next to the meditation room. "I had slippers at some point."

"We'll find them tomorrow."

I was still holding his hand when we boarded the elevator. Once in a while, I found myself squeezing it, still nervous and needing comfort.

By the time the doors opened onto the third floor I had regained some courage, and I was willing to walk to my room with John Dashiell's tall form beside me. "Will you think I'm a coward if I tell you I'm still afraid?" I asked.

"I will not. I'll think you're a regular person."

I managed a little smile. "I *am* a regular person. I'm going to have that put on a bumper sticker or something." I was babbling, trying to extend the moment so that he wouldn't let go of my hand and walk away, leaving me in the yawning darkness of the hallway.

"Open up your door," he said. "Let's get you safely inside."

I turned the knob with a trembling hand. We walked into the room, and he shut the door. Impulsive and nervous, I said, "What if you stayed in here? You could lie on my bed and I could sleep in my armchair there."

"I have no intention of leaving you alone. When your friends wake up, they can come and watch over you."

These words brought such relief that I almost began to cry. "Thank you."

He walked to my bed, smiled down at the kittens, and

said, "You climb back in. I have some texts to send, so I'll go over there by your TV. I won't make a sound."

I did as he said, feeling the warmth and comfort of my covers with sudden exhaustion and a new calm. I realized that I felt safe, and I sent him a look of gratitude that he did not see as he walked away.

He settled into the chair. "Good night, Nora. Put everything out of your mind. We'll deal with it tomorrow."

"Good night," I said. The only sounds in the room were the wind, the soft snoring of one of the kittens, and the gentle clicking of keys as Detective Dashiell texted some unknown person. I listened until all the noises seemed to blend together, and then I heard nothing at all.

10

The Legacy of Otranto

I WOKE TO THE sound of murmuring voices in the hall. I looked toward the chair, where my companion had been sitting, but he was not there. I sat up and rubbed my eyes; I didn't feel afraid anymore, just slightly uncomfortable, and I wondered who was talking outside my room.

A light knock sounded on the door, which was not entirely closed. It opened a bit more, and Connie's face appeared in the aperture. "Nora? Are you okay?"

"Yeah. What's going on?"

"Detective Dashiell was telling us what happened. He said we should keep you company. You might want to get dressed, because he's planning to ask questions."

"Is he out there?"

"He went to get some breakfast, he said."

"Oh. Okay." I jumped out of bed. "Give me ten minutes."

Connie agreed and closed my door. In a whirlwind, I put food in the kittens' bowl, went into the bathroom to wash myself and brush my teeth, then flew to my dresser to find a sleeveless denim dress, which I donned quickly. I combed

my damp hair and slipped into some sandals, then went to
the door and opened it, with only a twinge of anxiety as I
recalled the night before.

Connie's door was wide open, and she was sitting at her
desk, jotting something in a notebook. "Connie?"

She slapped the notebook shut. "Wow, that was fast."

"Yeah. Come on in. Are we supposed to meet in here?"

"I guess. I'll bring a couple more chairs."

She marched over with two wooden chairs, her ever-
present Connie energy on full display. She was dressed in
white capris and a pale yellow blouse.

"You look like a buttercup," I said.

"Yeah, that was my goal." She made a wry face at me,
and I laughed.

Elspeth's face peeked in my open door. "The cop told us
about your spooky visitor," she said. She walked forward
and perched on the edge of my bed, where the Brontës now
sat, looking sleepy and cute. Elspeth dangled the thin gray
braid in her brown hair, and Emily Brontë began to jump
at it, much to Elspeth's delight. Soon all three kittens were
cavorting around her.

"Yeah, it was really scary. It wasn't one of you, was it?"
I asked. Perhaps there was a rational explanation.

Connie snorted. "God, no. Why would I get up in the
wee hours to dress as a monster? That's super weird, Nora."

Elspeth looked thoughtful. "It was from the costume
room, you know. Derek wrote this awesome script last year
based on *The Castle of Otranto*. He had us all read the
book, and then we became characters in the castle."

Connie nodded, remembering. "That was a fun script! It
felt so authentic to this place."

Elspeth looked at me. "There's a scene in the book
where Manfred is walking down the hall, and he sees a
monk who he assumes is from the adjoining monastery.
The holy men are in the castle all the time in the story.

There are lots of religious references and visions of saints and stuff. Anyway, Manfred calls out to the monk, but it turns, and it's a skeleton."

"That is horrifying," I said. "Not just the idea, but the fact that someone decided to pop on that costume in the middle of the night. Why? Why would they do it?"

Before either woman could answer, Detective Dashiell walked in, holding a pot of coffee and some paper cups. He was followed by Tim and Renata, who had plates full of pastries. "That is a question we're going to answer very soon, Nora," he said. "And I asked your neighbors to be here so that I can ask a few questions."

Connie jumped up and helped Dashiell pour coffee; they handed the cups around. Renata and Tim brought us all little plates and then held out the pastry trays so that we could select one.

"Why are we meeting in here?" I asked, less offended than I was curious.

Dashiell sent me an apologetic look. "There is some value in asking questions as quickly as possible in the place where an event occurred. While it's still fresh in your mind and others might remember details. "

"It will always be fresh in my mind."

"Don't sound so glum. We're here to cheer you up!" said Tim, showing his dimples in a bright smile.

Connie and I had made a little circle of chairs for the guests, with a low table in the center where they could set down their food; Elspeth and I sat on the edge of my bed. Soon everyone was seated and companionably drinking coffee.

"I didn't know you had kittens in here," Tim said, darting forward to pet Charlotte before sitting down again.

"It's becoming the worst-kept secret of the year," I said.

Renata caught my eye and smiled her regal smile. She, too, left her chair to study the kittens. Annie was currently hanging from Elspeth's braid, so Renata picked up Emily and absconded with the kitten back to her seat, where she murmured into the gray fuzzy face that looked up at her.

"I need to know what you all heard last night," Detective Dashiell said. "At approximately two a.m. Was anyone awake at that time?"

Tim raised a hand. "I was, I think. But I had my earbuds in; I was listening to the latest Stephen King on audio. And I thought *that* was a scary experience." He sent me a sympathetic look.

"So you heard and saw nothing?" Dashiell said.

"No—sorry. I had no idea people were moving around in the hall."

Connie looked guilty. "I wish I could say I saw something. I sleep very deeply; it's hard to wake me up."

"But someone was in your room," I said. "Or they tried to go in it, at least. I heard your door close, and that's why I thought it was you."

Connie's face showed a strange flurry of emotions. For an instant it was bright, almost hopeful, then confused, then fearful. "I didn't let anyone in my room."

Dashiell pointed at her. "They might not have gone in there. Other possibilities exist. They could have opened your door and closed it again. Perhaps they had the wrong door."

"Except that my door was locked, as it is every night," Connie said, her voice crisp with anxiety.

Renata still held the kitten, who looked absolutely hypnotized. "There is a problem with these old locks and keys," she said. "I am afraid that one key is as good as another."

We all stared at her in varying levels of surprise. "That is not comforting," I said. "Does Derek know this?"

She shrugged. "I myself did have the wrong door once, after a bit too much wine with friends in town. I was able to open the door of a room that was not mine—a locked door. Luckily it was merely the costume room, and I didn't embarrass myself and someone else."

Dashiell made some notes. "We'll have the locks changed. The locksmith is coming today, anyway, for the south entrance door."

"Which means someone could still have come in that door last night," I said.

"Perhaps," Dashiell said. He turned to Elspeth. "Based on what Renata just said, everyone would have access to the costume room?"

She blinked. "Well—yeah. Sometimes I don't even lock it. It's just costumes and makeup and stuff, and I know everyone here."

"So whoever it was went in at some point, grabbed the monk costume, and decided to wear it—why? To terrorize someone?" Dashiell's face was almost fierce when he concentrated.

Elspeth removed Annie from her hair and set the tiny fuzz ball on the bed. "It's a baggy costume with a built-in mask. Maybe they just didn't want anyone to know, like—who they were."

Dashiell stared at her without seeming to see her; he was clearly in deep thought.

I said, "At this point, I almost hope it was someone from outside and that you catch him. I certainly don't like to think it was one of the people in this room."

This brought an uncomfortable silence. I ate a bite of the chocolate donut I had selected and realized that it was delicious. "Oh, *wow*! Did Zana make these?"

Connie shook her head. "No, that's from Balfour Bakery. Jade's mom made it all. I guess Zana grabbed the rolls on her way in today."

Renata was daintily eating some sort of croissant; Emily had climbed up to her shoulder and remained there like a little gargoyle. "The rolls are quite delicious. Detective

Dashiell, did you need any more information from us? I usually call my sister at this time."

Dashiell looked around the room. "I heard from Tim and Connie. How about you, Renata? Did you hear anything last night?"

Renata wiped crumbs from her hands with a brisk motion. "I sleep well generally, not to mention the fact that my hearing is not what it once was. I am afraid I can tell you nothing."

Elspeth looked apologetic. "Yeah, same here. If you hadn't told me this happened, I would have thought it was a very peaceful night. Just some wind outside, but that always helps me sleep. The contrast between the violence outside and the coziness inside is somehow comforting."

Dashiell said, "Anyone spoken with Bethany today?"

"I can text her," Connie said.

"Do that. Tell her I need to speak with both her and her husband. The sooner the better."

Connie nodded, her face solemn. "Okay."

"Meanwhile, Derek asked me to remind you all that his friend is coming to bless the chapel this morning." He took a sip of his coffee; his eyes looked a bit puffy, and I realized that because of me he had probably gotten very little sleep. He looked at me and said, "Nora, are you feeling all right this morning?"

"Yes, thank you." My voice was still a bit hoarse from the screaming. My vocal coach would have been horrified to hear what I had done to my "instrument."

Dashiell took two more gulps out of his coffee cup, then tossed the paper cup in the wastebasket near the door. "Good. I'll speak with you all later." He waved vaguely at the group and left the room, his footsteps heading in the direction of the costume room.

Elspeth stood up. "I'd better make sure he doesn't let

Ollie out. See you later." She patted her kitten friend on the head and headed into the hallway in Dashiell's wake.

Renata soon followed her, after reluctantly relinquishing Emily Brontë. Tim lingered long enough to eat another donut.

"These really are good," he said.

I pointed at the plates, which still held several rolls. "Take those with you, Tim. Connie and I don't want them, do we, Con?"

Connie leaned in and snagged a cinnamon roll. A sudden sunbeam shone on her hair and Tim's and made them look like two angels. "We want *one* more. Take one, Nora, so I don't look like a piggy."

I laughed and took a jelly filled donut. Then I waved at the plates. "All yours, Tim. You'll work it off riding your bike. And you can share them with your girlfriend. What was her name?"

"Amy," he said. "And I will be seeing her after the chapel blessing, so thanks." He waved and walked out, carefully balancing the plates as he moved through the doorway.

I stretched, then stood up. The kittens looked ready to jump, so I set them on the floor. "Anyway, I guess I should clean up these cups."

Connie was back to her bustling self. "Let me put this snack in my room and then I'll take the coffeepot back downstairs." She ran across the hall, then returned. She came close to me and touched my hair. "Are you sure you're okay? Dashiell said that you had a really bad scare."

"I *was* scared, Connie. It was terrifying. I wish you had been there to hold my hand," I said, only half joking.

For once her face was serious. "We'll do a better job of watching over each other now that there have been two . . . incidents."

"That's the thing. Those incidents have to be connected,

right? A murder one day and a weird ghost in the hallway soon after"

She shook her head. "That's for the police to figure out. I'll see you in a few; we can walk to the chapel together."

She whisked out of the room, holding the coffeepot, and I shut and locked the door. The book I had been reading the night before caught my attention. I walked to the bedside table and looked once again at the cover: a brooding castle, a woman running away with a terrified expression. I had mocked it as silly and Gothic and overly dramatic.

But last night, that fleeing woman had been me. What would have happened if John Dashiell hadn't been there to protect me?

I set the book on the table, facedown. Perhaps tonight I'd seek out lighter fare.

THE CHAPEL WASN'T as frightening as I'd feared. It was filled with morning light and the varicolored reflections from stained glass windows. The room had been cleaned thoroughly. I tried not to focus on the spot where Garrett had lain, but instead to look at the window above the altar, where a saint of unknown origin sat smiling at a dove perched on her hand.

Derek pulled me aside before I sat down. "Nora, I heard what happened. Let me assure you, I will get to the bottom of this, and the sun will not go down today before every door in this castle is secured."

For an illusory moment, I felt that Derek's handsome, impassioned face could have belonged to some distant king determined to ensure the safety of the people under his protection and to root out the enemy within his walls.

I patted his arm. "It was scary, but I'm over it. Thank God you put Dash in that room next door." I pointed to the hallway down which was the room where I had sat, shrouded in horror, while John Dashiell had pulled thorns out of my feet like a man in a fable.

Derek's brows rose. "You call him Dash?"

The heat in my face infuriated me. "Well—you had called him—I assumed that—"

He nodded, his face a reassuring mask. "Of course, I had forgotten that." He looked at his watch. "We're about to get started. Just have a seat anywhere."

I sat down in an empty row, and moments later Paul sat beside me. Like Derek, he apologized to me with an earnest expression. "If you want us to relocate you to another room, just say the word," Paul said. While Derek's eyes were a sort of dark gray, his brother's were a deep blue and compelling. I found it hard to look away once I had made eye contact.

"No, it's fine. Connie and I have pledged to watch out for each other."

Something flickered across his face, and then he smiled. "That's good, but you shouldn't have to worry about that. After this blessing, I'll need you to come with me to my office so that I can fill out an incident report."

"Oh—uh—I mean, I already told the police. . . ."

"This is for our records, Nora. Our business. In case you decide later that you wanted, let's say, compensation . . ."

"Oh, Paul, I would never—"

He patted my hand. "We'll just fill out the report and be done with it." Paul was clearly a man who liked things slotted into tidy rows. Perhaps these features were the perfect contrast with those of his creative, dramatic brother. He sighed, looking around. "Garrett and I had some great talks together," he said. "One of them even in this room. He was an opera enthusiast, did you know?"

"I didn't. I barely knew Garrett."

"Right, you're brand-new. Well, I love opera, too. We would talk about the various scores and the great composers. He was a Puccini fan. I lean more toward Rossini or Bizet as the best of all time. But we would debate and have great fun doing it." He gestured vaguely toward the altar. "We had talked once about arranging a mini concert in here, bringing in select members of the public—that is, people willing to pay a huge price to hear opera in a castle—and someone from the Lyric Opera to give a performance. Garrett was really excited about it."

"It's a wonderful idea."

He nodded, then focused back on me. "But you yourself have a beautiful voice. Maybe you could do a concert." His eyes started glowing as visions of PR danced through his head. "We could call you Nora of Castle Dark."

"I've certainly never been called *that* before. But I don't know—"

His attention was back on the front of the room. "Oh, it looks like Jim is starting."

The priest, an amiable-looking person with a mostly bald head and a gentle smile, said good morning to us and spoke in a quiet voice about the room he had come to bless. "Since the castle was built, the chapel has been a place of meditation, of refuge, and of peace. Two days ago, that peace was shattered by an act of violence that has harmed not just the victim, but everyone connected with him. Today we ask God to bring serenity back to this place and back to our hearts." He murmured some other comforting words, and I realized that this blessing had in fact been a good idea. There was a certain relief on all of the faces in the room. After Father Jim murmured his final prayers, I tuned back in to hear him say, "Many of you are familiar with Bonnie's Flowers in Wood Glen. Bonnie often works with Derek for castle events, and she knew Garrett well. She has sent this lovely arrangement today"—he pointed at a truly beautiful bouquet on the altar—"and also an individual gladiolus for each of you. Not only did Garrett admire this particular bloom, but in the language of flowers, the gladiolus means 'remembrance.' I will now give you each a single stalk, arranged by Bonnie, in remembrance of Garrett."

He reached behind him into a bucket that held beribboned arrangements that he handed to us one by one. The blooms were a beautiful creamy shade somewhere between yellow and peach. I studied mine while Father Jim held up a hand and said, "May the beauty of these flowers help us to focus on the beauty of Garrett's life rather than on the sadness of his death. And may the beauty of nature bring peace back to this quiet room."

"Amen," Connie said aloud.

Father Jim smiled and said, "One last thing: I spoke to Sora, Garrett's girlfriend, and to his family. They asked me to convey the information that Garrett's funeral service and interment will be a private affair, but at some future date, they will have a public remembrance ceremony."

Derek went to the front of the room and thanked Father Jim, his face solemn, and then we all milled around for a while, talking to one another and to the priest and sharing favorite stories about Garrett.

At one point Father Jim approached me and took my hands between his, which were large and warm. "I understand you found Garrett."

"Yes."

"You've been through a trauma, but God is a great healer. Turn to Him in distress, and you will find peace."

"Your words were very comforting, Father."

He nodded at me and released my hands. I felt a moment of regret; his warmth had been reassuring. He moved on to say something in Renata's ear, and I slipped out of the chapel, holding my flower. I wanted to put the gladiolus in water before it wilted; I peered behind me to see if Connie was also ready to leave and realized that she had already left the room. I wondered how I had missed her departure.

With a shrug, I went to the main stairway and began my climb. As I reached the second-floor landing, I glanced down the elegant hallway toward Derek's apartment, just in time to see the large wooden door closing. How had he gotten up here before me?

I kept walking until I reached my own floor. Connie's door was slightly open, so I pushed on it with one finger. "Connie? You sure got up here fast!"

She wasn't in the room, which looked just as I'd seen it last, neat and attractive, with her PR poster of Castle Dark, and her elegant cherrywood desk tucked against one wall. On its tidy surface lay the notebook she'd been writing in earlier. It lay open, with a pen lying on one page.

Still holding my flower, I edged toward her blotter to glance at the contents. She had listed a series of dates with notations beside them, starting in spring

MAY 25–30 *Promising: connection and good flow.*
MAY 31–JUNE 4 *Disconnect; avoidance. Very unhappy.*
JUNE 5–JUNE 10 *Carly leaving; new girl interview.*
JUNE 11–JUNE 16 *Nora Blake tours the castle. She might be a problem.*

I stepped away from the table so suddenly, I tripped over her carpet and almost fell. I straightened up and catapulted out of the room, pulling the door back to its almost closed position.

Stunned, I stood clutching my flower, not certain how to process what I had seen.

She might be a problem. Connie had written that about my first visit to the castle the day she had given me a tour. The day that had become the basis for our friendship and for my decision to take the job.

Elspeth and Renata emerged from the servants' staircase. Elspeth held my slippers. "Nora, we found these on the stairs. Are they yours?"

"Yes, thank you." I took them from her with my free hand.

Renata came closer. "Are you all right? You look upset."

"No—uh—I just need to get these flowers in water. And I just realized I was supposed to meet with Paul about something. I'll have to find him later, I guess."

Elspeth pursed her lips. "I'm pretty sure gladioli are deadly for cats."

"What?"

"Yeah, which is why I'm going to give you mine. Ollie would eat it right away." She tucked her flower against the one in the crook of my arm, and I automatically clasped it. "And you can put yours on your fireplace mantel. Those little stinkers can climb curtains, but they can't climb bricks. And they're too tiny to jump that high."

"Oh, right. Good idea."

Renata leaned in and took the slippers from my hand, then pressed her flower into my growing bouquet. "I will give you mine, too. I'm allergic, so eventually it would make me sneeze."

"But—"

"We can come and visit our flowers, right? Meanwhile you'll have a nice bouquet in memory of Garrett," Elspeth said.

The door from the stairs opened and Connie emerged; she looked surprised to see us all. "Hey," she said. She noticed that her door was ajar and said, "Did I leave that open again? Man, no wonder monsters are invading our rooms." She meant it as a joke, but it fell flat.

She studied our faces. "What's wrong?"

"Nothing," Elspeth said. "Where did you get off to? You whipped out of that chapel pretty quickly after the service."

"What? No, I just had to use the bathroom." Her eyes moved to me. "Nora, are you okay?"

I wasn't. "Sure, yeah. I've got to put these flowers in water and set them up high before the cats get them."

"Yes, do see that they're well out of reach," Renata warned. "I'll unlock the door for you and set these slippers inside." She took my key out of my hand and unlocked the Green Crown Room, then set my slippers on the tile in the hallway.

Connie looked blank. "Why do you have to keep them away from the cats?"

I glanced at her, then looked away. "Because, Connie, they're bright and pretty, but they're also poisonous."

I walked into my room without saying goodbye, and I shut and locked the door behind me.

11

Assailants

THURSDAY MORNING I listened at my door before exiting to make sure no one was nearby. Since seeing Connie's notebook I had suffered a severe loss of trust, not just in her but in everyone. Who was I kidding, thinking that I was in a castle full of friends? They were strangers, all of them, and one of them had killed Garrett. *Killed* him! And that person—or perhaps a second person—had donned a terrifying costume and stalked the hallway outside my room. From now on I would keep to myself, remain hypervigilant, and start reading the audition boards again.

I made it to the kitchen without seeing anyone; it was early, and Zana hadn't put out hot food yet, but I found cereal and milk and prepared myself a bowl of Cheerios with a banana sliced on top. I ate it in peaceful solitude in the giant dining room, feeling like a deposed queen.

Tim appeared wearing his biking attire. "Hey, Nora, I'm just headed out for a quick cycle. Amy can't come today—do you want to come along? Derek has a few bikes out in the shed; I'm sure he wouldn't mind if you borrowed one."

My mistrust was still there, but the idea of leaving the castle was a very appealing one. I studied Tim's open face, his embarrassingly tight bike shorts, his overall child-like aura and decided that he was not a danger to me—there was certainly nowhere he could have been hiding a weapon in that outfit. "I would like that," I said. I got up and brought my dish into the kitchen, where I washed it and my spoon. Tim followed me, talking about the various trails we could explore.

"I'll have to change—"

"You're fine. Leggings and gym shoes are perfect for cycling—nothing to get caught in the gears."

"All right, then!" I said. "You're officially my de-stressing coach at this castle. First the piano and now biking."

"I aim to please," he said. "Grab a bottle of water. Let's go look at the bikes."

Derek did in fact have a variety of bicycles in the shed. Tim wiped some dust off the seat of a black ten-speed. "He accumulated them so that when film crews are on the property, they can choose one and take a break. And he got them for us, of course."

"Of course. I think this one works the best," I said. It was a pearl pink touring bike with a wide white seat and a pretty white basket.

Tim was squatting down and putting air into one of his tires. Now he stood; he wasn't extremely tall, but he was taller than I. He pointed at the bike. "That one is popular when people want to go shopping in town. The basket holds a fair number of groceries. Derek's got some helmets here, too. This one looks like it would fit you." He handed me a black helmet and I strapped it on.

"Great. Are we going to town?"

He shook his head. "I like the back roads. There are some really gorgeous views around here."

"Sounds great, but don't go too far. It's been a while

since I rode a bike, and I don't want to have sore muscles for two weeks."

He grinned. "Just a couple miles, Scout's honor."

"Were you a Scout?" I asked as I mounted the bike and rode after him down the narrow cobblestoned walk.

"No—but I understand their honor code," he called over his shoulder.

I laughed and followed him down the path, then onto the road that curved into the trees, away from Castle Dark.

HALF AN HOUR later, I was starting to tire, although the scenery was as beautiful as Tim had promised. It had rained in the night; the trees hung heavy with water, and the air was fresh with the scent of rain-washed greenery. He led me down some country roads and allowed me to stop and photograph the cow that gazed mournfully at us over a farm fence. After the farmland came more forestland and roads that Tim seemed to know by heart; he twisted and turned with confidence, and I was sure that I would never, ever be able to find my way back alone. Images of the mythological Labyrinth rose in my imagination.

"Almost there," he called eventually.

"Almost where?"

"There's a fancy view I want to show you. A real showstopper. But we have to ride uphill."

"Ugh!"

"Just for a while. Here we go."

Moments later I was cursing Tim and hating myself for agreeing to go with him. I glared at his black-clad legs and his fancy blue biking shirt. Why would anyone enjoy biking while steep inclines existed?

I pushed hard, feeling suddenly oppressed by the drooping waterlogged trees around me; their heavy branches weighed on my spirit like disappointed ghosts.

"Just a few yards more, Nora. There! See that little gate? That's where we're going." I followed him as he turned onto a dirt road that led to a patch of grass. Some benches were arranged on the grass, facing away from us.

I rode up to the lawn, dismounted my bike, and took huge gulps of water. "I hate you now," I said.

Tim laughed. Was there something wrong with him that he was never in a bad mood?

"Come here, Nora." He walked to one of the benches and I stalked after him, trying to summon some appropriate insults.

He saw the look on my face, but just grinned and pointed outward. "Look."

I turned and realized why all of the benches were facing away from the path. We were on a scenic overlook, and from this spot, we could see much of Wood Glen—the rolling hills and the shady forested bluffs going on for miles, shining gold-green in the morning sun.

"See those rooftops and that white water tower? That's downtown. And the red roof is that antiques shop that Derek loves so much. Garrett loved it, too. He and I—" He stopped and shook his head.

"He and you what?" I sat down on the bench beside him.

"Nothing. I'm not going to bring up anything depressing. Just look at that view!"

"It's amazing." I got out my phone and snapped some pictures from a variety of angles. "Lots of Instagram fodder today," I said lightly.

He studied me for a moment. "I think you could be a huge Instagram star or a Broadway star, Nora. I think you would have been one by now if you had really gone after your auditions. But you have things holding you back."

I kept my tone light. "Really? You figured all this out about me, huh?"

He shrugged. "It's clear as day. You don't want to be far from your family, and you kind of like where you are. You're like me. I made it to New York, and I realized pretty fast that I wasn't really a New York guy." He pointed at the view. "I was this guy."

"It is lovely scenery, and I do like living here. I don't know if I'd like New York, but I guess it would be fun to find out. I did visit my sister there once; the city was very exciting. And I'm not looking to be an Instagram star."

"You could be. Just post a video of you singing a song every couple of days. You'd be discovered in no time."

"That's sweet. Thank you."

We sat in silence for a while, enjoying the quiet. Tim's blond hair lifted in the slight breeze. His face was good-natured as always, but I sensed some agitation beneath the surface. "Why aren't you riding with Amy today?" I asked.

He shrugged. "A bit of a misunderstanding between us," he said. For the first time since I'd met him, he scowled, and it made him look childish.

"I'm sure you'll work it out."

"Yeah." He continued to frown. "Hey, I meant to ask you something. That thing I told you and Elspeth about Garrett being my teacher—you didn't tell anyone, did you?"

The question surprised me, and I stared at him for a moment. Why would it matter if I had told someone or not? "No, I didn't. It hasn't really come up."

"What about Elspeth? Did she—"

"I have no idea."

"I never should have mentioned it," he said, almost to himself. His hands clutched nervously at his knees. "I need you to keep it to yourself. Elspeth, too."

"What does it matter? So he was your teacher. He taught a lot of people over the years."

"Yeah." He picked up his metal water bottle. "But there

was a reason I didn't tell Garrett I was his student." His voice had a weirdly ominous quality, as though he was about to confide something unpleasant.

My brain, sluggish until now, made me picture the hallway outside my room, the monk with the skeletal face who had been walking south. *Toward Elspeth's room.*

Was it paranoia that had me feeling so nervous about the fact that he hoped Elspeth would keep quiet? That he had asked if I had kept quiet, too? That he had led me through a twisting series of paths far from the castle?

I looked at my watch. "I need to get back, I think. I promised Elspeth I'd help her with a project."

He turned toward me and studied my face. It dawned on me that no cars had arrived to see the view and no other people sat on the pretty benches. "Is that a lie?" he asked, a half smile on his face.

"What?"

"Are you lying? I can't tell with anyone in the castle, because they're all professional liars. It gets frustrating after a while."

I had felt the same way, but somehow Tim's complaint was making me uncomfortable. Tim *himself* was making me uncomfortable. Why had he brought me here in the middle of nowhere? Why was he asking questions about Garrett? Why was he so concerned that I might be lying to him? Was there even an Amy at all? I had never seen her.

I stood up. "The truth is that I need to get back. You can stay and enjoy the view a little longer." I picked up my bicycle and mounted it.

He stared at me, his face chagrined. "Nora, don't go. I'm sorry if I made things weird. Come and enjoy the view. I want to show you something."

"I've got to be going. See you at the castle."

"Nora!" he called, and came striding toward me as if he was going to stop me from riding away. I pedaled rapidly, putting distance between him and me and then turning hard when I reached the road, riding until I couldn't see him when I looked back. But what if he chased after me? I didn't want to talk to him. And what had he wanted to show me about the view? Was he going to push me off the grassy hill and into the shrubbery far below?

I imagined the terror of falling, falling, grasping at air, screaming for help that wouldn't come. . . . How long would it take someone to find me buried in the foliage of a Wood Glen forest?

I pedaled faster, turning at a road that looked unfamiliar and realizing I had no idea how to get back. My phone buzzed in my pocket notifying me of a text. I pulled it from my pocket and glanced absently at the screen. It was a Gif from my brother Jay—some Monty Python clip—which made me smile. I put my phone back in my pocket.

My phone!

GPS had always been a lifesaver for me when I drove around Chicago; now it would help me get back to Castle Dark. I typed in the address (why had I not found it ironic that it was located on Apprehension Road?) and then listened to the comforting computer voice as it told me which way to turn and when.

When I had covered enough distance, I found time to scold myself. Had I not just committed to trusting no one? Had I not just realized that no one in this castle was what he or she seemed to be? Even John Dashiell had initially seemed to be someone else. Again that spiderweb feeling came down on me. I was an unsuspecting fly lured by the promise of no rent in a beautiful setting. I had seen murder, and a monster, and betrayal, and—what? What exactly had made me so uncomfortable about Tim? Was it just that he had called me a liar—or was it that he himself seemed to be hiding something?

And why had I suddenly felt it was imperative to put

distance between Tim and me? Was it an overactive imagination or a long-dormant instinct?

The voice on my phone told me to turn on Forest Road,
at which point I started to recognize my surroundings. Some
cars passed me, and ahead of me on the road a red-haired
man leaned on the side of a car parked on the shoulder,
looking at his phone. There was something familiar about
him, but I couldn't place it. I shrugged. He probably reminded me of someone I had seen on TV. I rode past him
and he nodded at me, smiling. Even this stranger's smile
seemed sinister, and I pedaled harder, putting distance between us and looking back once to make sure he wasn't
following. But his eyes were back on his phone, perhaps
consulting his own GPS for help in navigating the twisting
roads of Wood Glen.

Ten minutes later I was riding back onto castle grounds,
half relieved, half anxious. The castle sparkled in the
morning light, windows glinting like diamonds and welcoming me with no hint of the disturbances within its
walls. "Liar," I murmured to the building on the horizon.
Then I recalled Tim asking, *Are you lying?* I had been, of
course, but Tim seemed to have hinted that others had lied
to him in Castle Dark.

I dismounted, still a good distance away from the entrance, and stood staring at the castle. Aside from the police car visible at the east driveway, the building looked
utterly innocuous, like a beautiful picture from a calendar.

It was at that moment that I decided to leave. I would
break it gently to Derek and Paul, explaining that I was too
nervous to remain, and that they could find someone new
while the police had the castle shut down to visitors. And
what of Connie? Assuming I had misunderstood her odd
notes and she really was my friend, I would encourage her
to leave, as well. Castle Dark was dangerous, and the more
alluring it looked, the more it seemed like a bewitching

trap. I would be fooled no longer—not by scenery, or lovely objects, or smiling faces. I thought of what Renata had said about *Macbeth*, and a line from that play suddenly occurred to me, spoken by one of the sons of the murdered king. "Where we are, there's daggers in men's smiles." I understood poor Donalbain's words much better now. He felt the urgent necessity of leaving, and so did I. By the end of the day, I would be back in Chicago. I had any number of friends who would be willing to put me up for a night or two while I got my bearings; I could send a moving van for my things at a later date.

Pleased with this plan, I walked the bike back to the shed, took off my helmet, and hung it over the handlebars. As I moved through the shed doors and out onto the grass, a man appeared beside me—a youngish man with red hair. He was the man I had seen by the side of the road. A chill of caution made me take a step back.

"Good morning," he said with a pleasant expression. "I'm here to see Connie."

"Uh—okay. Is she expecting you?"

He smiled a bashful smile. "No, I'm kind of surprising her. But I wasn't sure which door to enter by, so I figured I'd go in with you, if that's all right."

That wasn't all right. Both Derek and Detective Dashiell had told us that absolutely no strangers were to be allowed into Castle Dark for the foreseeable future. "Um—I'm afraid I can't do that. You'll have to call the castle's main number and explain the reason for your visit. We have tight security here, and—"

"Oh, but that would ruin my surprise!" he said, looking chagrined yet still smiling.

"I'm sorry. I'm not allowed to let anyone in the building."

His smile disappeared. Something was wrong about him, something I couldn't pinpoint. He looked normal enough; he wore khakis and a green T-shirt that had *Grand*

Canyon on it. His hair was clean and he smelled like after-shave. No immediate red flags there; and yet he wanted to get in the castle at—I consulted my watch—nine thirty in the morning.

"There must be a way," he said. "I'd love to surprise her."

"I'll go in and ask my boss," I said. "You can wait here and—" But he was following me, his face confident. He obviously intended to force his way in when I opened the door.

I stopped, still far from the door. "Better yet, I'll text him," I said with fake pleasantness.

I took out my phone. I would message John Dashiell and have him take over. *Enough with the weird people at this place!* I swiped a finger across my phone, and then, to my astonishment, he snatched it from my hand.

"Just let me come in with you," he said.

"Give me back my phone." I could hear the cold fury in my own voice.

He edged toward me, his shoulders hunched, his arms flexing. I instinctively knew that his next step would be violence. My brain sorted through the possibilities in milliseconds. I recalled the "safety lecture" my brothers had given me when I moved to my Chicago apartment. They had created a PowerPoint presentation, which they accompanied by real-life demonstrations—Luke attacking Jay, Jay attacking Luke. Luke had become excited about his own oration. *You always go for what's vulnerable, Nor, because you don't have time when someone's attacking you.*

Jay flipped to the next slide, which said: *What Are Your Weapons?* Fingers, elbows, head. I could head-butt someone, my brothers said, but they didn't trust me to do it correctly or hard enough, and then I would just hurt myself. *The elbows are nice and hard, but the moves require practice and finesse, and he could bend your arm in a way you don't want him to,* Jay said, his face regretful. *So the fingers are the best bet. Bunch them together into a hard little weapon and go for the soft tissue: eyes or throat. Either way you can take him out long enough to run.*

Their words came back to me in that moment, and when the stranger moved toward me with a menacing expression, I went with my impulse: two fingers jabbed hard into the hollow of his throat. His eyes widened and he made a choking sound, then bent at the waist. He dropped my phone, and I leaned down to pick it up, my hands shaking. I turned to run and saw John Dashiell behind me, holding a gun.

"What—?" I said.

"Move, Nora," he shouted. He holstered his gun and strode swiftly forward, patting down the man who was still bent over and trying to catch his breath.

Scowling, Dashiell pulled a pistol from the man's waistband, and I gasped. *He'd been carrying a weapon.*

Dashiell pocketed the gun and produced handcuffs, with which he efficiently cuffed my assailant while he said, "Brent Trainor, you are under arrest. . . ."

I felt faint with the adrenaline of the moment, and I barely heard the words "stalking" and "felony" before more police officers showed up. Dashiell spoke to them briefly; the weapon he had retrieved was placed in an evidence bag, which one of the officers claimed, and the red-haired man was led to a police car.

"I'll be there in an hour," Dashiell called to them. Then he turned to me. "I'm sorry. I've been watching so closely, but I was just a minute too late."

"You were a welcome arrival," I said, slightly breathless.

He offered a tentative smile. "That was some move you used. I'm impressed. I thought I was going to have to tackle him."

I held up my shaking hand. "Carefully trained by teenage boys."

He nodded, grinning.

Something dawned on me as I watched the police car drive away. "Why did you know his name?" I asked.

"We identified him as a person of interest long ago, but we couldn't find him. Odds were he was going to show up here sooner or later."

"Uh—why?"

"I promise to tell you that, but I need to tell Derek first. Let's go inside." We started walking toward the main door, and he said, "What were you doing out here, anyway? Just roaming around?"

"I went biking with Tim. He said it would be good for stress. But he led me down all these twisty side roads and then he started acting weird. I'm probably overreacting, but—I came back alone."

His eyes, alert and focused, studied mine. "Are you all right?"

"Yes, fine. I see him coming back now." Tim's bike, still distant, had appeared on the periphery of the property.

Dashiell looked at him, then back at me. "We'll talk about this as soon as I finish with Derek. Okay?"

"Yes, sure."

We walked in together, and Dashiell pulled out his phone. He spoke brusquely to Derek; I moved away to give him privacy, but I heard him say, "Get Connie down here, too."

Moments later Derek came down the main staircase, accompanied by Connie, her blue eyes wide with surprise. She looked at me, perhaps for some indication of what was happening, and I shrugged. I knew only part of the story.

They reached us, and Derek said, "In my office."

John Dashiell touched my arm. "We'll talk afterward, right?"

"Yes. I'll be around." I watched them walk down the main hallway toward Derek's castle office, and suddenly Paul appeared beside me.

"Nora, so glad I caught you; we never did fill out that incident report yesterday." He was casual today in a pair of jeans and a blue polo. "Do you have a minute to come to my office?"

"Sure," I said, and I followed him to the chapel hallway, where it turned out one of the intriguing little doorways led to Paul's professional space, small but attractive with its large desk and built-in shelves. The first thing I noticed, as Paul slipped behind his desk and I sat in a chair in front of it, was that he had all sorts of office toys: a Newton's cradle, which I immediately set to clacking back and forth; an expandable plastic sphere, which Paul handed me and I rendered large and small like an accordion; a bowl of multicolored Koosh balls. The books on his shelves were interesting, too—there was an obligatory shelf of professional volumes about finance and management, but he had a big fantasy section, then mystery and biography.

"This room is great," I said, still playing with the sphere.

"Toys help with stress," he said.

I studied him. "Is this a stressful job?"

He smiled. "It can be. But my other job is even more stressful. That's why I'm hoping we can get the castle running to its full efficiency so that I can retire from Castor and Associates."

"Ah, that's a noble dream."

He rustled in a drawer and brought out a form. "Okay, here's our standard incident report. If you could fill it out, I'll put it in my binder, and—"

"You might want to give me two."

"What?" His eyes widened, then narrowed in anticipation of a blow. "What happened?"

I told him about the man outside the castle, my hands still shaking slightly as I related the traumatic events, and he slumped in his chair. "Oh, God, Nora—are you all right?"

"Yes. Mostly. Getting better."

He tossed me a red Koosh ball. "Play with that. It helps."

It did. I enjoyed the cool, silky texture of the rubbery tentacled sphere.

Paul sat thinking about what I'd said. "And Derek is in there now with Connie and Dashiell?"

"Yes."

He gave me a frank blue-eyed look. "Okay. This is bad, but also good in a way."

"If you say so," I said, trying to put the red ball inside the expandable sphere.

He sighed and contemplated his desk for a moment, then said, "Nora, do you like chocolate?"

"Of course," I said.

He rolled his chair toward a ledge under the window behind him and retrieved a blue-green glass bowl. He set it in front of me, and I saw that it was full of M&M's. "Stressful times," he said.

To my surprise, I laughed. "You are a man after my own heart," I told him, and we both took a handful of chocolate therapy.

12

Revelations

JOHN DASHIELL SPOKE to me only briefly after his meeting with Derek, saying he had to go back to the station, but would check in with us soon. "There are still police officers on the premises," he said. "Just be sure to stay in the castle."

I nodded.

"Do you want to tell me what happened with Tim?" he asked.

I shook my head. I had gone back over my conversation with Tim at the scenic overlook, and I couldn't pinpoint what it was that had made it feel so wrong. I was beginning to fear that I had overreacted. "No—it's embarrassing. I'm just going to avoid him."

He hesitated, then nodded. "I'll be back tonight. Derek is calling a meeting."

I waited until he met my gaze. "Thank you—for everything."

He stared at me for a moment, then touched my hand. "Text me if you need anything," he said.

* * *

THE MEETING WAS mandatory, and we gathered in the library, curious about what was to be revealed. I had avoided everyone for the rest of the day, and I was relieved yet surprised that Connie hadn't sought me out. The third floor had been quiet and restful, and I played with the kittens and read my book (not scary in the light of day), going downstairs only to grab some lunch to go.

The whole group was present again: Derek and Paul, Detective Dashiell, Zana, Elspeth, Renata, Tim, Connie, and me. Tim avoided my gaze, and Connie sat frowning in a chair in the corner.

Derek went to the front of the room and said, "Thank you all for coming. I wanted to fill you in about an incident that happened at the castle today, but before that I'd like to explain John Dashiell's presence." He took a deep breath, then said, "Close to four weeks ago, I received a letter that contained a very specific threat against someone in my employ. I can tell you now that person was Connie."

We turned to look at her, but she continued to frown at the floor. Derek saw this, and his face flushed. "I contacted the police, and Detective Dashiell came. He took the letter into evidence and instructed me to call him if the threat was repeated."

Derek scratched his arm with an absent expression. "From that point on, I monitored the mail closely. Another letter came the following week—a letter addressed to Connie. Because I recognized the handwriting, I kept the letter and turned it over to Detective Dashiell. He felt that the threat was escalating, and in fact the letter contained another specific threat to Connie, as did two subsequent letters." Derek stole a glance at Connie and said, "It was at that point that I hired Detective Dashiell to remain on the premises as castle security."

"But he pretended to be a gardener so that I could be kept in the dark," Connie said in a thin voice.

"Dash didn't know that you hadn't been informed. That was my call," Derek said.

Dashiell stepped forward. "Derek decided to keep me undercover so that castle personnel would not be nervous. My team was able to pinpoint the perpetrator fairly quickly. He didn't sign his letters, but he used distinctive stationery that we were able to trace to him in South Bend. He went to school with Connie several years ago."

"I barely knew him," Connie said. Her face was blurry with a blend of emotions.

"The problem was that when we contacted the South Bend police, they investigated and informed us that he had disappeared from his residence. At that point we felt it was likely that he would try to come here, and we've been watching for him."

Dashiell looked at me. "Unfortunately, he decided to come this morning when Nora was returning from a bike ride. There was an altercation, during which he threatened Nora and seized her phone. Nora was able to briefly disable him, which allowed me to disarm him. He has been arrested and charged with several crimes, one of which is a felony."

His comments were met by surprised murmurs and rustling. Tim caught my eye, looking remorseful.

Dashiell said, "Apparently the offender approached Nora and asked her to let him in."

"He said he wanted to surprise Connie," I said. "I told him he couldn't come in and that he had to go through castle security. That's when he got belligerent."

A hush fell on the room. Derek said, "Now that Connie's stalker has been arrested, we felt it was appropriate to let you all know what we could not tell you before."

Connie's voice cut through the silence. "Could not or would not? I'm still not clear how you decided to keep information about a stalker from the woman who was being stalked." She was truly angry, her blue eyes glittering as she glared at Derek.

Derek held out his hands in a beseeching manner. "It was a judgment call, Connie. Detective Dashiell told me it could be a long time before this person showed his face, and I didn't want you to be living in fear, or losing sleep, or wondering what was waiting around the corner."

"So you didn't want me to be able to protect myself," she said, her voice furious. "And you took the liberty of reading my mail."

Derek looked wounded. "I'm sorry, Connie. I didn't want this to stress you out." He looked around the room, seeking support. While I understood Derek's desire to protect Connie and everyone, I agreed with her. She had deserved to know.

Connie contemplated him with a stony gaze, not backing down.

Something in Derek seemed to crumple. He said, "Constance, you have to understand. I didn't want to see your eyes filled with fear every day when you came downstairs. You're always so happy, such a bright, blithe spirit. I couldn't let him ruin that. I couldn't let him hurt you that way. . . . You deserve only the best, only contentment. . . ." He was almost babbling now in his effort to win her back.

I exchanged a stunned look with Elspeth, then looked around and saw that everyone in the room could see it, except for Connie: Derek was in love with her.

She stood up. "What I deserve is my privacy, and no one tampering with my mail, and a home in which *men* don't make decisions on my behalf." She glared at Derek and then at John Dashiell before she swept out of the room.

Renata looked confused. "But, Derek, who was this man?"

Derek sighed. "Connie was never romantically involved with him. They went to high school together—that was all.

Apparently he recently saw an advertisement for the castle that included a picture of Connie dressed in costume—a princess with a crown. You've all seen that brochure." We nodded. He gestured to Dashiell. "John thinks that might have been the trigger for whatever obsession he had. His letters suggested he believed he had a relationship with Connie, and he was angry at her for neglecting it."

"That is so creepy," Elspeth said.

Dashiell tipped his chin at me. "We're lucky that Nora had the proper instincts for dealing with him."

Renata was persistent. "And how can Connie be sure that this man won't be let immediately out of jail on some technicality?"

Derek's expression grew dark. "The police will be monitoring him very closely, as will I. Detective Dashiell has promised to keep me in the loop."

"And Connie, as well?" I prompted.

Drooping slightly, Derek said, "Yes, of course. Dash will share the information with Connie and me."

Zana said, "What about Garrett's murder? Are you getting any closer to solving that?"

Dashiell turned his quiet gaze on her. "We are following several leads. Meanwhile we're counting on your cooperation—all of you—in reporting anything you recall that might be significant."

Derek said, "Thanks, everyone. I'll update you soon about our performances and when they might resume."

People stood and milled around for a moment, murmuring in low voices. John Dashiell made eye contact with me; he still wanted to discuss my interaction with Tim. A moment later Derek pulled him aside and they started what seemed to be an intense conversation. Suddenly tired, I decided to return to my room and call my sister.

Normally the castle stayed relatively cool despite the summer heat, but tonight the air around me felt close as I climbed the dim stairs, the castle itself seemed determined to oppress me. I paused on the second floor, tempted to run to the piano, but I didn't want people to flock around me, requesting their favorite tunes. More than ever, I wanted to be alone.

In my room I found the kittens playing on the floor of the kitchenette. I filled their bowls with food and water and watched them tumble comically toward their dinner, their tiny tails pointing at the ceiling. I went to my armchair and watched some mindless TV for a couple hours, trying to clear my mind of all the conflicts in the castle. Eventually I went to bed, expecting to toss and turn, but I fell asleep almost instantly.

I had barely dressed on Friday morning when there was a tap at my door; I opened it a crack to see Connie in the hall. She had obviously been crying. "Do you have a minute?" she said.

"Sure. Are you okay?"

She shrugged, walked across the floor, and flung herself into my easy chair. I grabbed a chair from the kitchenette and sat across from her. She wiped at her eyes and said, "I've been better."

Connie had always been a pretty charismatic personality, but a sad Connie was impossible to resist. "Listen, is this about yesterday? What he did was out of line. But I think he had a very compelling reason."

She waved these words away. "Oh, *Derek*. I could murder him right now. But I just can't believe this—that someone out there wanted to hurt me, that he wrote threat after threat—and I didn't do a thing to encourage it! I don't even know him, Nora!"

"He's mentally ill, Connie."

"Well, it's horrifying. And then to have it kept from me. This is a bit much, coming on top of—"

"On top of what?"

More tears leaked out of her sky-colored eyes. "Okay,

well—it seems like you've been mad at me. And I've been racking my brain, trying to figure out what I did."

I handed her a box of tissues, and she wiped her eyes and blew her nose. Then she looked at me and said, "Did I do something to upset you, Nora? Because it kind of feels like I've lost my only friend."

"Connie, this isn't the time—"

"The time for what? What did I do?"

She seemed poised to become even more emotional, so I held up a hand. "On Wednesday, I went to look for you in your room. You weren't there, but your door was open and your notebook was there on your desk. I glanced at it and saw my own name. You wrote that I was a problem."

"What?" she asked, eyes wide and innocent. Connie, ever the ingenue.

I shrugged. "I was shocked. And then I didn't know what to think."

She stood up and raced across the room and out the door. Moments later she was back, holding the notebook. She was reading what she had written, her eyes widening. "Oh, I see. I guess that looks sort of bad, right? But it wasn't about you, Nora."

"Oh?" I knew my voice was cold, but I couldn't help it.

She went back to the easy chair and sat down. Shuddering out a sigh, she said, "Do you know how long I've tried to get Derek to notice me?"

"What?"

"At least a year. I mean, I wasn't here long before I had developed a huge crush on him, but over time it just got bigger and bigger. I realized how good he was, how kind and compassionate and—noble, not to mention how gorgeous and sexy the man is."

"Okay—"

"I did all sorts of things to get him to like me back. I made him little treats in the kitchen with Zana. I sat and worked with him on his scripts, offering constructive criticism. I went antiquing with him. I flirted my head off. And sometimes he seemed to be really responding. And I'd get my hopes up, and then he'd sort of go blank and practically ignore me. Up and down, up and down. For a *year*. And I keep saying, 'Give up on him, find someone else.' But here I am in a castle with a prince. Who else is going to appeal to me?"

"What are you saying?" I looked at her in real confusion, surprised by her unsolicited confession.

She stood up and put the notebook in my hands. "I was keeping track. Look, it goes back way farther than the page you were on." I turned to the page before and saw entry after entry, going back to May of the previous year, where she had written, *I think I like Derek*. And then by December, an entry with a little heart: *I am in love with Derek*.

I flipped back to the page where she had written about my interview, my arrival. "So why did you write that I might be a problem?"

She shrugged. "Because there was the chance that he would like you as much as I did," she said. Her bottom lip quivered slightly, and I relented in a rush of affection and relief.

"Connie, Derek doesn't like me. And I don't like him, not that way."

"I don't know anymore. For a year I've tried to figure out if there's some other woman, someone he keeps secret." She sent me a guilty look. "I actually hang around his room, Nora, trying to listen at the door. Sometimes if it's unlocked, and I know he's not around, I even go in."

"You need to stop doing that."

"I know," she said. "It's crazy."

My eyes opened wide with a realization. "You were in there Wednesday. When I thought you were in your room, you were in his."

"Just for a second," she whispered.

I folded my arms. "And did you ever find a sign of this mystery woman?"

"No. There is a picture of him and a woman, but he and Paul have a sister somewhere, and I think it's her in the photo."

"Yeah, probably. There is no mystery woman, Connie, and he's not going to fall in love with me. He's already in love."

"What?" Her watery eyes were impossibly blue. No wonder she had Derek enthralled.

"You were too angry to see it, but all the rest of us did. He was practically groveling at your feet!"

"What? He just feels bad." She folded her arms. "Which he should."

"He loves you, Connie. I'd bet my sweet little Brontës on that fact."

A gleam of hope entered her eyes, but her face remained stony. "If he loved me, he would have told me so. He's had a year. With no distractions, no other men in the picture."

"I can't explain that. Maybe you should ask him."

Now her lip curled and her pretty face became sardonic. "Yeah, I'll just go up to him and ask if he loves me. When's the last time you asked a man that?"

"I did it in a play once," I said meekly. "It had a happy ending."

"Well, this is real life," she said. "And I think it's time for me to move on."

"Move on to other men or—"

"I think I need to leave the castle." She was the picture of melancholy, drooping in the chair.

"You can't make that decision right now. You're upset, and decisions shouldn't be made when you're emotional. On the other hand—"

"Yes?" She sat up in her chair.

"Well—it's dangerous here."

She nodded. "I know. There are so many reasons to go

now. Except that you just got here, and I'm just getting to know you, and I . . . *like* it here." Her eyes grew wet as she gazed out one of my giant windows.

I stood up and clapped my hands together. "Like I said, you can't make decisions now. You need some therapy, and I happen to know the best therapist in the castle. He has toys and chocolate."

Connie turned back to me, her expression reclaiming some of its usual brightness. "I like both of those," she said.

"Come with me." I held out my hand, and she stood up to clasp it. "We'll get things sorted out."

She walked with me into the hallway. Annie the kitten marched beside her and tried to leave with us, but Connie tucked her safely into the room and shut the door.

As we approached the staircase, she sighed and said, "I'm so glad you don't hate me anymore."

I laughed. "I didn't hate you. I distrusted you."

Her face was solemn. "That makes sense. But just so you know, you *can* trust me. I'm terrible at lying."

"I know that now."

Her pale brows rose. "Why?"

"Because I saw your face when you said you were done with Derek."

Connie pursed her lips and marched determinedly down the stairs, ignoring my teasing smile.

PAUL WAS STILL in his office, and he looked concerned but also amused at the idea that I had brought Connie to him for "therapy."

"My toys are your toys," he said. "Any psychologist will tell you that play is healthy." He retrieved the glass bowl full of chocolate and held it out while Connie and I dove into it like children.

"Listen," Paul said. "This afternoon I'm heading to

town to get a couple things for Derek at the antiques shop. Do you want to come along? Have a change of scenery?"

"Absolutely," I said at the same time that Connie said, "Yes, please!"

Paul laughed. "Great. Meet me here around two, and we'll head out. Sound good?"

We nodded and left him to his paperwork. Back in the main hall, Connie murmured, "I should have fallen for Paul instead. He's almost as gorgeous as Derek."

I nodded. "But maybe not as exciting."

She sighed. "What do we do now? Do you want to forage in the kitchen?"

"Let's go to the library," I said. "We never got to go the other day. I really do want some reading material. Plus I told my mom I'd send her a picture of it. She works at a library, you know."

"I didn't know that! How neat. Your family sounds so nice." She bounced along beside me like a happy Tigger, revived by chocolate and our repaired relationship.

"They are nice. What about your family? Do you all get along?"

She shrugged. "My brothers are all older. I was a sort of last-chance baby. So my parents are kind of old, but they're sweet. And my brothers dote on me from a distance. None of them lives nearby, unfortunately. I don't even want to tell them about this stalking thing, because they'll lose it."

I would have "lost it," too, if Gen told me someone had stalked her in New York or if one of my brothers was being stalked. "You have to tell your family. Just let them know that the police have the guy."

She was still worried, and her face showed it. "Charges like that never seem to stick, do they? I feel like he'll get out."

I put a hand on her arm. "We'll talk to the police. You don't have to worry about anything right now. He trespassed on this property with a weapon and assaulted me, and he wrote threatening letters. He's under arrest and I'm guessing he's sitting in jail."

We had reached the library; Connie peeked in the doorway, then turned back and made a face at me. "Oh, man. Zana is in there again, doing that weird thing. Should we leave?"

"No. Let's just go in. If she's uncomfortable, then she'll stop what she's doing." I walked into the library, enjoying the slightly musty smell and the way the walls of books looked in the stippled sunlight. I snapped a couple of pictures to send to my mother; then Connie and I walked farther into the room. Zana sat at her corner table with a stack of books, fanning the pages of a large tome, holding it upside down and shaking it.

"Hi, Zana," I said loudly.

"Hey," she said. She didn't stop her strange behavior; she merely set the book down and picked up the next one.

We walked toward her table and sat at two chairs across from hers. "What are you doing?" Connie asked.

Zana grinned at us. "Something my grandma taught me long ago. She called it Treasure Hunt—probably her way of keeping little kids occupied in a library. You go through every book to see what people left inside. I know librarians do that when books are returned, but Derek got this whole load from private donations, so who knows what people forgot? It's fun. Try it!"

Connie shrugged at me, and I laughed. We went to a nearby shelf and each grabbed a stack of books. Then we returned to Zana's table and began riffling. I raised an eyebrow at Zana, "Doesn't Eric miss you?"

Zana shook her head. "He and our baby girl are at the movies tonight. I'm just claiming a little me time. This library has always relaxed me." She smiled at Connie, who had just found a bookmark.

"There, see—treasure already. We'll compare at the end of this pile," she said.

A couple of minutes later we showed our individual discoveries: Zana had a bookmark with a kitten on it, a note that read: *9 PM*, and a sticky note with someone's shopping list. She shrugged. "Not my best haul ever, but my daughter will like the bookmark."

Connie showed us her little pile: a gas station receipt, a pressed rose petal, and a photo of someone's beagle.

"Pretty good," Zana said. "It's a cute dog. You can put him up in the costume room."

Elspeth did have a photo-sharing wall in the costume room, and people routinely tacked up pictures of family, pets, scenery—whatever they felt like posting. "I will!" Connie said. "What did you find, Nora?"

I showed them my two items: a dollar bill and a hand-drawn cartoon of a person with a two-sided face, half human and half monster. The human side was an attractive-looking face of indeterminate gender, with a large eye and full lips. The other side was a gory, terrible image of that face seemingly decayed or transforming into something else. The caption read: *Castle Dark's Jekyll and Hyde.* The artist had obviously dashed it off quickly, yet there was real talent evident in the sketch. It was signed with the initials G.P.

"Oh, I like that," Connie said, "even though it's gross."

Zana nodded. "Yeah, Nora wins this round. That's a real conversation starter."

I studied it more closely. "I think Garrett drew it," I said.

"What?" Connie leaned in and saw the initials. "Oh, my gosh! He was a pretty good artist. He always helped to paint the scenery at the community theater."

A sudden memory came to me. "He said something about being an artist the night we all introduced ourselves. He said he liked to draw up in his room. And he was doodling on a napkin—some kind of amazing tree."

Zana was studying the picture; she had an odd look on her face. "You need to give that to the police."

"Why?"

She pointed. "Who was he drawing? Who turned into Hyde? He says this person is in Castle Dark."

We sat and considered this with solemn expressions. "Yeah, I think you're right," I said. "I can send it right now." I took out my phone, snapped a picture, and texted it to Dashiell.

I think Garrett drew this.

Then I explained where I had found the drawing. Moments later he texted back:

Got it. Thanks, Nora.

I lifted my pile of books and brought them back to the shelf. Then I returned and said, "Zana, I have to admit, that was an interesting game."

She nodded. "Shades of my childhood, but I still enjoy it."

"Childhood is a recurring theme today," Connie said. "Paul has an office full of toys."

Zana thought about this. "Someone famous said that when we're children and young people, we have our most important experiences, and that we spend the rest of our lives remembering them. I wish I could recall who it was. I think about that concept a lot."

"Huh," Connie said. "Well, I like to think I'm still having the experiences."

Zana sighed and said, "Well, that's my little treat for today. There's something really addictive about hunting for treasure, no matter what kind of prize it is. Don't you think?"

My mind flashed to Garrett's room with his items thrown all over the floor. Could Zana have been hunting for treasure up there? Or could Hyde have been searching for something? Maybe for this cartoon?

"I think you're absolutely right," Connie said. "I've been hunting for my own kind of treasure for more than a year. And it is addictive."

"But duty calls," Zana said. "I need to put out lunch and get started on dinner." She put her books away and walked back to the table. "By the way, my daughter said that you are both pretty."

"Oh, that's sweet," Connie said.

"Your daughter is the pretty one, Zana. She reminded me of a cartoon with her big eyes," I said.

"Yeah, she got those from Eric. They both have Bambi eyes," she said, laughing.

Connie put her books back on the shelf, and the three of us walked out of the library together. "What's on the menu tonight?" Connie asked.

"Chicken stew and corn bread," Zana said. "And lunch is tuna salad croissants."

We made appreciative noises and she smiled. We walked her to the kitchen and I said, "Thanks for inviting us to the treasure hunt."

Zana waved and disappeared inside. I realized that I still hadn't actually taken a book out of the library.

"I should go call my mom and dad," Connie said. "I've put it off, but you're right. I need to tell them. My dad is going to want to tear Derek's throat out."

I nodded. "Maybe. Or maybe he'll appreciate Derek's intention, which was to protect you. And to hire private security for you with his own money."

Connie stopped walking. "That cost Derek money? Don't the police do that for free?"

"No, Con. Lots of people could benefit from the police just hanging out on their grounds, but that wouldn't happen unless they were posted there by their bosses. I think Derek's been losing money and sleep over this. And I think I know why."

Her face flushed for a moment, and then she lifted her chin. "Well, he didn't need to spend a dime on me. He could have told me the truth, and I could have protected myself."

"True." She was right, of course, but I couldn't help but think that Derek had been blinded by love, and that his choices, while irrational, were genuinely made with Connie's welfare in mind. "I need to check on my little fuzz girls before we leave. They need some playtime."

We climbed up to our rooms, huffing slightly with the effort. Connie said, "Let me know when you're going down for lunch." She looked at her hand and said, "Oh, wow. I've been clutching my 'treasure' this whole time. I'm going to run and post the beagle on Elspeth's photo board. I think I'll name him Charlie. Do you want me to post your cartoon?"

"I'd better not," I said, "in case the police need to see it. I wouldn't want it to go missing. I'll put it in my room somewhere."

"Okay, cool! See you in a few for lunch and antiques!"

She ran down the hall, and I watched her, smiling. It was barely past noon, but it seemed a century since I had ridden my bicycle into the sinister woods, and a man with a gun had lunged toward me with a menacing expression. I needed to tell my brothers that they might actually have saved my life.

I turned to the Green Crown Room, prepared to face whatever tiny mischief the Brontës had been up to.

13

Relics

PAUL ENDED UP being just the companion that Connie and I needed; he was calm and cheerful, and the change of scenery he promised seemed to be the antidote for all of our troubles. Connie climbed into the front, I tucked into the plush backseat of his black Lexus (just how much money did Paul and Derek *have*?), and we pulled away from the castle. The day was bright and sparkling now, with no more traces of the previous night's rain. We glided through the twists and turns of a forested pathway, and once again the scent of gardenias filled my senses. I closed my eyes and leaned my head back on the seat, enjoying the fresh summer air through my open window.

"You two look like you needed a break," Paul said.

"We did!" Connie cried. "I think Nora and I should both live in a spa somewhere for a while, until we recover from the—events—of the past couple of days."

"Yes," Paul said, his face troubled. "I don't even know what to say about that. I hope the police get to the bottom of things soon. I feel bad for Derek. He's trying to be everything to everyone and still hold the business together."

"Do you think the business is in danger?" I asked.

He shrugged. "It shouldn't be. Time passes, people forget. But we've been in the papers now and on the news. Who knows what effect that will have?"

"So it has been on the news?" I asked. Oh, God. I hadn't told my parents; they had enough going on with Luke's hospitalization. Only Gen knew about the murder. But I certainly didn't want my family to find out about it on the TV News. . . .

"Are you okay, Nora?" Paul's intense blue eyes met mine in the rearview mirror.

"Yeah. I guess I hoped it would just be in the paper and not on television. But of course it would be televised. It's a big story."

"Let's not think about that right now," Paul said. "This is our escape."

I wondered if Paul needed to retreat, as well. What stresses did he face with two jobs and constantly traveling back and forth?

Connie turned to Paul, her face bright and curious. "Do you have to go back to Indianapolis again?"

"In about a week," Paul said. We had reached the end of the curving driveway, and now he pulled onto Apprehension Road.

"Is there someone special waiting for you there?" Connie asked, ever the romantic.

Paul grinned. He really was handsome; I wondered what the parents of Derek and Paul looked like. "There was someone. We ended things a few months ago."

"Oh!" Connie's face fell. "I'm sorry it didn't work out."

"I think we knew for a while that it wasn't right. We just sort of stayed with each other out of habit." He shrugged. "But she was perpetually disappointed with me. Either I was too neglectful or I was too attentive. I think she just liked being upset with me."

Connie wrinkled her nose. "Oh, she sounds horrible."

"She was okay. We just weren't a good match. I'm taking a break from that scene right now, just focusing on the business."

Connie drooped slightly. "You're a great catch. I'll bet Nora and I could find the perfect woman for you."

He laughed. "Let's hold off on that for now. I'm in dormant mode at the moment."

"I can relate to that," I said. "I've had my fair share of relationships that didn't quite fit."

"Yeah?" His eyes shone again, glowing blue in the mirror. "Lots of actors, I bet."

"Yeah, most of them. Actors shouldn't date actors—that's what I've learned."

Connie grew quiet in her seat, turning her head to look at the passing scenery.

Paul smacked his hands on the steering wheel and said, "We need to liven up this car! We are three adventurers going into town!" Suddenly he began to sing in a silly falsetto "Three Little Maids from School."

Connie and I burst into laughter, but soon we were singing with him, inserting *La La La* when we didn't know the words.

We finished, and I wiped some tears of laughter out of my eyes, but Paul had started up with "Brightly Dawns Our Wedding Day," which I had sung with my high school choir and apparently Connie had once sung, too. We did a creditable version of it, Paul revealing his lovely true baritone and Connie taking alto as I soared above with the high notes.

"That was fantastic," Paul said at the end. "We really should start some sort of castle choir. Wouldn't that be fun? Audition some locals, as well, maybe. I'll have to ask Derek what he thinks. . . . Meanwhile, here we are!"

He pulled into a public parking lot at the end of Barnaby Street, the main drag of Wood Glen. We climbed out and surveyed the vista before us. I had been here only once, with Connie, when she had taken me to a pub to celebrate my arrival. The downtown area was a nice blend of elegance and old-fashioned charm, with little shops nestled together on red cobblestone sidewalks adorned with potted pines and tubs of summer flowers. I could see the antiques shop at the very end of the road, its red roof rising above the rest in a distinctive square shape.

"I see our destination," I said, pointing at it.

"Yes, eventually," said Paul. "But first, Connie, I think we need to introduce Nora to Dorian's. Don't you?"

"Oh, yes!" Connie said, brightening. "Come on, Nora, you will love this. I hope you haven't had too much sugar."

"I am absolutely positive that I have," I said. "We decimated Paul's M&M's bowl!"

"You're young. You'll recover," Paul said, and he and Connie led me to a maroon doorway with a placard above it reading: DORIAN'S DELIGHTFUL ICE CREAMS.

"Ahhh, ice cream," I said.

And then they bundled me inside, where we went to the front to order our cones (Blue Moon for Connie, Raspberry Ripple for Paul, Chocolate Chunk for me). Then we sat in a cozy booth and Paul challenged us to share one interesting little-known fact about ourselves.

"I'll start," he said. "When I was younger, I loved tennis. I was quite good for a while, even played in some professional tournaments. I had a trainer and everything."

"Why did you stop?" Connie asked, catching some drips on the side of her cone with her tongue.

"My father died," he said. "Then my priorities shifted."

We were both about to say something to him, but he held up a hand. "No serious stuff. Connie's turn."

"Oh." Connie licked her cone for a moment, thinking.

Then she said, "I can speak two languages. My mother is French."

"I didn't know that!" I said. "That's really cool. How do you say 'I love ice cream' in French?"

"J'adore la glace," she said with a lovely French accent.

"Very good," Paul said. "Nora's turn."

"Oh, well, I don't have any cool secret talents like you two. But I was in a viral video once."

"Oh?" Connie looked particularly intrigued; she leaned in and dripped some Blue Moon on my shoulder.

"When I was a toddler, my sister, Genevieve, who was four, loved to teach me things. Eventually she decided she would teach me how to sing. She sang 'My Bonnie Lies over the Ocean' line by line, and I sang it back to her. My mom recorded it because she recorded everything back then, but it turned out so cute that she and my dad showed it to his college roommate who works in advertising. They ended up using it in a TV commercial for cereal."

Paul nodded. "I remember that. It was adorable."

Connie thrust the cone into Paul's free hand. "Hold that a minute." She tapped furiously on her phone to bring the commercial up on YouTube. Then she looked at me, her eyes enormous. "You're one of the Singing Babies? Oh, my gosh, you're as famous as the 'Charlie Bit My Finger' kid!"

I shrugged. "Luckily no one knows it's me. Gen and I prefer our privacy these days." I grinned at them, but Connie was watching the video again.

"Nora, even then you had practically perfect pitch. It's amazing. And you and your sister were such cute babies."

"Yeah, well, clearly my mom thought so."

Paul handed back Connie's cone and shoved the rest of his into his mouth, smiling while he savored the last bites. Then he said, "That was wonderful. I feel like I know both of you better already. We should do this with the whole castle staff sometime, right?"

We agreed and thanked Paul for the ice cream, which had been his treat. As we left in high spirits, a part of my brain was wondering what secrets the castle staff had and if we would really want to hear them.

BEFORE WE REACHED the antiques shop, Paul said he needed to stop in at Balfour Bakery. "I promised Zana I'd get her a couple loaves of bread and a coffee cake," he said. "Won't take more than a minute."

We followed him inside a room fragrant with baking and bright with summer sun. Jade herself was behind the glass counter, beneath which I glimpsed a wondrous array of pies, cakes, and donuts. Her hair was tied back and she wore a crisp white apron, but her dark glasses were still perched on her nose. "Hey," she said, "I know you guys."

"Hi, Jade," Paul said. "I need two loaves of your country white and a raspberry coffee cake."

"Sure," she said. "Hey, Mom!" she called over her shoulder.

A woman came out from a back room; she was auburn-haired, like Jade, and wore a similar apron. Her face was attractive but serious, and she seemed a bit nervous. "Have you been waited on?" she asked Connie.

"We're all together, Mara," Connie said. "This is Nora, our new member of the Castle Troupe."

"Oh, nice to meet you," she said. "Is Jade taking care of you all?"

"You can get the coffee cake," Jade said. She had climbed on a stool to get loaves of bread from a high shelf and now came down to wrap them. "He wants raspberry."

"Of course," Jade's mother said.

"How are the kittens?" Jade asked.

"Fine," I said, stealing a glance at Paul. His eyes stayed on Mara, but his brows rose at the mention of the cats. "They're wonderful."

"Yeah, they were really cute. I might come by this week to say hi."

"Text first to make sure we're not busy," Connie said.

"Yeah, okay," Jade said, shrugging a casual teenage shrug. She handed over the bread bag, and Connie took it. Paul went to the register to pay Mara Balfour, and Jade squinted at us. "Are you guys okay and everything? Eriza's mom told me about the guy who got killed. And I saw it on the news, too."

Connie and I nodded. "We really can't talk about it," Connie said.

Jade was undeterred. "He used to come in here a lot with his girlfriend. They both liked the Balfour Bites." She gestured to some delicious-looking cookies that seemed to contain both chocolate and butterscotch. "He was always nervous, though. I always thought he must have been a soldier."

"Why is that?" I asked.

"I don't know. It was almost like he had PTSD. He was always looking over his shoulder and stuff, like the mob was after him."

"Maybe he just didn't want to be seen with his girlfriend," Connie said.

Jade bristled. "That's silly. Sora is awesome. She's a highly respected businesswoman here in town."

I edged a bit closer to her. "Oh? What does she do?"

"She has a little café on Porter Street, a couple blocks over. High school kids love hanging out there during the school year, and she's really nice and motherly to everyone."

Sora actually sounded like a great match for quiet Garrett. "Did you tell the police this, Jade? That Garrett seemed nervous?"

"What police?" she asked with a blank expression.

Paul had been chatting with Mrs. Balfour, but now he held up his bag and said, "All set, ladies!"

We waved to Jade and her mother and left the bakery.

Connie offered to put the baked goods in the car; Paul gave her his key, and she ran back to the lot.

As we waited for her, Paul looked pointedly at me and said, "Kittens, huh?"

I looked up at him, stricken with guilt. "They needed a home. And they're behaving like little angels."

He laughed. "I have no problem with it. Does Derek know?"

I bowed my head. "No. And he's probably the only person in the castle who *doesn't*, thanks to the grapevine."

"How many kittens are we talking about?" he asked.

"Three. They're all gray; I named them after the Brontë sisters."

He nodded. "How fitting."

"I'll tell Derek," I said. "I'm just working up the courage."

His smile was slightly mocking. "Haven't you learned yet that my brother is a pushover? Especially when he's talking to an attractive woman."

Connie ran back to us, bursting with enthusiasm. "And *now* we can look at some truly beautiful junk," she said. "I love this store so much." She and Paul rapid-walked down the sidewalk and I did my best to keep up; finally we reached the building with the red roof, called Relics Antiques. A gold placard on the wall beside the door read: THERE IS VALUE IN AGE, AND TRUTH IN THE RELICS OF OUR PAST.

We walked in, past a gorgeous green velvet throne chair of an unknown era; a sign on the chair read: I'VE BEEN MARKED DOWN!

"I want that chair," Connie said, flipping her blond hair over her shoulder.

I laughed, and we moved deeper into the dark, wood-paneled room; it was cool in here, with a slight lavender scent. I suspected there was a bowl of potpourri somewhere on the premises. I soon saw why everyone at the castle loved Relics Antiques: every surface looked like a delightful prop table.

One table near the door held every imaginable piece of costume jewelry; we lost Connie there immediately. The next table was a hodgepodge of old clocks, ornate pipes, vintage toys, a Victrola, and some carved wooden Santas. After this came several tables of china and glassware, from Wedgwood to Spode to Royal Doulton.

Paul and I turned a corner to see rack upon rack of vintage clothing. "Oh—I see why Derek loves it here," I said, touching the delicate lace on an old wedding dress.

"The best is yet to come," he said. He led me to some tables along the back wall of the store. "Look," he said.

It was an actor's paradise: vintage swords and scabbards, enough hats to fill a millinery shop, helmets and armor, antique boots and shoes, pageant sashes, military regalia, and a basket full of watches.

"Heaven," I said.

Paul had found an elaborate beard somewhere and he held it up to his face. "Nora, look!"

I laughed. "Truly villainous."

"Ladies like villains, don't they?" he said lightly. "Or so they say."

"I don't think you need a beard to attract ladies," I said, trying on an arm-length black glove.

"Good to know." He put the beard down, grinning. "Anyway, have fun. Derek wants a couple of crowns for the costume room, so I'm going to see what they have on that other table."

He drifted away, and I began taking a tour of the hats, some of which were beautiful and laced with delicate scarves. I tried on a sunbonnet and looked in a mirror above the table, then laughed at my reflection. Perfect if I was going to play Rebecca of Sunnybrook Farm.

I put the hat down and wandered over toward the swords; any one of them would have been perfect as one of "Uncle Harold's" collection, but I supposed we wouldn't be returning to that story line (assuming that Connie and I stayed at the castle).

Farther down the table were some inlaid wooden boxes, intricately carved and brightly painted. I opened one of them and admired the red velvet interior. To my right glinted some lovely Shakespearean-looking daggers and Jocasta-style brooches. That reminded me of the pin Renata had given me; I had set it on my dresser for safekeeping, but I realized I should wear it soon to show her that I appreciated the gift. Perhaps I would wear it to dinner.

I wondered if I should get Derek a little gift. He truly did seem to be under a great deal of strain, especially now that Connie was angry with him, but he had been nothing but gracious and generous to me. Even if I ended up leaving, I wanted to show my gratitude to Derek Corby.

The daggers seemed a likely possibility; they would all look good in his apartment full of treasures or somewhere in the castle as an objet d'art. One of them was especially appealing, glinting gold and sporting a lovely emerald-like stone. It would have made a perfect replacement for the missing dagger, in fact. I wondered if Derek would even want one or if it would simply remind him too much of Garrett.

I leaned closer to the knife. It really did look like Garrett's dagger; it had a distinctive design that I recognized from John Dashiell's slideshow, and the emerald was cut in a diamond shape. What if someone had brought it here? It would have been easy enough to put it on this prop table and not have anyone find it for weeks. Better yet, some patron might simply buy it and take it away; even if the store had no record of it in their computer, mightn't they just shrug and make up a price on the spot?

I took out my phone and photographed the dagger from several angles; I sent the shots to John Dashiell with the message:

Is this the missing dagger?

Less than a minute later, I got his message:

Where are you?

I told him; he wrote back:

Be right there. Don't let anyone touch it.

I hovered at the table, deputized to protect possible evidence. Paul walked up to me, holding a grand gold tiara. "How do you like this one?"

"Beautiful," I said. "Listen, Paul—the police are coming."

"What?"

"I think I found Garrett's missing dagger."

His brows rose. "*Here?* But why would—?"

The gleaming knife now looked almost obscene to me on the black velvet cloth. "Do you know how many castle staffers left the grounds in the past two days?" I asked.

Paul shrugged. "I'm afraid that's not going to help us. Everyone left at one point or another. But why bring it here? Why not just chuck it into the woods?"

I shook my head; I had wondered the same thing.

By the time Connie sought us out, her hands full of jewelry, John Dashiell and another official-looking man were walking toward us, their expressions grim.

Our Relics playtime was over.

14

The Dark Hallway

I DIDN'T GET A chance to speak to John Dashiell; I heard him murmuring to Paul that he would see us at the castle later. I got one intense look from him before he and his companion became absorbed in their task of photographing the knife where it had been left. Soon they would dust it for fingerprints and then take it away.

We went to the front register, where a white-mustached man, whose name tag read: *Griff*, was clearly fascinated by the fact that the police were in his store; he kept craning his neck, trying to get a view of the men at the back table.

Paul had selected a couple of crowns and texted photos to Derek, who had approved them. Paul paid for these, along with some bracelets that Connie had selected (he insisted that she let him pay) and a large inlaid box I had chosen because I thought the kittens might like to sit inside it.

"That wasn't necessary, Paul," I said. I had received only one Castle Dark paycheck so far, but I had a bit of money that I had been saving for my Chicago rent, so I had a small nest egg.

"You both deserve a treat," he said. "Derek and I feel terrible about all that you've been through. From this point on, things will be looking up."

Connie and I approved this sentiment with hearty nods, but as an actor, I felt superstitious about the fact that Paul had said those words out loud. Connie's face told me that she felt the same way. One must never tempt fate by claiming that everything was fine—in the world of theater or any other world.

On the sidewalk Paul suddenly raised a hand and waved to a woman across the street. "Hello, Sora!" he called.

The name alerted me, and I turned to see Garrett's girlfriend, a slight woman with blondish gray hair and a kind face. She crossed the road to accept Paul's hug; he murmured the usual platitudes about being sorry for her loss and her letting him know if there was anything he could do.

"It's hard, I must admit," she said, her gray eyes filling with tears. "We were planning a trip at Christmas. I'm sad we won't get to go. But you and Derek have been lovely, and I appreciate your support. When all is said and done, I'm grateful for the time Gar and I had together. "

"I know the funeral will be private, but do let us know when the public commemoration will be," Paul said.

She nodded. "Of course." She turned to Connie and me. "You two worked with Garrett?"

Connie held out her hand. "I'm Connie. I worked with him for almost two years. I remember him saying complimentary things about you after he met you—it was at your café, right?"

She smiled. "Yes, he came in for lunch one day and we got to talking." The memory obviously brought both pleasure and pain.

"And the rest was history," Paul said in a gentle voice.

She shook her head. "We started dating, but we weren't exclusive at first. At one point I found out that he was seeing someone else—a woman here in town. I asked Garrett point-blank if he wanted me or her. He chose me, and we were dedicated after that." She pointed at Paul. "He talked a lot about your castle and how much fun he was having and how he never would have found it if a friend of his hadn't tipped him off about the job."

"We loved working with him," Paul said, a consoling hand on Sora's arm.

She turned to me, and I said, "I'm Nora. I'm brand-new, but I got to know Garrett a little bit. I'm sorry about what happened."

Her face paled. "Nora . . . They said— You're the one who found him, right?"

I dipped my chin in acknowledgment, uncomfortable with this distinction.

She wore a brave expression. "Did he look peaceful?"

A sudden vision of Garrett's sightless eyes staring at the chapel ceiling. "Yes," I said, and I was telling the truth. "And he was in the chapel, which is a peaceful place."

She reached out and took my hand in hers. "Thank you for that."

Paul gave her another half hug and said, "We have to go, but reach out anytime you need something, Sora."

She nodded and gave my hand another squeeze. We said our goodbyes and she walked back across the street, returning to whatever mission she had been on when Paul called her name.

Our drive home was a more solemn affair; we sat quietly, thinking our own thoughts, and no one had the impulse to burst into song. By the time we reached the turning for Castle Dark, the sun had gone behind a cloud, and the twisting drive was cast into shadow.

* * *

DINNER WAS A rather tense affair. We sat at the long dining table like the characters we played in the game, eating Zana's stew in relative silence and staring into the flickering candles that she had placed in the center of the table. Derek stared mournfully at Connie, who looked mostly at her plate. Paul got a phone call and disappeared into the hallway, and Tim and I avoided each other's gaze. I had put Renata's crown pin on my lapel and I saw her eyeing it approvingly when I reached for a piece of corn bread. Bethany was present because Derek had told us it was a dinner meeting; she and Elspeth murmured to each other while they ate, Elspeth's latest headdress—a pink-sequined slouch hat—glinting in the light of the chandelier.

Eventually Zana came in to clear our plates; I got up to help her, carrying the dishes near me into the kitchen. "Boy, it's really somber in there," she whispered as we set the plates in the stainless steel sink.

"I know. I think we might all be having a delayed reaction to the events of the last couple days."

She nodded, her expression thoughtful. "Here, since you were nice enough to help me clear, maybe you'll also carry in some dessert for me."

"Of course," I said.

She got out some cake plates and began slicing a chocolate pie. "Here you go—take these three, and I'll get the rest. Thanks, Nora."

I walked into the moody dining room and set pie in front of Derek, Elspeth, and the newly returned Paul. They murmured their thanks, and Zana came in to serve everyone else. "I'll bring in the coffee," she said quietly, and disappeared again.

Derek cleared his throat. "I may as well get started with my announcements. First of all, Detective Dashiell has said we should be able to open up in about ten days. I'll be doing a couple of interviews with the media between now and then, clarifying our sadness over the loss of Garrett and our desire to put our energies back into our work. Paul will be helping me with the PR." He sent a grateful glance to his brother. "If we do this with dignity and sensitivity, our re-opening shouldn't be a problem."

Bethany raised a hand. "Who will be playing Garrett's part?"

Derek shook his head. "The old script is done. I've written a new one, and I'll give you your role descriptions tomorrow. Elspeth will have an individual makeup meeting with each of you to plan your look for the new story. She and I have already brainstormed and come up with some exciting ideas."

Elspeth nodded her sparkly head.

"Next," Derek said, "the locks have now been changed on both the back entrance and your individual rooms. If Paul has not already given you your new key, he will do so after dinner. The locksmith has assured me that the new locks are excellent and tamperproof. I hope this will allow everyone to sleep a bit easier."

"Thank you," I said.

Derek nodded at me. "Another agenda item," he said. "Dash has asked that each of you who left castle grounds in the last two days to please provide a list of the places you went and the exact time you spent in each place"—he held up a hand as people began to protest—"to the best of your recollection."

Tim looked indignant. "Why do we have to do that?"

"Because the police *want* us to," Derek said. "And once again I'll remind you that the police are trying to find out who murdered our friend Garrett. I'm sure we'll all be happy to cooperate in any way we can." His gaze took in everyone. "And if you can all do that tonight, I would appreciate it."

Connie met his gaze for the first time and nodded solemnly.

"Finally," he said, "you all know that we had a recent incident involving someone walking around at night in a costume. I can't begin to guess what that was about or whether there was an evil intention behind it. So I'm going to ask—I don't want to use the word 'curfew'—but I'll ask that you all remain in your rooms after midnight. If this is somehow a hardship for anyone, let me know."

He looked around the table with his searching dark eyes, his hair drooping dramatically over his forehead, as though he were auditioning for the part of "man under extreme stress."

Paul folded his hands in front of him on the table, his expression calm. "That's not a lot to ask. If anyone needs to leave their room, they can call Derek or me to explain. Then there won't be any misunderstanding."

Tim frowned. "Do you really want us calling you at two in the morning?"

Paul was unfazed. "If it means avoiding a terrifying incident, then yes."

People were looking furtively at me. I wondered if now, with some distance, my encounter with the skeletal vision seemed like melodrama to them, something that I had manufactured for attention. Even I had trouble understanding, in retrospect, why I had been so frightened that I stopped thinking rationally. It was impossible to quantify terror.

"Well, that's it," Derek said. "If anyone needs me, I'll be in my room."

Bethany said, "I assume that I can leave now." Her face was slightly petulant.

Derek stared her down. "Right after you account for your whereabouts for the last two days. Leave the document with me."

She bristled. "This is getting pretty ridiculous."

Connie sat up in her chair, her face flushed. "I think everyone needs to remember that Garrett was *stabbed to death* in this building. One of *us* might have done it. And I think Derek has done a great job of remaining friendly and polite while he tries to figure out if he has a murderer on his payroll. So maybe we should all show him a little gratitude, instead of making his life harder than it already is."

Bethany paled, and everyone else avoided Connie's gaze.

"Sorry, Derek," Tim said.

Connie stood up and said, "I'm going to my room. Nora, will you go with me?"

"Of course," I said. I looked at Derek to see if he was finished, and he nodded. I stood up and took my cake plate to the tray on the sideboard. The pie had been delicious; I'd been planning to peek into the kitchen to see if there was any more, but Connie was saving me from my sweet tooth.

We left the kitchen and went into the hall, where Paul caught up with us. "Don't forget your new keys," he said. "Connie, this is for Blue Crown. And, Nora, you're Green Crown, right?"

I nodded and accepted my new key with relief.

"Thanks, Paul," Connie said.

"Thank *you*," he said, "for defending Derek. I know you're not thrilled with him right now, but he really was trying to do the right thing. He always does." Paul's face held a mixture of pride in his brother and apology for what Connie had endured. She nodded. Then we said our good nights to Paul and walked to the main staircase, at which point I said, "It *was* nice of you to stand up for Derek that way."

She shrugged. "I'm sick of all the complaining. I'm still mad at him about the other thing, but he's way too accommodating of all the whining. He could have told the police to just question us down at the station instead of letting us all wander around here."

We turned on our flashlights and began ascending the stairs. "Do you think we should leave?" I asked.

She didn't answer at first, and I couldn't see her face clearly as she climbed the stairs at my side. "I don't know. I guess I still would like to stay, assuming this stuff can be cleared up soon. This is my home, and—you know—I care about Derek. It would feel weird being away from the castle. And him."

"Well, that's honest."

"What about you? I know it's selfish, but I would hate it if you left, Nora. It wouldn't be the same without you."

"I don't know. I don't really feel safe here, Connie. Garrett's dead, and that thing in the hall was chasing me. And then—well, you know what happened with that guy on the lawn."

She pondered those words for a while. In the meantime we had reached our third floor hallway. "Even now," I whispered, "I'm halfway afraid I'll see a ghost." We beamed our lights into the darkness, first one way, then the other. "And I'm getting tired of not being able to turn on a light."

Connie summoned up some humor as we walked to our rooms, clutching each other's free hand. "You probably didn't realize you had to take Castle *Dark* literally."

"No kidding," I said.

We reached Connie's door, and something cold touched my arm. I screamed, and Connie jumped, but then she said, "It's just Hamlet. He must have followed us up here."

I looked down to see Hamlet's dark eyes glowing in the beam of my flashlight. "You have to stop scaring me, dog," I said, my heart hammering in my chest.

Another figure loomed up in the dark. I grabbed Connie's hand; she tensed, and the figure materialized into Tim. "Hi," he said. "Nora, can I talk to you for a minute?"

No, absolutely not. "It's pretty late," I said.

"I know. I just— I feel like I need to clear some things

up." It didn't endear him to me that he used so many personal pronouns. Connie didn't look impressed, either.

"Maybe in the morning, Tim," she said crisply.

"Just for a second. We can talk wherever you want."

"I won't talk to you alone," I said. "Talk in front of Connie or not at all."

He looked wounded. "Okay, that's fine."

I turned to open my own door. "I have to check on my cats. We can talk in here." I turned on the lights and we all walked into my living space with Hamlet at our feet. I grinned when I saw Emily Brontë rise up on the bed, looking fluffy and blinking at me as though to assure me she hadn't been sleeping. Charlotte sat like a tiny boat in front of the fireplace, but Annie was not in sight.

I did a quick search of the rooms, not finding any ghosts or monsters, but not finding Annie, either. "Help me," I said to my guests. "Annie's missing. Oh, I hope she didn't somehow get in the hall."

Tim and Connie got to work. Tim lay on the floor and looked under my bed, Hamlet snuffling at his ears, and Connie began a search of the pantry compartments. "Sometimes cats can get into drawers from the back," she assured me.

After ten minutes I was starting to panic, picturing the tiny kitten lost and afraid in a giant castle with a million hiding places. I would never, ever find her. My eyes filled with tears. Tim saw this and said, "Now, don't give up. She could be any number of places. Where were they the last time they were missing?"

"Climbing the curtains," I said, wiping my eyes.

Tim went to the curtains and peered behind them. "Okay, no one climbing here." I wilted slightly, and he said, "No, wait—I spoke too soon." He pulled the left curtain back with a flourish to reveal a tiny gray ball on the windowsill—a gray kitten still fast asleep.

"Oh, Annie," I said, rushing forward and scooping her up. She gazed at me with bleary eyes, her whiskers twitching above her white chops. "You silly girl! Why would you sleep there when you have all these other comfy places?"

Tim and Connie laughed, each of them picking up a kitten of their own.

"I almost forgot," I said. "I got a gift for my little Brontës." I went to my bag from Relics Antiques and pulled out the velvet-lined box, the dark wood inlaid with turquoise and jet. "Look, girls." I set Annie on the bed, then opened the hinges so that there were two distinct compartments: the lid and the box. Annie climbed into the box immediately, testing the felt with her claws.

Connie and Tim set down their kittens, and they also immediately climbed into the box, where the three sat looking at one another.

"Hilarious!" Connie said, laughing. "Your three little daughters."

"A box of fun," Tim said. He seemed like the same old Tim again, friendly and likable. Had I imagined his sinister expression, his underhanded intentions?

"Does anyone want something to drink?" I asked. Connie went to pull a couple of wooden chairs across from my armchair.

"Not I," she said.

Tim patted his stomach. "No. I'm full, thanks."

We sat down and entered into an uncomfortable silence. Finally Tim scratched his arm in a nervous gesture and said, "I wanted to apologize. Looking back, I see why you were scared at the overlook, and I realize I was acting like— I don't know what. A weirdo or an idiot."

"What happened?" Connie asked sharply.

I said nothing. Tim sighed and said, "I invited Nora to go biking. I took her to the overlook to show her the view, but I was in a weird mood. I had a fight with Amy last night, and—" He saw my expression and almost laughed. "You don't think there is an Amy, do you? I freaked you out that much?"

I shrugged, and he took out his phone, poking it a few times to bring up his photo screen. Then he handed it to me. "Scroll left," he said. "There are a few there."

I did as he suggested and saw several pictures of Tim, smiling his dimpled smile, standing next to a pretty chestnut-haired woman in a variety of poses: next to their bikes, in front of a birthday cake, with a smiling family group. "Okay," I said.

"So what did you *do*?" Connie asked.

"He took me to a totally deserted location," I said. "He said he didn't want me or Elspeth repeating something he had told us, but he made it sound creepy, like he wanted us silenced."

"No, I—," Tim said, crestfallen.

"And he called me a liar. He said everyone in the castle was a liar."

"What the heck, Tim?" Connie said, glaring at him.

He looked at me. "Were you lying, though?"

I met his gaze with some defiance. "Yes, I was, because I wanted to get away from you."

"Okay, so I was right. We all lie, and we make it look convincing. That's what we *do*. That's why I was feeling weird. My girlfriend was mad at me, and I was living in a castle full of people wearing masks."

I narrowed my eyes at him, considering. Then I turned to Connie. "Tim had Garrett as a teacher in high school."

Connie turned to Tim, her mouth open in surprise. Tim gave me a wry look. "Okay, I guess I deserved that."

"He was your drama teacher? Why didn't you ever tell us?"

Tim shrugged. "Garrett didn't remember me. I didn't want to make a big deal of it."

"Why?" I said. "You hinted that there was a reason, and it wasn't just that you were embarrassed that he didn't remember you."

He shook his head. "No, it wasn't just that. I didn't want him to remember something else. I had this new adult relationship with him, and I didn't want it to be ruined—"

"By what?" Connie asked.

He sighed. "Garrett was a really popular drama teacher. All the kids loved working with him. But sometimes there would be grudges. Kids didn't get the parts they wanted, or they felt Garrett showed favoritism or something. Anyway, at one point a rumor started going around that Garrett was having an affair with one of the other teachers, Mrs. Spellman, in the world languages department. It was eventually quite a scandal, and I think a few parents complained and there was some kind of investigation. Ultimately Garrett was exonerated. It seemed like the rumor was the work of a disgruntled student, but his reputation had taken a hit. And I guess it also made things rough for the other teacher. I don't think she came back after that year. And Garrett left teaching pretty soon after."

"So why does that matter? Were you the disgruntled student?" I asked.

He looked miserable. "No, but I did my fair share to spread the rumor around. I'm not proud of it. But I was a high school kid, and I guess there was kind of a feeling of power in 'having something' on a teacher. Later I felt terrible because I had really liked him and learned a lot from him. Our next drama teacher wasn't as good. Garrett was talented."

"Wow. I'm surprised he gave in so easily," Connie said. "That doesn't seem like him."

Tim shrugged. "I think he just felt he had lost the confidence of the students, which he really hadn't. It was just a bad scene. I still feel guilty about it. When I got here and saw that Garrett was in the cast, I was relieved that he didn't remember me. It had been almost ten years, after all. So I wasn't in a big hurry to remind him of that time or to have him wonder about my part in it all."

"There's always the chance he did remember you but didn't say so for similar reasons," I said.

Tim thought about this. "I don't think so. There would have been some awkwardness. Plus I look different. I've filled out and grown a couple inches."

I studied him. "But that doesn't explain why you wanted Elspeth and me to keep silent. Garrett can't learn anything now, so what does it matter?"

He sighed. "I don't know. I just felt like I opened a box I shouldn't have." For some reason we all looked at the box on my bed, still filled with kittens that had now made themselves comfortable inside it. "And I didn't want it getting back to Sora or anyone who might have questions."

Connie folded her arms and stared at Tim. "Well, it sounds like you acted like a real weirdo this morning and I can understand why Nora took off."

"I'm sorry," Tim said. "And I was especially sorry that I wasn't with you when that guy confronted you outside the castle."

"It sounds like Nora handled herself really well," Connie said. She turned to me. "You'll have to show me what you did. That cop said you 'incapacitated' him. What exactly did you do?"

"Fingers in the soft part of the throat," I said.

"Oooh!" Connie said, impressed.

"Ouch," Tim added, looking pained. "But good job."

"My brothers taught me everything I know. As teenage boys, they have a special fascination with all brands of violence."

Connie giggled. "We should have them here in the castle as our guards."

"They would truly like nothing better," I said. "Which reminds me, I need to call them and see how Luke is doing."

Tim leaned forward. "Do you forgive me? I don't want things to be weird between us."

"I guess," I said. "You can prevent that by not acting weird anymore. Did you make up with Amy?"

Another sigh. "I hope so. I sent her flowers and an apology. It's my day of apologies."

"What was your fight about?" Connie asked, oblivious to her own rudeness.

"It's a long story. But essentially she wants me to leave Castle Dark and get a 'better job.' I told her this isn't a bad job, that I like it and I'm good at it. She seems to think a person isn't a professional unless they're working in an office somewhere."

Connie stared at him. "Then why are you apologizing? Tell her you want to keep your job."

"Well, I did. But I apologized for getting upset. We were both pretty intense, which is why we needed the time apart."

I stretched, suddenly tired. "I know we're all actors and we're paid to act, but there's a little too much drama in this castle."

Connie and Tim agreed with fervent nods of their heads. Hamlet sidled up to me, panting and smiling, and I patted his big head. He still wore the ruby that was meant to be a clue in our mystery. I took it off his collar and handed it to Connie. "You can give this back to Derek. I don't think Hamlet needs it anymore."

She took it and studied it in her palm. "It's pretty," she said. "Derek has such an eye for pretty things." She stood up and said, "Good night, everyone. Nora, I'm glad you found your kitten. Tim, come and make sure no one murders me in the hall."

Tim stood up. "See you tomorrow, Nora."

"Yeah, see you, Tim."

He held out his fist, and I bumped mine against it. I gave him credit for apologizing. I had met very few men who were willing to do so.

I watched them go into the hall, and I didn't close my door until I saw Connie ushered safely into her room, Hamlet at her side. "Good night," I said again.

I clicked my new lock into place and realized that I felt quite secure. I knew there was no one hiding in my room, thanks to my search for Annie, and I trusted Derek and John Dashiell when they said the new locks were good.

The Victoria Holt novel still lay facedown on my bedside table. Despite the frightening events of the day, I felt drawn to it. I wanted to finish the story.

After brushing my teeth, washing my face, and putting on pajamas, I fed the kittens, set their box on the floor, and climbed into my comfortable bed. I grabbed the book from my nightstand and put it on the pillow beside me. But, first things first, I picked up my phone to call my brothers, and it rang in my hand. It was Jay.

"Hello, brother."

"Hey," he said. "Sorry to call so late. We brought Luke home and then everyone was running around doing his bidding." I could hear relief in his voice under the supposed aggravation.

"I'm glad he's home."

"Yeah." He yawned hugely in my ear. "Listen, I wanted to check on something. Is it your castle where a guy just got murdered?"

"Where did you hear that?"

"I saw it on a news brief on YouTube."

"Okay—yes, it is this castle. It was a man I worked with."

"Whoa. That is *crazy*. You are in a *castle* where a guy got *murdered*."

"Yes, Jay. Do Mom and Dad know?"

"No, but I'm going to tell them!"

"Jay, don't. You know they'll freak out. The police are looking into things. We're all hoping this will be resolved soon."

"It's kind of a big secret to keep," he said.

"Tell Luke, then. You two can talk about it between yourselves. Mom and Dad have enough worries right now."

"Yeah, but if you get murdered, they'll be very angry that I didn't tell them so that they could drive out there and demand that you come home."

"I thought about coming home. But I want to give it a couple of days, see if they catch whoever did it. We're supposed to reopen in a week and a half. I have to learn a new script and stuff."

"What if Luke and I came there? We could patrol the halls with baseball bats."

"I know you guys would actually do that, but number one, Luke is a convalescent. Number two, you need to be there for him. And number three, if Mom and Dad don't want me at the site of a murder, they definitely don't want their teenage sons there, either."

"Oh, man, how cool, though. Hunting a murderer in a dark castle."

"You don't know the half of it," I murmured, picturing the skeleton with a frisson of remembered horror.

"There's *more*?"

"Not that I'm going to tell you right now. To be continued," I said.

"We have to come there soon," he said, and suddenly I missed him terribly, missed all of my family.

"I agree. Do talk to Mom and Dad about that. See when they're open to a visit. I'll find out when Derek thinks it might be okay."

"All right. But I'll have to tell them before I get them to agree to enter the premises of your death castle."

"Yes. In a week or so you can tell them. Just wait a little while."

"Okay. Do *not* get murdered in the meantime. Send a daily text."

"I will. Hey, you know those self-defense moves you and Luke taught me?"

"Yeah. That was a great presentation. We should put it on YouTube."

"I used one of them, and it helped."

"What? You had to fight someone?"

"Sort of. That's for the to-be-continued story, too."

There was a pause. Then Jay said, "Do I have to reassess my entire view of you? Are you some kind of badass? I thought only Luke and I got that gene, and that you and Gen were more like butterfly princesses."

"Yeah, I guess we're a combination," I said drily. "Go give Luke a butterfly princess kiss from me and tell him to feel better."

"He's fine," he said. "He just ate lasagna."

"Good night, Jay."

"Don't get murdered," said my little brother.

I ENDED UP finishing the book; it had a satisfying ending, which I read aloud to the Brontës, who had returned to the bed and purred in trio on my lap. I set it aside and turned off my lamp. I could see the dark silhouette of the tree outside my window, illuminated only by some pale moonbeams. There was no wind tonight.

I had expected the events of the day to torment me, replaying themselves again and again in my memory, but I was surprised. My mind was blank as I lay back on my pillow, and I fell almost instantly asleep.

Sometime later I woke again. I peered at the clock: two thirty. The room was still and quiet; I felt all three kittens as separate balls of fuzz on my bed. What had awakened me? I lay still, listening, and there it was—a faint shuffling sound and a beam of light visible under my door. I stiffened. Was someone trying to get in? Trying to lure me once more into the hall?

But I had learned my lesson. Whatever it was, I would not be investigating. Someone was clearly breaking Derek's curfew, but I was going to trust my new lock. Let someone else confront the person in whatever costume they had chosen tonight. Anger rose in me as I stared at the weak beam of light, which gradually moved to the right and then disappeared from view. Whoever had stood out there was walking southward, just as the skeleton had been walking when I looked out of my room.

I lay awake for another hour, listening for any rustling, half expecting to see more light under my door and half fearing that I would hear a loud bang as someone tried to batter it down.

Nothing happened. Eventually, despite my vigilance, I fell back to sleep, and I didn't awaken until the sun poured into my room.

15

Lover's Torment

WITH OUR BOOKS tucked under our arms, Connie and I took our breakfast sandwiches outside, through the south exit, where we sat on the edge of the fountain and listened to the gurgling water. The naiad beamed down at us with her peaceful smile.

"This is nice," Connie said, looking up at the blue sky. "We should be doing this every day while it's still summer and the mornings are so mild."

"I agree," I said.

We had brought books to read, as well; we both wanted a break from the castle without having to leave castle grounds. I was still eating Zana's creation. "This sandwich is delicious. What did she put in here besides eggs?"

Connie poked at her food. "It looks like red pepper. Maybe some kind of cheese."

"Mmmm." I took my last bite and chewed contemplatively, taking in the beautiful view. "It really is lovely here."

"Harder to leave than you might think," Connie said, trailing her fingers in the cool fountain water.

"But at some point I have to tell my parents what's happened here, and they're probably going to come and physically remove me."

"I know. My parents were tempted, too, but I told them that Derek is being super protective. They like Derek. Even after I mentioned—" She glanced at me with a wry expression. "You were right. They took his side for the most part. Said that it was noble of him to try to protect me. Which it would be, if this were eighteen fifty."

"I know. I get that." Over her shoulder I saw Derek emerge from the south exit, looking ridiculously handsome in a blue linen button-down shirt and a pair of white summer trousers. He approached us with his usual friendly expression, but he was nervous, as well.

"Good morning," he said.

We both greeted him, and his dark eyes locked on Connie's. I felt suddenly superfluous and longed to be gone. I stood up, gathering the little plates from which we had eaten our breakfast, and picked up the new book I had selected from the shelf in my room, the first in the Sue Grafton series. "I'm going to run this stuff inside. I'll see you later, Connie."

She looked surprised. "Uh—okay. Could you take my book, too, Nora? I guess I'll read inside later if you're not staying."

I took the book she offered and made a quick exit, sensing that some sort of confrontation was on the horizon. I set everything down to open the back exit with my new key, and then I carried it all inside. I set it down again on the window ledge so that I could peer out at Connie and Derek. He stood in front of her where she sat, saying something with a polite expression. His body looked awkward and gangly.

Connie regarded him in silence, her face inscrutable, and then she stood so that their faces were closer together.

She had to look up at him, but then she spoke with great animation, gesturing with her hands.

Derek put a hand on her arm and said something back. He looked as though he was assuring her of something.

She removed his hand from her forearm but continued to hold it between her palms. She said something that seemed to surprise him—oh, God, had she finally told him how she felt?—and he stared at her, stunned.

With a sudden lunge he took her in his arms and brought his mouth down on hers; Connie's arms went over his shoulders and her hands linked behind his head. They were so beautiful together that I couldn't stop watching, as though I were in the audience of a romantic play. "Oh, yay, yay, yay," I said happily, my face pressed to the window.

"You always look slightly suspicious when our paths cross," said a voice behind me. I jumped half a foot in the air and turned to face John Dashiell, who was giving me his raised-eyebrows smile. "Are you spying on someone?"

I lifted my chin. "As a matter of fact, I am. Connie and Derek have spent a year lusting after each other and everyone figured it out except them. They finally caught on," I said, gesturing to the window.

He peered out and said, "Ah. Good for them."

My gaze had returned to the window. Derek had lifted Connie so that she was sitting on the table. He was saying something, his face very close to hers, and she was laughing with an enviably carefree expression. "Yeah. I'm really glad. They make a sweet couple. It's nice to think of the castle as a place of romance instead of— You know."

"Yes." He waited until I looked at him again; he seemed suddenly tall and official, and my heart sank.

"Oh, no. Why are you here? Did something terrible happen?"

"Just asking some follow-up questions. How are you doing today?"

"I'm fine."

"Can we talk for a moment?"

I pointed at the dishes and books. "I just have to put those in the kitchen and take the books upstairs."

"I'll grab the dishes. You get the books. We can talk while we walk."

With one last peek at Connie and Derek (still kissing, still Hollywood-caliber visuals), I grabbed the books and joined John Dashiell as he walked toward the kitchen.

"Anything happen recently that I should know about?" he asked.

I struggled to keep up with his long stride. "Derek set a curfew for us."

"Good."

"And last night someone broke it."

His head whipped toward me; his eyes were almost glowing. "What happened?"

"I didn't even get out of bed. I had locked my door, and I've learned my lesson about going into the hall. I just heard a kind of shuffling, and I saw a light under the door-frame in that tiny crack between the door and the tile."

"It couldn't have been Connie?"

"I guess it could have been anyone, but the individual in question was moving southward. The same way as my skeleton friend."

A ghost of a smile appeared on his face, then vanished. I studied him for a moment, appreciating his strong-looking shoulders and his sharply carved jaw. I said, "What's happening with Connie's stalker? Is he in jail?"

He nodded. "He is, and he'll stay there because his bail was denied. Apparently Connie is not the first person who has reported him for stalking, which puts him at a class-three felony. He's going to do time, maybe as much as five years. Whenever he gets out, Derek and I will both know about it."

"Ah. That's good." We had reached the kitchen, and Dashiell brought the plates inside, where I could hear him talking to Zana. I peered into the dining room and saw Renata and Elspeth eating with Bethany and her husband, Tyler. I waved at him, and he held up a hand in greeting. She leaned over to talk to him, her red head a stark contrast with his dark one, and I realized that they, too, made a handsome couple. That reminded me of Connie and Derek. Were they still kissing back there?

Renata saw me and beckoned with a royal hand. "Come and have breakfast with us," she said.

"I just finished. Thanks." I moved my hand in a general farewell, then went back to the hall, where Dashiell joined me.

"Why are you grinning?" he asked.

"Am I? I was still thinking of Connie and Derek."

"You're a romantic, I guess."

"I absolutely am. I just think— Oops." I had adjusted the books in my hand, and Connie's bookmark fluttered to the floor. I picked it up and saw that it was the photo of Garrett and his girlfriend. "Oh—Connie must not have had this with her yesterday," I murmured. Then I looked more closely at the shot.

"Something wrong?" my companion asked, leaning in to study my expression.

"Dash," I whispered. I looked behind me at the dining room doorway, then said, "Come here." I walked rapidly away, toward the main staircase, and climbed to the second floor. Dashiell followed me.

When we got to the quiet landing, I said, "Connie was going to give this picture to Garrett's girlfriend, Sora."

"Yes, I remember."

"Yesterday we saw her unexpectedly, and I guess Connie didn't have it with her. But that was the first time I ever met Sora."

"Okay."

"You've met her, right?"

He nodded.

I held up the photo. "This isn't her."

He looked more closely, his face alert. "Are you sure? They're pretty far away—"

A sudden inspiration struck. "You took a photo of it on your phone. Can we look at that?"

He nodded, taking out his phone and finding the picture in question. He used his fingers to pull the picture into a larger size, focusing only on the faces. They were closer now, but more pixilated. Still, what I saw made me gasp, and John Dashiell swore under his breath.

The woman standing beside a younger Garrett Perth, with his arm slung around her, both of them smiling and relaxed, was definitely not Sora.

It was Renata.

16

Chronicle

I MET THE WIDE eyes of John Dashiell. "Did she ever mention—?"

His jaw tightened. "No, she did not. Do you know where she is?"

"I just saw her in the dining room."

He turned and began jogging down the steps; I left my books on a dark wood buffet that held some castle pamphlets and flew after him.

I caught up to him just as he reached the dining room; Renata, Bethany, and her husband all looked up with shocked faces. Dashiell's expression was intimidating.

"What's going on?" Bethany asked nervously. Tyler looked ready to jump out a window.

"Could you two excuse us?" Dashiell said. "I'd like to speak with Miss Hesse."

The young couple left so quickly, I almost laughed. Zana's shocked face appeared briefly in the doorway to the kitchen, and then she, too, disappeared.

Dashiell turned to me and held out his hand. "Do you still have that photo, Nora?"

I did, and I handed it to him.

He put it on the table in front of Renata, then sat down across from her.

She glanced at it, unsurprised, and smiled briefly. "So you know," she said. Her eyes met mine with something like resignation.

FOR REASONS UNCLEAR to me, Renata asked if I could stay for the interview. Dashiell said, "I have no objections," although it looked as though he did.

Renata sighed. "What did you want to know?"

Dashiell's lips were a thin line. "Let's start with why your past relationship didn't come up in our earlier talks."

She shrugged, seemingly weary. "It *was* in the past, so long in the past. We were just friends now. I helped him get this job, actually."

I remembered Sora saying that Garrett would never have gotten the job if not for a tip from a friend.

Dashiell didn't relent. "Were you jealous of his new relationship? Did you resent him for dating Sora?"

She shook her head. "No. I was happy for him. She was mellow, kind, not mercurial the way we actors are. He needed someone to balance him that way. He and I were too similar."

I nodded, seeing the logic of this.

"When did your relationship begin?" Dashiell asked.

"Years ago," she said. "Ten, eleven years ago now. It didn't last. It was a workplace romance."

I thought of what Tim had said: that Garrett was rumored to have had an affair with a foreign-language teacher. Renata was German. I gasped. "Oh, my gosh—are you *Mrs. Spellman*?"

Both Dashiell and Renata looked at me, surprised by my outburst. Renata said, "How did you know—?" just as Dashiell said, "What are you talking about?" He then swung toward Renata and said, "She's right?"

Renata sighed. "I was Mrs. Spellman. In another lifetime. Garrett taught drama at the same school where I taught German. A group of faculty members went out once after one of Garrett's shows. We ended up being the last two to leave the pub, and it . . . started something. I was estranged from my husband, and Garrett brought out the actress in me. I was still acting, taking parts in whatever productions I could get into, but it didn't pay a regular salary. That's why I started teaching. He encouraged me to keep pursuing my art." She turned to me. "How did you know—?"

"Tim told me that Garrett left his job because there was a scandal about his affair."

"Tim?" she said, her brows high.

"He was one of Garrett's students back then."

"Really? I did not know it. How strange . . ."

Dashiell had taken out a notebook and was jotting rapid notes. "So Tim has a connection to both Garrett and Renata?" he asked me.

"Yes. He just told me last night. He was—apologizing for the scene during our bike ride."

"Uh-huh." Dashiell's eyes were steely when he turned them back on Renata. "And what else should we know, Renata? Because I think there's more."

Renata sat up straight. She should have been wearing the crown that looked so good on her. "I went into Garrett's room after his . . . murder. I was afraid to face—well, this. Interrogation. So I thought I would remove evidence of our past affiliation. I found a photo in a frame; I was going to take it out of the room, but I heard a noise. I tossed it out the window."

Dashiell acknowledged me with a nod. My theory had been correct.

"The next morning I retrieved it. Nora saw me coming around the corner, the evidence still in my pocket, and I told her I had taken a walk."

"I should have known," I said. "You didn't smell like the outdoors. You smelled fresh, as though you'd just had a bath."

She nodded. "But what you should know, Detective, is that when I went into his room, it had already been ransacked."

"Oh?" Dashiell's pen paused above the paper.

"It frightened me. I didn't know who had been in there, and after I threw the picture out the window, I thought I heard people coming up the stairs. I escaped to my room, but on the way out of Garrett's space, I saw our old yearbook from West Vale on a shelf—Vale was the school where we taught—and I grabbed that, too." She met Dashiell's steely gaze. "Just as I was leaving, though, I thought I heard a sound."

"People coming up the stairs?" Dashiell asked.

"No—a sound in the wall."

Dashiell became very still, and I stared at Renata. Realization dawned. "Oh, my gosh—Elspeth told us that there was a secret compartment that abutted Garrett's room. She lets her cat walk around in there."

"*Show me*," Dashiell said, his face intense.

And then we were back in the hall, back on the staircase, bound for Garrett's room on the third floor. Renata set a slow pace, and Dashiell was clearly impatient, but he remained politely behind her.

When we reached the third floor, Renata pointed. "There are three ways to access the little passageway. Garrett was very excited about it when he was assigned this room. First, through the costume room." She led us into the costume room and to a panel covered by a mirror. A small lever to the right of the panel had it swinging outward and revealing a narrow hallway. She pointed again. "That goes across the hall and comes out in the little broom closet just before Garrett's room. Unless you keep going, in which case there is another exit in Garrett's room itself."

Dashiell found a pair of latex gloves in his pocket, pulled them on, stepped into the passageway, and disappeared. Renata and I walked across the hall and peered past the police tape into Garrett's room; moments later the wall near Garrett's wardrobe opened, and Dashiell walked out. He was furious. "We could have searched here on the night in question. And no one thought to mention it?"

"I didn't know," I said meekly.

"I wasn't there when you searched," Renata said. "But I did keep things from you. I'm sorry."

"I'll take the yearbook, please," Dashiell said, his voice still icy. He pressed a button on his phone and said something about needing "the team" again.

Renata went into her room and returned with a book called *The West Vale Chronicle*, dated 2011. "Here it is," she said.

She still had an aura of quiet dignity, despite Dashiell's constant glaring. She opened the book to the theater page and pointed to Garrett's picture. It was a standard faculty shot: Garrett wearing a suit jacket and a white shirt, his blue tie not entirely straight. There were candid shots, as well, and I spotted one in which Garrett was leading some sort of creativity exercise with a drama class: his hands were high in the air, his expression animated, and the students around him were laughing. A couple of kids on the outskirts of the group scowled in typical teenage fashion. What had Tim said? *Sometimes there would be grudges.*

Renata tucked the picture of her and Garrett into the book and snapped it shut. "I've bookmarked it for you," she said.

Dashiell nodded.

I noticed that Renata, for the first time since I had met her, looked uncomfortable. Nervous even. A moment later Dashiell noticed it, too. "What else?" he said.

She cleared her throat. "I thought, when you came downstairs, that it was about the curfew. Derek asked us not to leave our rooms."

"Was that *you* last night?" I asked.

"I couldn't sleep." She studied her hands. "I was worried about the girls." It took me a moment to determine that by "the girls" she meant Connie and me. "So much has happened, in such a short time, and I feared that somehow they had become targets. I'm afraid my anxiety got the better of me. I had to make sure that their doors were locked."

Dashiell's face softened slightly. "I think they were quite safe."

She nodded. "Yes, yes. I'm glad to say that both doors felt solid."

"And that was all you did? Walk down the hall to their rooms and back to yours?"

"Yes. I had my cell phone light on so that I could see."

"And did you see anything out of the ordinary?"

"No," she said. "But that hall is full of shadows at night; it's quite frightening. 'Hell is murky,'" she quoted shakily. And she had been like Lady Macbeth, walking with her candle in the darkness, plagued by guilt or anxiety.

I reached out and squeezed her arm, trying to reassure her. "Thank you for checking on me."

Dashiell cleared his throat. "I have to ask, Renata. Was it also you in the monk costume the night that—"

"No!" she cried, looking scandalized. "I would never terrorize this poor child that way." She sent me a look of motherly concern. "Besides which, I don't act with masks. Talented actors use facial expressions."

Dashiell looked at her, his face blank. "That person

wasn't *acting*, Renata. She—or he—was hiding. Anyone can hide."

She waved a dismissive hand, back to her regal self. "It wasn't me, I can assure you."

Dashiell nodded, all business now. "If you'll return to the first floor or to your rooms, perhaps? We have work to do now."

He turned away from us, but his manners had him turning back briefly to say, "Thank you for your help." Then he went to the end of the hall and began to talk into his phone.

17

Unrequited Love

FOR A FEW days, life seemed to return to normal at Castle Dark. June turned to July, and the days grew steamy under perpetual blue skies. We were working on our new scripts. Derek had indeed created a scenario in which I played a singer—in this case a singer in a cocktail lounge. Elspeth and Bethany were waitresses, Connie was a bartender, Tim was the club accountant, Renata was a regular customer, and Derek owned the club.

Derek had decided that instead of eating with the Inspectors in the dining room, we would create an actual cocktail lounge in the second-floor ballroom and its foyer, where the piano would be authentically a part of the scene. For the dinner portion, I was supposed to play and sing, and Inspectors would be allowed to make requests and put tips in my jar. Then a "policeman" would come in (a rare appearance by Paul) to announce that a man had been found murdered outside—a fictional man named Chip Gillespie, who happened to be Renata's stepson, Connie's fiancé, Elspeth's college friend, Tim's roommate, Bethany's crush, my sometime lover, and Derek's enemy. We all had motives for wanting Chip dead, but ultimately it was Elspeth who killed him after she found out that he'd broken up her college romance by telling her boyfriend a lie. She had never found anyone quite like him. . . .

Clearly, I mused as I read the script, Derek's writing had been influenced by his own romance, which was now the talk of the castle. Connie floated around on clouds of happiness, grinning at everyone, and Derek wore a stupid smile almost constantly. At dinner the two of them gazed dreamily at each other and never noticed that the rest of us were good-naturedly poking fun at them.

One night, after a late rehearsal, they left the table early because Connie said she needed to "proofread Derek's notes," and we managed to wait until they were gone before we burst into laughter.

Elspeth wiped her eyes. "Oh, but it's sweet. Clearly they were made for each other."

Renata nodded. "I am glad their great unspoken passion has finally been revealed. The castle was heavy with their angst."

"What about you, Elspeth and Renata?" I said, spooning into my dessert cobbler. "Zana and Bethany are married, and Tim is spoken for, but you're the mysteries. Do you have some secret grand passions?"

Renata laughed. She was wearing a sleeveless blue blouse and a white skirt, and some blue stones glinted in her ears. "Oh, 'passion' is a word for the young."

Elspeth snorted. "There are tons of guys in town who have the hots for Renata, ever since they saw her in the community theater version of *Cabaret*. And a certain guy named Rafe sent her flowers just last month."

With a wave of her hand, Renata dismissed Elspeth's assertions, but she was smiling and blushing.

Elspeth pointed at her. "Yeah, she knows it's true." Then

she sighed. "I, on the other hand, have relentlessly pursued a guy who teaches at Wood Glen High, but so far he is not picking up on my signals."

"Maybe you need different signals," Tim suggested. "Like neon signs."

"Worth a try," Elspeth said, patting tonight's tiara into place.

"What about you, Nora?" Bethany asked. "Are you dating anyone?"

I shook my head. "No, but I've had many an unhappy love affair."

"Oh, come on," Zana said as she came in to clear the table. "I can't imagine a guy letting you get away."

"Lots of guys let me get away," I said, "even when I wasn't trying to get away. My big college romance was initially dreamy—we fell in love when we were cast in a play together—until I realized that he had a habit of falling in love with his leading ladies. When he was cast in a new play and fell for a new girl, I protested, and he called me melodramatic."

"Ironic," Tim said.

"Yes. I must confess to some Schadenfreude when I learned he did not become the big Broadway star he told everyone he would be. I think he works at an office supply store."

"Karma," Elspeth said.

"Very good German pronunciation, Nora," Renata said approvingly, and I laughed.

"Anyway, there were others like him. I made the mistake of falling for actors, and as I told Connie the other day—actors shouldn't date actors."

Renata nodded sadly; her relationship with Garrett had not survived. I wondered if they, too, had found that actors were incompatible.

Bethany had donned one of her exaggerated expressions, this time one of disdain. "That's ridiculous. Tyler and I were both drama majors in college, and we are perfect for each other."

I bowed my head in acknowledgment of this. "I stand corrected," I said.

Tim was grinning at me, but furtively. He had confided, on a recent and much more enjoyable bike ride, that he found Bethany's histrionics "insufferable."

"Tim," I said, tired of talking about my love life, "how did you and Amy meet?"

He grew bashful. "Oh, I don't think you romantic ladies will be all that impressed by this. We met online."

Elspeth held up a finger. "Almost forty percent of couples meet online."

"Really?" Renata said, turning to her. "How very interesting."

Tim nodded. "It wasn't a dating site; it was a video game. We both played it, and we did a lot of chatting in the game. It was fun. Eventually we exchanged e-mail addresses, and we started chatting there. Then we exchanged photos, and a few weeks later, we decided to meet. We had immediate chemistry."

I said. "I disagree with you, Tim. That's very romantic."

He shrugged, blushing slightly.

Zana appeared in the doorway, leaning on the jamb. Bethany said, "Sit, Zane. We're talking about relationships. Tell us how you met Eric."

To my surprise, Zana smiled and sat down. She shook her head, still smiling, and said, "We were so young. So young."

"Did you attend school together?" Renata said.

"Yes, but we didn't know each other in high school. It was after we graduated; Eric was a student at U of I, and I was in culinary school. His family had a party, a big birthday party for his dad. I was working part-time for a caterer, and we got hired to do the event. Eric and I recognized each other from school, so we got to talking. He told me later that he had just thought I was so pretty in my little caterer's outfit. Just a little black dress with a white apron. He asked if I would go to the movies with him the next day, and I said yes. Before I left that party, he pulled me into a hallway and stole a kiss."

"Oh, my," Elspeth said. "Fast mover."

"But so romantic," said Bethany with a misty expression. "Ty and I went to school together, but the funny thing is, we didn't meet on campus. I met Tyler at a concert. We were at Lollapalooza in Chicago. I couldn't see the band, and I was jumping up and down. He asked if I wanted him to lift me up, and I said yes, and he put me on his shoulders. It was amazing."

"That's cool," Tim said.

Paul had been sitting at the end of the table, eating cobbler and quietly listening to all the stories. I turned to him and said, "Paul and I should start a club. The Happily Unattached."

"I'll join," Elspeth said cheerfully.

"As will I," said Renata, her expression placid.

Paul grinned. "I'll be in charge of the T-shirts."

We laughed, and Zana said, "I better get started on those dishes."

"I'll help you," Tim said. He stood up and accompanied Zana into the kitchen.

Elspeth and Renata rose, murmuring about phone calls they needed to make, and they said their good evenings.

Bethany looked at her watch and said, "Oh, gosh. Tyler will be home from work. I have to run, too. See you!" She whisked out of the room as though she were walking off a stage.

Paul and I were left alone. He said, "Our club theme song could be 'All by Myself.'"

"Ha ha! That's a great song, though."

His expression became mischievous. "Fancy playing it for me on the piano? I wasn't at the other concert."

I had been yearning for a reason to return to Derek's Steinway. "I could be persuaded," I said. "I only charge a thousand dollars."

He nodded, considering this offer. "How about a handful of M&M's?"

"Deal," I said.

Moments later we were climbing the stairs to the second floor, beaming our lights ahead of us. I looked for Hamlet this time before he could terrify me, and sure enough, he was following us up the stairs.

We reached the landing, and Paul flipped on a light I didn't know existed, illuminating the hallway. "Ah, this castle," he said, gazing down the red-carpeted expanse. Hamlet found a toy and brought it to Paul, who patted his head. "It's always been such fun. I can't wait until this terrible event is resolved, and we can build our way back."

"Back to what?"

His blue eyes held regret. "To being happy again."

ON JULY 3, Jade came to visit the kittens. She had brought a ball of yarn, and we spent a good half hour watching the Brontës tumble over their new toy, flipping their little bodies this way and that as they attempted to conquer the large yellow ball.

We were sitting on the floor in front of my fireplace. Jade rolled the ball of yarn to me, and the kittens chased it. Charlotte pounced with spectacular form, Emily pounced on Charlotte, and Annie fell on her fat little belly.

Jade laughed, and said, "This is a really nice home for them. And I'm glad they got to stay together. I like what you named them, too; I read *Jane Eyre* in school. It was pretty good in between the boring parts."

I stared at her, scandalized. "There are no boring parts."

She shrugged. "Like I said, it was pretty good. Do you read a lot?"

"I do. Books, and scripts when I audition for things."

Her eyes took on a gleam of interest behind her dark glasses. "I would love to audition for something in the city. That sounds so awesome!"

"It can be. It can also be very nerve-racking and heart-breaking. Right before I got the job here, I thought I had a part in the bag. I had two callbacks, but they ultimately said no. That hurt."

"Oooh, I bet. You are going to try out for our next community-theater thing, right? I think there are auditions for *Fiddler* in the fall."

"Hmm. Maybe. If we're not too busy here."

Jade picked up Annie and held her high in the air. Annie gazed at her, utterly trusting. "I love cats," she said, setting Annie down near the yarn.

"Do you have one at home?"

"If by one you mean four, then yes." She grinned. "And we'll end up with more. My mom and I are suckers for strays."

"You and your mom are pretty close, huh?"

"Well, all three of us, really. I'm an only child."

I grinned at her. "I had kind of guessed that."

"Yes, yes. I'm a precocious child, blah blah. Like I haven't heard that all my life." She was trying to line all three kittens up for a picture, but Emily kept wandering away. "My parents are pretty cool, though. My dad is a real feminist, not a fake one. And he isn't like those jerks who say 'I'm a feminist because I have a wife and daughter.' That's still sexist. He's a feminist because he believes all human beings have rights."

"Good for him."

"Yeah. Got it!" she said, finally snapping her picture.

She showed it to me. It was a remarkably good picture—well framed and lighted and capturing the sweetness of each face.

"Oh, could you send that to me?"

"Sure. Give me your number. You can make it your profile picture or something." I gave it to her and her thumbs flew on her keyboard, and she said, "There."

Now the kittens were staying in the little pile Jade had posed them in, and I realized they were getting sleepy. "I love the way they just nap right in the middle of things. I aspire to be like that," I said.

"Yeah, it's great." Jade sighed and stretched, then snapped a few more pictures of the Brontës. "I should probably go soon. I have afternoon shift at the bakery." She pushed her glasses up on her nose and sent me a quizzical glance. "Are you guys any closer to getting the killer? Or am I not allowed to ask?"

I shrugged. "We can all ask, but the police aren't saying anything. I think they're working hard, though." There was still always at least one police officer on the premises, and I had seen Detective Dashiell more than once, either talking with Derek or stalking around the grounds for reasons unknown.

She nodded, looking thoughtful. "My mom says I have too big an imagination. I think that's kind of a compliment; shouldn't all imaginations be big? Anyway, I kind of came up with my own reason why any person in the castle could have done it."

"Really? Why might I have done it?" I asked, genuinely curious.

"That's easy. You have a secret, and Garrett found out. Simple."

I laughed. "And what is my secret?"

Her smile held a hint of evil. "You're planning to kill that lady who got your part."

"Oh, my," I said. "Even I am not that competitive. But in a story, that would work. What else have you got?"

She started counting on her fingers. "It could have been Derek because he and Garrett had a fight one time. Maybe it wasn't resolved."

"What?"

"Yeah, like a yelling match. It was at Wood Glen Gardens, which is like a restaurant/pub in town. It was the talk of the neighborhood for a while."

"When was this?"

She shrugged. "A couple months ago."

I had never heard this. Had Derek mentioned it to Dashiell? Perhaps I could ask Connie. . . . Jade had moved on without me, immune to my shock.

"And then Connie, because maybe Garrett made a pass at her. I assume guys do, simply because she's pretty. The curse of beauty, right? You probably get that, too."

"Well, thanks. And Connie doesn't strike me as the murderous type."

She pulled down another finger. "Then there's Renata. My mom saw her one time when she got 'overserved.' That's what Mom called it. Maybe she and Garrett got drunk and did something they regretted, and she killed Garrett so he wouldn't tell."

Renata had mentioned, when she said the keys could open other doors, that she'd learned it after having too much to drink. But I had never seen her looking inebriated. . . .

"And of course Bethany, because she was mad that Derek didn't hire her husband. She was always moaning about it when we did a play together last year."

"Wasn't there only one opening?"

"Yeah, I don't know. Maybe she thought Derek should have made one? She was like 'People refuse to see Tyler's talent,' which I took to mean he has none."

I couldn't resist a giggle at that, and Jade looked pleased.

"Then of course Elspeth could have done it because Garrett came into the costume room and caught her in the act."

"The act of what?"

Jade shrugged. "That's for the police to figure out. She was doing something, Garrett saw her, and she killed him."

It was chilling, the way she said it in such a matter-of-fact voice.

"I think you've covered everyone," I said, stroking Emily's soft ear with one finger. Charlotte had curled into a ball, Annie was stretched out next to her, and Emily was a foot away from them, belly up and snoring.

"Nope. Two more. Zana could have done it because Garrett wanted his own girlfriend to be the chef at Castle Dark and was advocating for it. Zana was furious because he was threatening her job."

I stiffened. "Is that true?"

She shrugged. "I don't know. I remember Sora said something once, when my friends and I were having sundaes at her shop, that her boyfriend worked at Castle Dark and that it would be a fun gig for a chef."

Jade was a surprising storehouse of information. I needed to let Dashiell know about her.

"And then of course there's Paul. That one's easy. He's always been jealous of his brother, and he wants to take over his role. So he kills Garrett and frames Derek for it, then takes over the castle as the noble and grieving brother. And he ends up getting more business than ever because of the murder."

I recalled Derek's words at the dinner table, right after Garrett's death—that the Inspectors had been even more thrilled because someone had actually died.

I studied Jade's face. "And what about Tim?"

She shrugged. "I don't know, maybe Garrett made fun of his bike pants."

Normally this would have made me laugh, but Jade's theories had disturbed me too much. I rubbed my hands on my legs and stood up. "This is getting a bit depressing," I said.

Jade looked up at me, surprised. "It's only fake stories," she said. "I'm just a child." She batted her eyelashes at me, and I laughed.

"You're hardly a child. And I doubt anything gets by you."

She sighed. "Meanwhile, time to make the donuts. My mom showed me this old commercial on YouTube where a guy just says that over and over. 'Time to make the donuts,'" she said in a zombie voice. "We joke about that all the time."

I held out my hand and she took it, standing up and slinging her little purse over her arm. "Jade, it has been a pleasure," I said.

"Yeah. Thanks for taking such good care of the kittens. They like it here."

"I love them."

"See you soon! Come to the bakery—we've got some really good Fourth of July treats, and we're open in the morning."

"I'll try," I said.

She walked to the door, waved over her shoulder, and walked out, shutting the door behind her.

The Brontës remained in sweet, furry slumber. I lay down beside them on the rug, gently scratching Annie's tiny head and thinking about everything Jade had said.

I closed my eyes for a moment and didn't wake up until Connie came to walk me down to dinner.

AT THE DINNER table, Derek looked happy and excited, the way he had when I had first arrived at the castle. "We have an announcement," he said to us after we were all seated, "and this is a good one."

"About time," Tim joked.

Connie looked ready to burst with the news. "Derek had the best idea, and then Paul made it even better."

Derek put his arm around her. *The king and queen of the castle.* My brain studied that idea for a moment, even as Derek went on talking. "As you know, tomorrow is July Fourth. We used to have a big fireworks show, but that won't happen for two reasons. One, we are still in mourning and it would be inappropriate. Two, the Wood Glen Ecology Commission asked us last year to consider alternate celebrations, since fireworks are actually rather devastating to the birds and animals in our woods."

"So what are we doing?" Elspeth asked.

"A bonfire," Derek said. "We'll put up a poster in town, charge some minimal fee for tickets on entry, see if any locals want to come out. Paul used to build big fires all the time at his fraternity bonfire parties, and he knows how to do it safely. We'll light it well away from any forestland. People can come and enjoy an hour or two on the grounds, and hopefully it will help to minimize the stigma that we've gotten in the last week or so. Then a day or two later, we'll open up our website to reservations again and we'll get to work on building our cocktail lounge."

Tim looked dubious. "Isn't it kind of late to expect anyone to attend?"

Derek shook his head. "I'll plant the information tonight with people who might be able to spread the word over most of Wood Glen by morning. A lot of people in this town wouldn't turn down a chance to hang out at the castle on a holiday."

"Derek, I think it's a good idea," Renata said.

"Assuming that Garrett's attacker was an outsider," I said, "do we have to worry that person will take this opportunity to come back and attack someone else?"

Derek grew solemn. "Paul and I have talked with the police. They'll be on the premises, as well."

"It sounds kind of spooky," I said.

"Which is good publicity," Paul said. "That's sort of our claim to fame."

We ate our dessert in a festive mood, planning the details of the bonfire and feeling a certain shared relief at the prospect of something positive on the horizon.

Connie tended to linger with Derek these days, so I walked up the stairs on my own. Even Hamlet had deserted me this evening, which was oddly depressing. I followed the brave beam of light to my door and locked myself securely in my room. Charlotte strolled up to me on crayon-sized legs; she had obviously been drinking water, and it had given her a pointy gray beard. "You look very wise, Charlotte," I said, and she began to purr. I scooped her up and took her to the bed.

I had been wondering whether or not I should contact John Dashiell about Jade's revelations. It felt rather tattly, but at the same time some of her details had seemed important. I set Charlotte down and lifted my phone. I found Dashiell's number and typed:

Dash, you should talk to Jade Balfour at Balfour Bakery.

I pressed SEND before I chickened out and set my phone down. It buzzed a moment later, and something in my stomach turned over with a ticklish sensation.

I picked it up, opened the screen, and read:

Hello, Nora. Why should I do that?

I was talking to her today, and she knew some things I'd never heard.

A moment later my phone rang. I panicked; I hadn't

planned to talk to him. Then I took a deep breath. "Don't be a fool," I said to myself, and I slid my finger over the ANSWER button. "Hello?"

"Nora."

Oh, God. Had I never realized how sexy his voice was? "Yes, hello."

"What did this young lady tell you?"

"Well, she was being kind of—whimsical—and making up motives for everyone in the castle. And in the process she told me that Derek and Garrett had recently had a loud and public fight."

Rustling on his side. "When was this?"

"She said maybe two months ago. And that it was the talk of the town or at least of the theater crowd."

"Did she say what it was about?"

"She didn't know."

He was tapping keys in the background. I tried to picture him at his desk. What did it look like? How big was his office? Did he have a window? "What else?" he said.

"Oh, uh—she hinted that Renata might drink a lot. And she suggested that Garrett was trying to replace Zana with his girlfriend, Sora."

"And are these just the gossipy assumptions of a teenager?"

"Probably. But I thought she might be worth talking to nonetheless. She works in the bakery and sees lots of people, and she misses nothing. Oh, she also said that when Garrett came in with his girlfriend, he always looked nervous. Looking over his shoulder, she said. I mean it—she's sharp."

"Hmm," he said, typing again. "Well, thank you for this information. I will follow up on it."

"Okay. I assume you know about Derek's bonfire?"

"I'll be there. Will I see you?"

"You probably will. Derek is asking us to mill around in

the crowd, talking up the mystery parties. He's asked El-speth to dress us up in something 'patriotic but dramatic.'"

"I can't *wait* to see her interpretation of that directive," he said. His voice was wry, but also held a touch of flir-tation.

"I'll see you then, Detective Dashiell."

Something in my voice must have encouraged him, be-cause he was chuckling as I ended the call.

18

Fire in the Dark

I SMELLED THE FIRE long before I left the castle. Paul, Derek, and Tim had been visible outside Connie's window earlier in the day, building the wood-and-stone structure that would contain the bonfire. Derek had notified the fire department, and a representative came out to make sure that everything was far enough away from both the castle and the woods.

Elspeth showed up at my door with a costume draped over her arm and a happy smile brightening her face. She held up her "patriotic yet dramatic" design, and I said, "No."

"Oh, come on! Derek has already approved it, and you and Connie will match. It's kind of an homage to the disco era."

"Connie!" I yelled.

Connie came out of her room, holding her book, and Elspeth held up the costumes.

"Seriously?" Connie said. "You expect us to wear those? Did you want people to think we were members of ABBA?"

"Sort of," Elspeth said. "I was going for that look."

She had found slinky one-piece jumpsuits with low necklines and bell-bottom pants. They looked like something from a production of *Hair*.

"You'll be amazed by how they look on you," she coaxed. "Connie, I think the white one for you, and the red one for Nora, and then I have a blue-and-white polka-dot neck scarf for both of you."

I stared at Connie, who was smirking at the outfits. "Okay, I'll wear it," I said.

"Great!" said Elspeth.

"If *Tim* does."

She looked like the proverbial cat that had dined on a canary. "You think you caught me out with that, don't you? Tim's is blue. Derek says they will be fantastic eye-catching costumes, and he figures the three of you can pass out pamphlets for the castle. So everyone will know you're in character."

"It's asking a lot, El," Connie said.

"Wait till you see the awesome platform shoes I found," she said, clearly excited. "Nora, you're a size seven, right?"

I stomped my foot. "No. I'll wear the costume, but I won't wear high heels. We'll be on the *grass*, in the *dark*. And there are, like, gopher holes. I'm not risking my life for a photo op."

Elspeth sighed deeply. I had tampered with her creative vision. She gave me a sorrowful look and said, "All right, ballet flats it is." She handed me the red suit. "Try this on so I can see if it needs hemming."

She turned and began plodding toward her room, acting the part of the dejected artist, but I said, my voice suspicious, "Hang on! What are you and Renata wearing?"

With a shrug, she said, "Derek made this a ticketed event, even though the tickets are free. Renata and I will be at the front gate taking tickets, so he told us to wear our Castle Dark T-shirts and Fourth of July hats."

"Convenient," I said.

"You're going to look amazing," she assured me.

Two hours later Connie and I stood next to each other, clad in formfitting pantsuits that made us look like Elton John's backup singers. We had tied on our blue scarves and wore our hair down and straight, at Derek's request.

"Your boyfriend is going to owe me one," I said, feeling moody.

Connie started leaping around. "It's actually really comfortable material, Nora! Almost like pajamas. It's growing on me."

"That's because you look outrageously sexy in yours. I look like some weird holiday prostitute."

"Come here. I'm taking a selfie." She pulled me toward her, and I managed not to frown into the camera while she took pictures of us together.

"Send that to my sister," I said. "I'll ask for her fashion opinion." I gave her Gen's number.

Her thumbs moved rapidly on her phone. "Gen? That's a neat name. Is it short for something?"

"Genevieve."

"Oh, how pretty! Your parents were good at naming kids."

"Yeah, I guess." My phone buzzed, and I saw I had a text from Gen:

Those are amazing! Retro but somehow nouveau. Love it.

"Huh," I said, showing it to Connie.

She laughed. "See? Derek knows his stuff."

"Let's get this over with," I said. It was the best I could do in the circumstances.

* * *

THE FIRE CREATED a dramatic tableau: orange flames shooting toward the star-filled sky, people jostling against one another, sometimes holding sparklers that briefly illuminated laughing faces. The castle loomed behind the flames, a dark and Gothic silhouette looking like a burned-out shell of itself. In the firelit dark, our costumes were less garish and more festive. Derek's vision had been right. Even Tim, in his blue pantsuit that Renata said "made him look like a Bay City Roller" (whatever that was), seemed to get into the spirit of the thing and tried out some disco moves as he engaged the crowd, handing out pamphlets and chatting with visitors.

Connie found me at one point and spoke close to my ear so that I could hear her over the noise. "I'm so glad that we can do something happy and positive. Derek is brilliant. The people are having fun, and the bonfire is fantastic!"

It was a beautiful fire, a big, bright, and gorgeous study of heat and light and combustion. It was the heart of history and mythology and folklore. It was primal, a key element in every story ever told. . . .

"You have a weird look on your face," Connie said.

"I'm just enjoying this. The fire, the sky, the night air. I'm used to the city. This is the best part of my move to Wood Glen."

"That and your friend Connie."

I put an affectionate arm around her. "That's true."

She looked around with an eager expression. "I'm going to pass out some pamphlets and find something to drink. Zana has a refreshment table over there. Do you want anything?"

"Not right now," I said.

She nodded and skipped off in her effervescent way.

Prompted by Connie, I made a halfhearted journey

through the crowd, passing out Derek's pamphlets for the castle. I saw various couples on the outskirts of the group kissing in the shadows. What a romantic evening this would be, really, if someone was dating. I tucked the rest of the pamphlets into a little bag I had slung over my shoulder and let myself be a bystander once again. My fascination with the fire continued, and I didn't even notice the person next to me until he touched my arm.

"The costume has exceeded my expectations."

I turned to face John Dashiell, the former gardener of Castle Dark. He wore a pair of blue jeans and a dark shirt. "Hmph," I said. "I will be charging Derek money for every mosquito bite that I get in a weird place."

He grinned. "Hello, Nora."

"Hello, Dash."

We exchanged a look in the smoky orange light. "Have you captured some business?" he asked.

"I think so. Have you found any criminals?"

"Not so far. The night is young."

I laughed and looked back at the fire. Dashiell's hand brushed mine, a tentative gesture, and then it curved around my palm and squeezed. I returned the pressure and experienced a sudden sensory overload: bright orange flames, murky smoke, a woodsy scent, the warm pressure of his hand, a burst of euphoria. . . .

Turning, I met his eyes and opened my mouth to speak, but was jostled by a man who staggered past, smelling of beer. "Hey," I managed, and then a teenage girl jogged up and handed me a sparkler. I said, "I don't have any way to light it."

Someone in the crowd said, "Here, light it on mine." A hand held out a lit sparkler, and I automatically put the fuse of mine against it. It was Tim; I noticed his school ring, with a stone that was blue and square, glimmering in the light. But then I happened to see someone disco-dancing in the midst of a group about thirty feet away—someone dressed in blue with a cap of blond hair. *That* was Tim.

I looked back at the man next to me and saw that it was Tyler, and he was standing next to Bethany, who had somehow escaped having to wear a costume at all because she had told Derek that she wanted to come as a visitor with her husband.

Tyler. Tyler was wearing a ring identical to Tim's, which meant that Tyler had gone to Tim's high school. Tyler had known Garrett Perth—yet Bethany had never once mentioned it. Perhaps she didn't know; she said they had met after college, at Lollapalooza. Now the two of them stood talking, their heads close together, their words inaudible. Was it my imagination that they looked sinister? Was that simply an effect caused by the weird light?

John Dashiell bent toward me. "Are you all right?"

I turned so that Bethany and Tyler were behind me and leaned closer to the detective so that I didn't have to raise my voice. "Dash, there's something weird here."

"What?"

"Hang on. I have to ask Tim something." I moved toward Tim, picking my way through the crowd and holding my sparkler as I would a strange candle. I thought of Renata playing Lady Macbeth. Of her saying "Hell is murky." The smoke was growing more plentiful, and Derek and Paul appeared out of the thick air to throw more wood on the fire, looking like dark, handsome devils. I reached Tim; Dashiell was close behind me.

"Tim," I said.

He turned, surprised. He looked a bit disheveled and sweaty from all his dancing. "Hey, Nora. Hey, Detective. What's going on?"

"Come over here," I said, and I pulled him away from the crowd to a spot where no one was standing, farther from the fire. Dashiell followed. "You never told me Tyler went to high school with you," I said. Dash stiffened beside me.

"Who?" Tim asked, his face blank.

"Tyler. Bethany's husband. He has the same school ring as you."

"What? I don't know him very well. Are you sure it's not just a similar—" He was looking through the crowd, and his eyes lighted on Tyler and Bethany. "Oh, my God," he said.

"What?" Dashiell prompted.

"There *was* a kid named Tyler at my high school. He was in drama, actually. He was kind of a joke, a terrible actor. He applied for a scholarship to Juilliard, but of course he never even got an interview. If that's him—wow, he looks different. He's bulked up. He was a skinny kid back then."

"So he knew Garrett in those days?" I said.

"Yeah, sure. He took a bunch of drama classes. He hero-worshipped Garrett, but he ended up hating him because—" His eyes grew wide as he realized what he had just said.

"Because what?" I said.

"Because Garrett refused to write him a recommendation for Juilliard. Tyler threw a fit."

Dashiell said, "Excuse me," and started walking toward the newlyweds, except that they had disappeared. Dashiell, too, was soon lost in the crowd. Moments later I got a text from him:

I don't want you actors out here. Get everyone you can back in the castle until I find this guy.

Mildly alarmed, I showed the text to Tim, who looked stunned. He scanned the smoky darkness and said, "I'm going to tell Derek; he's not going to want to leave while all these people are here. And he and Paul won't want to leave the fire unattended. But maybe he'll help me round everyone up. Go find Connie, and I'll meet you at the entrance with whoever I can find."

I nodded and plunged into the crowd, scanning for Connie's white pantsuit. I didn't see her. Might Derek have already whisked her inside? And was Dashiell perhaps being a bit too melodramatic? Maybe I had misunderstood about Tyler. Maybe his ring really was from some other school. Even if he had gone to Tim's school, it could mean nothing—just be a coincidence.

It was odd, though, that so many people from the same school hadn't recognized one another in the castle. Garrett hadn't recognized Tim, nor had Renata. Tim hadn't recognized Tyler—had Tyler recognized Tim? He certainly could have recognized Garrett, which gave him a motive to kill, assuming that he had held a grudge for almost ten years. Was it possible to maintain that level of anger?

I still couldn't see Connie; the crowd seemed to have grown larger in the last half hour, and the lawn was thick with bodies. I struggled away from the bonfire and moved toward the castle entrance; I would text Connie to meet me there.

Despite the large fire, the front steps were dark and shadowed. I shivered a little, finding Connie's number and sending a text:

Meet me at the front entrance.

I heard footsteps in the dark; I stiffened. A young couple wandered past hand in hand; they were clearly looking for a place to kiss. They saw me, and I pointed toward the fire. "That's the public event. This is the owner's private property," I said. "Visitors should stay on the back lawn."

Clearly not pleased with me, the two turned and stalked back toward the south entrance. A moment later Bethany appeared, looking confused. "Nora, have you seen Tyler?

He said something about getting a drink, but then he disappeared. And he's not answering my texts." She stared at her phone as if surprised by its silence.

"Uh—no, I haven't seen him. Bethany, you should probably wait here with me. Tim and Connie will be here soon, and some others. Dashiell wants us—"

"What?" She blinked at me. "I'm ready to go home. I have to find Tyler; we came here together as visitors. I'm not on the castle staff tonight."

"I understand that, but listen, Bethany, I'm just putting some things together, and I think that Tyler might be a danger to you."

She laughed. "Tyler? Don't be ridiculous. He's wonderful and very protective. I told you, he knows martial—"

"I think he may have had a grudge against Garrett."

"What? Tyler didn't know Garrett." She ran a hand through her red hair, which glowed like the fire in the darkness. She stared at her phone again, shrugged, and slipped it into a pocket of her purse.

"Tyler was there on the night Garrett died, right?"

"Just briefly. He dropped off my jacket."

I had seen him; he had peeked into the room where I was rehearsing.

"Does he have a quick temper? You said once he didn't know his own strength."

She stared at me, then put her hands on her hips in one of her dramatic poses. "Are you accusing my husband of *murder*?"

I was still trying to fit pieces together. Why would Tyler kill Garrett? "Tim went to the school where Garrett taught. He said that there was a kid named Tyler in his drama department. You told us Tyler loves acting. Tim said that this long-ago Tyler was a joke because he couldn't act. That he wanted to get into Juilliard but couldn't get a recommendation from Garrett."

Bethany's eyes widened; she seemed to realize something. "It— He did have something like that in his past: a teacher who refused to help him. It ruined his dreams."

"What if he ran into Garrett the night he brought your jacket? What if he realized for the first time that his old drama teacher was working at the castle? Perhaps they got into an argument. Maybe Tyler lost his temper. Is that possible?"

She shivered. "I— No, it's not possible. You didn't tell this to the police, did you? I don't want him to be in trouble." Her face, frightened and vulnerable, was closer to mine now. She was on the verge of tears.

"Bethany, if he's guilty of murder, he has to face the consequences. And you could be in danger. I don't think you should go near him until this is resolved."

She seemed to crumple a bit then. "Okay. I'll stay here for a few minutes. But I know you're wrong. Tyler would never do something like that."

I turned and unlocked the front entrance with my key. "If that's the case, I'll be the first to apologize." I peered into the darkness. "What is taking them so long? I wonder if Derek talked Tim out of going inside."

"Maybe we should go back out there," she said, her voice hopeful.

I turned to look at her. On the shadowy steps she looked as ingenuous as Connie always did. She reminded me of someone else, too, but I couldn't place it. I was starting to have second thoughts; the Tyler theory seemed nebulous now that Bethany stood before me looking like a regular person who wouldn't have a homicidal spouse. "Well, there's no point waiting out here. It's actually getting a little chilly." I swung open the door and we entered the dark foyer. Blindly, I patted the west wall, looking for a light switch.

Bethany started digging in her purse. "I'm going to text him. I'm sure he has an explanation for everything."

"I don't think you should, not until Detective Dashiell talks to him." I still hadn't found the light. I turned back to Bethany. "I guess we'll just have to make do with our flash—," I began, but I faltered and stopped.

Even in the dark, I could see that Bethany held a gun, and it was pointed at me.

19

Castle Walls

I STOOD, STUNNED, HORRIFIED not so much by the gun as by the look on Bethany's face. Her pale skin made it easier to see her mocking expression, even in the gloom; her head seemed independent from her body, floating there in the darkness and laughing.

"What— I don't understand."

"I don't want you sharing your theories with the police. They're wrong, anyway. Tyler didn't do anything, except tell me who Garrett was. He saw him in the hall that night, and then he found me and told me—that was the man who ruined his life."

"No one can blame his life trajectory on one person," I said. Distantly I knew I was afraid; I heard my own voice talking as though it came from someone else.

"No. But I'm as protective of my husband as he is of me. And Garrett refused, simply *refused* to write him a letter of recommendation when he was young. It broke Tyler's heart. So that night I found Garrett in the hall, while the Inspectors were chatting after dinner, and I told him who my husband was. I asked him, 'Why didn't you write it?' Do you know, he almost laughed. He said, 'Because I didn't want to lie.'"

"So he was honest," I said. "How does that lead you to grab his knife and plunge it into him?"

She shook her head. "I had to make it up to Tyler. He didn't deserve—" Her expression was profoundly guilty, but seemingly not about Garrett's murder.

Her eyes were wide, her full lips pouting. Suddenly I realized why she looked familiar. "Oh, God," I said. "You're Hyde. From Garrett's drawing."

"What drawing?" Her voice was blank. *Of course,* I thought, *he didn't show it to her.*

"So you had to make it up to Tyler. But that sounds like it's about something *you* did, not something ten years in the past. . . ."

My mind was teeming with images. Sora saying that Garrett had slept with a woman in town. Bethany saying that she and her husband were utterly devoted to each other, the night we introduced ourselves. She had smiled right at Garrett—defiantly, I realized now. And there was the cartoon of Jekyll and Hyde. Hyde's expression had resembled the slightly unfocused one Bethany wore right now. . . .

"You had an affair with him," I said with sudden certainty. "With Garrett."

Her eyes narrowed. "It was before I knew who he was to Tyler."

"But after you were married."

Her lips pushed outward in a pout. "I thought Garrett *got* me. He said I had acting skill, and he gave me tips. We were lovers in Derek's script, and we had to practice together. Then we started meeting in his room. I thought we had something special, something I could have on the side, just for me. It was kind of glamorous, having a young husband and an older lover. But he ended it. Can you believe that? An old man like Garrett telling a young, pretty woman that it's over?"

She was still angry about it. No wonder Jade had said that Garrett looked hunted when she saw him in town. Perhaps he was afraid that unstable Bethany would confront him and his girlfriend. "Put the gun down," I said.

"No. You know things the rest of them don't. So we're going to take a walk up the main staircase. You go first."

She cocked the gun in the darkness, an obscene and terrifying sound, and I screamed.

"Go."

I moved on leaden feet to the staircase and then up the stairs one at a time, my mind racing. Where were the others? Would I have time to run when we reached the top? Why did we have to go upstairs for her to shoot me? Would I be able to find a way to text for help? My phone was with the pamphlets in my little shoulder purse.

I thought of all the castle hiding places. Could I find one of the fake walls in the dark? But Bethany knew about them all, didn't she?

Stalling for time, I said, "So it was you in the costume. The monk."

"Yeah," she said. "I had hidden Garrett's knife in that wall by the costume room. I had to get it out, but you managed to ruin things. I scared you away and then had to go retrieve it with no costume on. That was scary, but nobody appeared. Just Elspeth's ugly cat, staring at me with his moon eyes."

"Why did you go in Connie's room?"

She shrugged. "I thought that after I retrieved the knife I might plant it in there. I wanted to see if I could get in. But after you saw me, I knew no one would think she was guilty." Her voice sounded bored. Why would she have wanted to frame Connie? Everyone liked Connie.

Thoughts kept tumbling through my mind. I remembered Connie telling us that Garrett had asked, *Do you trust him?* He must have been looking at Tyler; perhaps on some level he had recognized the young man, and it had made him distrustful.

I remembered Garrett's room on the night of his murder. "Why did you ransack Garrett's room?"

"I had to make sure he didn't have anything in there that linked him to me. No diary or something. I know old people keep things like that. Keep moving, Nora." She shoved my back and I almost fell.

"Why did you bring the knife to the store?" I asked. I wanted to get as many answers as I could. Then I would try to get away and tell them all to Dashiell. But she was so close to me, and she had a gun. . . .

"Because they would have found it out in the woods. They have equipment. But who would look in a store? I thought it was the perfect hiding place. Stop stalling."

"If you do this, it will be bad for you. You'll have killed two people, Bethany. You'll go to jail forever."

"No, I won't. I'll tell them you pulled the gun on me, and I pushed you down the stairs. I'll say you killed Garrett because he attacked you or something."

She was truly unhinged; she sounded almost cheerful. I wondered what sort of weird scene she must have made with Garrett to make him view her as Hyde.

"They won't believe that. Where would I have gotten a gun?" I reached the top stair and walked swiftly to the middle of the landing so Bethany couldn't easily send me tumbling to my death. "Besides, Detective Dashiell is looking for your husband. He'll find him, and he'll learn that Tyler was there the night Garrett died. That he told you Garrett was his teacher."

"So? That's not a motive."

"No," I whispered, "but shame and regret can be overwhelming." I understood it then in the dark of the castle, where I was about to meet my death: the motive had been her realization, in one terrible instant, that she had betrayed her husband with the very person he felt had already ruined his life. And her guilt and dismay in that moment had made her plunge a knife into Garrett's chest.

Bethany edged closer; the castle walls seemed to be closing in on me, and I thought I might faint. Something moved in the darkness behind Bethany, and I could hear my brothers saying something in my ear, something they had taught me long ago and for which I had yelled at them. . . .

"Go to the top stair, Nora. I'll shoot you if I have to, but I'd rather go with my first plan."

I bent over at the waist. "I'm going to be sick."

"Stop being so dramatic," Bethany said in the ultimate irony, and I lunged forward and pushed her backward into the large, solid body of Hamlet. She lost her balance and fell over the dog. Her gun fired somewhere toward the ceiling, and her head hit the floor with a *thunk*.

I ran; soon Hamlet was running beside me, and we sailed up another flight of stairs and straight to my room. I fumbled with my key, which I had worn on a little wrist bungee so that I wouldn't lose it. Soon I had unlocked my door and secured the dog and myself within my chamber. I grabbed my phone and dialed John Dashiell.

"Nora. Where are you?"

"I'm in the castle with Bethany; she has a gun, and she's hunting me. She killed Garrett."

"Where are you now?"

"I'm locked in my room. I'm afraid she'll come up here."

"We're on the way. Stay there."

I hung up and hugged Hamlet with trembling hands. He licked my hair. Foggily I realized that my brothers had inadvertently saved me once again. They had demonstrated "table topping" to me, a supposedly funny gag in which a person knelt behind an unsuspected dupe and another person pushed that victim from the front, making them fall over the body behind them and potentially hurting themselves. Luke and Jay had laughed, calling it hilarious, and I had shouted at them, telling them I never wanted to hear that they had done that to anyone. "Someone could get really hurt!" I insisted.

I wondered now if Bethany had been hurt. Might she be unconscious? Or was she even now creeping closer to me, ready to shoot my lock open and corner me in my own bedroom?

My room was dark and terrifying, but I didn't dare turn on a light. Perhaps she wouldn't know that I had chosen this haven. Maybe she was checking the exits. . . .

A tiny kitten climbed up my leg. I held it up and saw that it was Emily. I set her down and petted her; soon the other two joined her and created a purring mass in my lap. Their presence calmed me down, and I tried to breathe through my anxiety. In, out. In, out. The police were coming. My friends were coming. I just had to stay put.

And then I heard it—a light knocking at my door, so light it was barely there. "Nora?" said a whispering voice. "Nora, open the door. I want to apologize."

I shivered in the dark and reached for Hamlet. There was no way she could know I was in here. She was guessing. I simply had to wait. . . . But if she somehow got the door open, I was a sitting duck.

As silently as I could, I stood up, clasping all three kittens against my chest. I moved toward the window and the Brontës' favorite hiding place—my long red curtains. If she got in somehow, perhaps she would think that she was wrong and that I wasn't in my room at all. Then she could wander the castle and peer into its many hiding places until they found her there, gun in hand. . . .

I tucked behind the curtains, setting the kittens on the

wide windowsill. Then I beckoned to Hamlet, who came to my hand, and pulled the curtains together, cringing in place, peering through the small space between the panels and waiting for the sound of a bullet piercing my door. Instead, I heard voices. Renata's voice and Elspeth's, chatting happily. Oh, God—somehow they were coming back from their ticket table without knowing what was going on.

"Hey, Bethany," Elspeth said. I could see beams from their flashlights under my door. "What are you doing here?"

"Nothing" came Bethany's voice. It sounded odd, dull. "I'm looking for Tyler."

"Elspeth, come here." It was Renata's voice. She knew something was wrong. "Come into my room. I want to show you something. Bethany, we'll talk to you later." There was a slight scuffling sound, and then voices farther down the hall.

Elspeth was saying, "Renata, what the heck?" and then the sound of a door opening and closing. Thank God. Renata must have seen the gun or simply seen that Bethany wasn't right. Not much got past Renata. It sounded as if she had literally dragged Elspeth out of harm's way. Might she have guessed that I was in here? That Bethany was chasing me?

The light knocking began again. "Nora?" she whispered. "I think they're coming. You have to let me in. You have to protect me, Nora."

Hamlet nosed past the curtain, and suddenly his tail began to wag. He wanted to welcome whoever was at the door. I reached out and patted his head. I whispered, "No." He seemed to understand; he lay down quietly in front of our hiding place.

Suddenly a bright light shone under the crack in the door. "Drop it," said John Dashiell's voice.

"I didn't do anything," said Bethany in an odd whining tone.

"Drop the gun, or I'll shoot."

A pregnant moment. I didn't breathe.

Then the sound of a shot. I moaned softly. What if she had shot Dashiell? What if she was going to shoot her way into my room?

A high-pitched screaming filled the hallway. Scream after scream, and then Bethany's voice crying, "You've killed me!"

Dashiell's voice, closer now, saying, "It's a flesh wound. Stop being melodramatic."

I DIDN'T COME out of my room. I did emerge from behind the curtains and flip on my lamp; I set the kittens on the floor and plopped down next to Hamlet, slipping a hand beneath his collar so that he would stay by my side. I waited until I heard Derek's voice, and Paul's and Connie's, and then those of the ambulance attendants. I heard them carry the moaning Bethany away, and only then did I unclench my hand from around Hamlet's collar. He and I walked to the door. "Is it safe?" I asked.

John Dashiell's voice said, "You're safe, Nora. Let me in."

My hand trembled as I fumbled with the lock and turned the knob, and then Dash walked into my room and I plastered myself against his chest, clinging to his reassuring form for the second time in my life.

"I'm sorry," he said. "We were pursuing Tyler. It took a while before I realized he had no involvement in Garrett's death. And then I got your call."

"She's insane. She had an affair with Garrett just for fun, but then Tyler told her Garrett was the man who supposedly ruined his acting career. The man who hurt him deeply when he was young. She killed Garrett because she felt her betrayal of Tyler was too much to forgive. She was trying to kill her own indiscretion."

John Dashiell's hands rested on my shoulders: warm, comforting hands. They moved to my back, and he gave me a reassuring hug.

Derek peeked into the room. "Nora, I'm so sorry. Are you all right?"

I turned my face slightly toward him and said, "If it weren't for Hamlet, I'd be dead. I love that dog."

Derek beamed at the thought of his heroic Labrador, then frowned. "I can't believe Bethany did this. I can't believe it was one of our actors."

Connie appeared and tucked herself under his arm. "We'll recover from this," she said. "We'll be fine."

I sighed. "Weirdly, it turns out that Bethany was a really good actress, because she was hiding the fact that she was unstable. Garrett knew; he drew a picture of Jekyll and Hyde. Bethany must have been one scary affair."

"What? He had an affair with her?" Connie said.

"We can talk about this later," Dashiell said. "I need to get a statement from Nora, so if you can all wait somewhere . . ."

Connie and Derek murmured about informing the others, and they went back into the hall. Paul appeared in my doorway, looking chagrined. He moved toward me holding two cups. One held tea, and the other held M&M's. "Food is comfort. Isn't that what Zana said?"

I thanked him and smiled. Despite my fear and horror, despite my still trembling limbs, I felt happy in that moment. I had so many friends in the castle—friends I now knew that I could trust.

John Dashiell led me to the little table in my kitchenette. He ushered me into a seat, and I set down the cups Paul had provided. I took a sip of tea. Dashiell scooped up the kittens and put them in the center of the table. "Some moral support," he said.

"And my contraband," I murmured.

"Doesn't everyone know by now?"

"Not Derek."

He smiled. "I think he does. They were strolling around while we all stood in the doorway. He raised his eyebrows at them."

"Oh!" I looked at my little charges, who wrestled half-heartedly on the table. Then Emily decided to give herself a bath, and Annie and Charlotte stared at each other fiercely before Charlotte decided to clean Annie's ears. "I hope he lets me keep them."

He took out his phone and touched some buttons. "Is it okay if I record our conversation? I need you to take me through what happened step by step."

I held his gaze for the first time since he'd arrived in my room. "Remember when you said you'd show me the creek?"

"I do."

"I still haven't seen it."

His hazel eyes held some apology. "It's the next thing on my agenda as soon as I close this case."

"Okay. Is Bethany all right?"

He gave a short nod. "She will be. She aimed at me; I had no choice."

"I understand." I looked at his tape recorder. "Where should I start?"

"Start with me joining you at the bon fire."

I reached out to hold Charlotte's soft paw and made myself think back to the bonfire: the light, the heat, the chaos. A blue ring glinting on the wrong hand. Bethany's face so fearful and innocent, then mocking and cruel. The dreadful ascending of the stairs. The risky lunge and Hamlet's providential arrival. The terrified flight through the dark castle to my room.

I told him what Bethany said, her strange assertions and justifications, and he asked questions.

Finally he turned off the recorder on his phone and said,

"We're finished. You can eat your candy and be with your friends."

"That's what every girl wants to hear."

He laughed, then stood up and gathered his things. He stayed for a moment, looking down at me while I looked up at him. He was about to say something, but Connie peeked around the door and said, "Are you done with her? We want to claim her and spoil her a little."

"I am finished, yes. Nora, I'll see you soon."

I waved, and he walked away.

Then the room was suddenly full: Connie, Renata, Elspeth, Tim, Derek, and Paul were all there, and Elspeth showed me a text from Zana:

Glad you're okay, Library Pal! I'm making a torte for you.

I nodded, smiling. "Thanks, Elspeth."

Derek looked solemn but relieved. "I am not going to try to process this betrayal tonight. A double betrayal of Garrett and of all of us who called Bethany a friend."

"Why did she do it?" Tim asked; he still looked a bit shell-shocked.

I rubbed my arms. "She and Garrett had a brief affair." I thought of the Jekyll-and-Hyde drawing once again. Garret's artistic response to the mercurial nature of Bethany.

Derek looked chagrined. "I had heard a rumor in town that Garrett was sleeping with a young woman. For some reason I thought—" He turned red and looked at his shoes.

Connie, who seemed to be able to read his mind these days, said, "You thought it was *me*?"

He nodded. "I had a fight with him about it, and he denied it. He said I should stop believing gossip. Eventually I apologized to him, but now I find there was at least some truth to it."

"But I think Garrett was loyal to Sora once they committed to each other. He thought Bethany was just a mistake," I said. I pictured the drawing, the sweet, peaceful face and the malicious, scowling monster. I wondered if that second drawing was his vision of Bethany when he ended things with her.

Derek clamped a hand on my shoulder. "Nora, you've been scared too many times in this castle. So we're going to change your vision of it. The police are clearing the grounds for us. We can clean up the bonfire and the lawn tomorrow. Tonight we need to be here for you, for one another. It's not that late—who's up for a movie in the media room?"

"Only if it's a comedy," Connie said, looking like an extra from *Star Trek* in her weird white pantsuit.

"And only if I can change," I said, pointing at my own attire.

Renata nodded. "You put on your comfy clothes, and Elspeth and I will go make some popcorn." She took my hand and held it between her own for a moment. "You should know that when I saw the gun, my first thought was to get Elspeth out of the hall."

"Of course."

"But we went in the room and immediately called Derek. He said the police were on the way."

"Thank you, Renata. Your quick thinking probably saved lives."

She shrugged and patted my shoulder, then bustled out with Elspeth and Tim.

Connie said, "I guess I'll change, too. Derek, come help me pick something out."

Derek grinned like a fool and turned to follow Connie, but I put a hand on his arm. "Derek, you've obviously loved her for a long time. Why didn't you tell her ages ago?"

He nodded, then sighed. "I have loved her for a long

time. I fell in love with her almost immediately. I mean, you can see why."

"I absolutely can."

"But I was never quite sure if she—reciprocated my feelings. And it got to a point that I feared that if I confessed how I felt and she didn't feel the same, she would want to leave. And I ultimately felt that I'd rather see her every day, even if I couldn't have her."

"Derek, you were so dumb," I said affectionately.

He laughed. "Connie has already made that very clear. She showed me her little notebook where she recorded what she calls my 'torment' of her. I'm just—I'm so relieved. And so happy."

"Derek!" Connie yelled from her room.

"Coming!" he said.

Paul came jogging back in the room; I hadn't realized he had gone somewhere until he returned. He approached us in time to hear Derek say, "Nora, I know you've been through a lot. But you fit in perfectly here, and of course the next script is centered around you. Connie told me you had thought about leaving, and I understand why."

I needed to talk to Connie about confidentiality.

He touched my hand, his dark eyes beseeching. "Will you think about staying?"

"You have to stay," Paul said.

I pointed behind me, where the Brontës sat on the table, staring at us with glowing eyes. "Can I keep my cats?"

Derek pursed his lips. "I didn't know about these little fellows until this evening."

"They're all female, and they're sweet. Hamlet loves them." Hamlet was still in the room, sitting at Derek's feet.

This had been the right thing to say; Derek loved his dog. "Really? So they're friends? I did wonder if he could use a companion in the castle." He played with Hamlet's ears. Hamlet closed his eyes.

"He could use three. He'll show them the ropes." I wouldn't mention Ollie the cat just now. Derek was dealing with enough this evening.

Connie was back, wearing a pair of shorts and a blue-gray T-shirt that read: *Oxford.* "I couldn't wait for you. Nora, you get in your play clothes, too, and we'll go relax in the media room."

"Okay. Someone hang around so I don't have to walk down there by myself."

Paul stepped forward. "I'll stay. I'll wait for you in the hall."

"Thanks, Paul."

Derek left with Connie, and Paul stood guard outside my room. I went to the little bathroom and looked at my reflection. The face that stared back at me looked pale and slightly haunted by the night's events, but it was also smiling.

The words of Father Jim came suddenly to mind. He had said something about how an act of violence had shattered the peace, and we needed to bring serenity back to the castle and back to our hearts.

I washed my face and took off my weird costume, donning in its place a pair of pink sweatpants and a black T-shirt that read: *Goodman Theater.* I combed my hair and tied it back with a scrunchy, then slipped into some gym shoes and went into the main room, feeling refreshed. I fed the kittens and helped them get down from the table so that they could tumble toward their bowls.

The wind had risen outside, and once again the branches scratched against my windowpane. Their clacking would not frighten me tonight.

I went to the door, where Paul and Hamlet were waiting. "Thank you, gentlemen," I said.

As we walked toward the staircase, Paul said, "What's your favorite musical? Do you know *Brigadoon*?"

"Of course."

"Do you know this one?"

He started singing "I'll Go Home with Bonnie Jean" in his attractive baritone. I joined him with the words I remembered, and when we got to the refrain, we started skipping down the hall.

By the time we reached the media room on the second floor, we were wiping tears of laughter from our eyes.

20

Recapturing the Castle

THREE WEEKS LATER, life was different. We were on the verge of August, and mid-summer heat sat on the castle grounds and made everyone lazy. We had launched our cocktail café mystery dinner, and it had been such a success that Derek was considering extending it beyond the two-month limit. One of our Inspectors had been an arts reviewer for the *Tribune*, and he had written a complimentary article about the castle and its troupe that Paul said was, in PR terms, "better than gold." A picture of me at the piano had appeared with the article, along with the caption *Mystery and music make for enchanting fare in the new show at Castle Dark*.

My mother had immediately texted me a picture of that photo and caption in a frame on her living room table. My brothers sent me the same picture, with the text:

Castle Dark? More like Castle dork.

Paul had also put some of the songs from our mystery

night on YouTube, and he and Derek were working to lure more castle visitors via the clips. Paul said things were going very well, and our tragedy had not ultimately put the castle's existence in danger. He had left a week after our movie party, bound for the job that he no longer really liked, but he promised he would return on weekends. Before he departed, he christened Connie and Derek "Conder," and the rest of us had taken to calling them that for ease of reference (and to tease them).

After a successful three-day run of summer dinners in the "cocktail lounge" ballroom, Derek gave us a day off, and I invited my family to come for a Sunday visit. Luke was no longer sore, and he showed me his scar the moment he emerged from the car (this surprised no one). I took my parents on a tour of the grounds while the boys went with Tim for a bike tour of the area.

"This is lovely," my mother said. "Nora, we were so worried about you, but I can see why you want to live here. And your boss is so handsome! Has he asked you out?"

"No, he's going out with Connie."

"Oh." This disappointed her. "What about his brother?"

"Paul? We're friends. He came back from Indianapolis to meet you guys."

My parents exchanged a glance.

"No, really. No romances in the castle except for Derek and Connie. We're all like a big bunch of siblings."

My mother adjusted her purse on her shoulder. "What about that girl we saw on the news, the one who killed the poor man in the chapel?"

"She's in jail. I heard her husband has asked for a divorce. I feel sort of bad for her, but not really. She made a series of terrible choices."

We ascended the stairs of the main entrance and my father, cavemanlike, pounded on the wall. "How long did it take to build this place?"

"Seven years, Derek said."

"Huh. This is good brickwork right here," he said, trying to pry some old mortar out of the wall.

"Dad, stop touching that. Come on, I want to show you the portrait gallery." We went in the front door and were immediately greeted by a giant hound. "Oh, and this is Hamlet." My parents, both animal lovers, made much of Hamlet and his gentle, massive head.

The next several hours were spent in fun pursuits. My parents joined the "Castle Gang," as Derek called us, for lunch in the dining room. The twins reappeared with Tim and wolfed down some food before Derek took us all on a tour. We finished more than an hour later, on the main floor, and Derek said, "We haven't even toured the catacombs; Nora hasn't had the courage to go down there yet."

"That would be awesome!" Jay said.

But Paul appeared like a savior at that moment, holding bows and arrows. "Anyone up for some archery?"

My brothers practically tackled him in their enthusiasm, and he led them out the south entrance and onto the back lawn, where he had affixed a target to a distant tree. Derek, Connie, my parents, and I sat at the table near the fountain, chatting and laughing at the boys' primal cries as they tried to kill imaginary foes.

At two o'clock I got a text:

I'm here!

I ran through the main entrance hall to meet my sister, Gen, fresh from New York in a blue rental car and looking like a summer dream in a peach floral dress and some flat white sandals. In childhood we had nicknamed her Nancy Drew because she actually had titian hair, and today it shone in the sun like a red-gold crown.

I gave her a giant hug and said, "I missed you!"

"Oh, my gosh, I love New York, but I would quit in an instant to live in this place! It's crazy, like traveling into a storybook."

"You have no idea. Come on in! We're in the back."

I led her through the main hall, letting her *ooh* and *ahh* about all of the castle's charms, to the south patio, where she greeted my parents, Derek, and Connie.

"You'll meet the rest of the troupe at dinner," I said.

Derek poured Gen some lemonade, which she brought to a seat next to me. She leaned in and whispered in my ear, "Who is *that*?"

I stared at her. Derek and my father were talking loudly, so I was able to murmur, "That's my boss. He's spoken for." I frowned at her; she had just been introduced to both Derek and Connie.

"Not him," she said. *"Him."* She pointed toward my brothers, who were still hollering and shooting arrows like crazed Robin Hoods, guided by Paul, who had grown hot, removed his shirt, and stood gleaming like a young god in the sun. Wow.

"That's Paul. He's Derek's brother and my friend. Should I introduce you?"

She nodded, looking a bit starstruck. Gen had broken a series of hearts in New York, so this was new for her. And interesting.

I led her out onto the lawn, where the boys greeted her enthusiastically, and Paul quickly donned his shirt. "Excuse me," he said as I called him over. "Archery can be sweaty work."

"Sure. Paul, this is my sister, Genevieve. Gen, this is Paul Corby."

Paul shook her hand, and she smiled at him with her pretty Gen smile.

"Gen just arrived," I said, "so she missed the castle tour. I need to stay with my mom and dad; I wonder if you'd show her the sights."

"I would be happy to do that," Paul said. "Give me a minute to clean up, and I'll return for you. We men have been at this for a while."

Gen nodded and thanked him, and she watched him walk away.

We persuaded the boys to lay down their arms and join us for some lemonade. Luke regaled us with tales of his appendectomy, starting with his realization that something might be wrong. "It hurt like a—" He looked at Connie and her sweet, inquisitive face, and said, "It hurt a lot."

Jay was studying the back of the castle with a look of pure joy. "We have got to play some Murder Ball in this place."

Derek grinned. "What exactly is Murder Ball?"

"It's like hide-and-seek, except the goal is to kill the person you find with a Nerf ball."

I stiffened; this wasn't the kind of talk Derek wanted to hear after a man had been murdered in his castle.

To my surprise, he laughed and said, "We *absolutely* have to play that. But the castle is so big, it would be impossible to find someone. You'd have to set parameters. And of course the secret passageways would be out-of-bounds."

The twins looked at him, their mouths gaping. "*What* secret passageways?" Luke said.

By nightfall my brothers had exhausted just about everyone in the castle with their boundless energy, but not one person was immune to their youthful charms, especially (to my vast surprise) Renata. At dinner she sat across from them and continually burst into gales of laughter, wiping at her eyes and telling them they reminded her of a school friend she once had. Later, in the hallway, I saw her slipping them both a twenty-dollar bill and telling them to have "summer fun" with the money.

AT EIGHT O'CLOCK, Castle Dark was quiet. Teams had been pulled from a hat: Tim and my mother, Derek and Elspeth, Paul and Gen (I suspected that Paul had cheated to get this result), Renata and Luke, my father and Zana (who had stuck around for the fun), Connie and me. Each team had been supplied with a Nerf ball (which the boys had brought in hopes of playing the game), and we were in quest of one Jacob "Jay" Blake, who was hiding somewhere between floors one and three. I had made a no-catacombs rule that the boys were willing enough to accept with the rest of the castle at their disposal.

At one point, as the teams formed and the balls were distributed, Luke pulled me aside. "You can never quit this job," he murmured. "Your brothers are counting on you."

I laughed. "I plan to stick around," I said. "I like it here."

"How could you *not*?" he said with feeling.

"You have to visit me a lot. I missed you."

"We could stay over," he said hopefully. "I'll bet you have a ton of extra rooms."

"I can talk to Derek. Maybe during a vacation period."

"Yeah. We could help with chores and stuff. Zana said we could help her in the kitchen. She said her daughter would like us."

"I can think of another person who would like you," I said, thinking of Jade Balfour and her perky little glasses.

Soon we were all armed and ready to hunt. The boys had declared that the game had to be played in the dark, so once again Connie and I were clutching each other and holding our cell phones, this time in quest of my little brother. "I hate this game," Connie said. "I feel tense for no reason."

"I know. It's impossible not to feel that way. I don't even care if we find him. Maybe we should just go to the media room and watch a movie until it's over."

Hamlet bumped against my leg and I managed not to scream. "He has *got* to stop doing that," I said, petting his head.

Connie's beam of light shone on a suit of armor Derek had purchased in Chicago. "He couldn't be *in* there, could he?"

If anyone could achieve it, Jay could. "No, I don't think so." We poked it halfheartedly until we were sure no human being was inside. We were on the second floor and moving toward the ballroom, which was still a cocktail lounge. The beautiful piano gleamed in the narrow beam of light.

Connie touched my arm. "You should play some ghostly music, just to freak everyone out."

That sounded like fun: to be the ghost rather than to fear one. I went to the piano and set my phone on the music stand so that it could illuminate the keys, and I played the beginning of Bach's Toccata and Fugue in D Minor, something I'd learned for a piano competition when I was a teen. It was a song that seemed written to be played in a castle in the dark.

Connie stared at me with wide eyes. "That's wonderful," she said. "It's so scary."

We laughed, and I stopped playing when the piece got too complicated; I remembered only the beginning without sheet music.

"Maybe it will lure out our quarry," I said. "Do you have your Nerf ball ready?"

"I do. Your brothers are so fun," she said, putting an arm around me. "Your whole family is. And your sister is gorgeous." We sat together on the piano bench, uninterested in hunting for the moment. She touched my hair. "How did you get this dark hair when everyone else in your family has light hair?"

I shrugged. "I don't know. My parents endured a lot of child-of-the-mailman jokes when I was little. I think my grandfather had very dark hair."

Connie sighed. "I'm so glad you're my friend, Nora."

I rested my head on her shoulder. "Same here." Then I lifted my head to look at her. "How are things with you and Derek?"

Her smile was dazzling. "Wonderful. Perfect. I knew they would be, if I could ever get him to—"

"Yeah, he wins the award for slow mover of the century."

She giggled, then grew thoughtful. "I think your sister likes Paul," she said.

I nodded. "I think Paul likes my sister." I wasn't sure what I thought of this, but it seemed positive. Except that Gen would never want to leave New York to date some guy in the middle of nowhere in Illinois.

A sudden shout reverberated down the hall, a chilling and terrifying cry that made Connie jump and caused me to emit a small scream. Then Luke's voice. "*Got* you, Jay! Murder ball! You die!"

Jay groaned, and there was some good-natured brotherly shouting.

Distantly, I thought I heard Renata laughing.

MY FAMILY STAYED the night because Derek said they shouldn't make the long drive home in the dark. They were pretty easily persuaded because of the boys, who looked so happy at the thought of sleeping in the castle that my parents couldn't resist.

In the morning I found my parents in the dining room

having coffee with Elspeth and Zana. They informed me that "one of the castle men" had taken my brothers out in the woods in search of the deer the boys had heard about.

"They don't have—arrows, do they?" I asked, worried.

My mother laughed. Her blond-gray hair was tied into a neat ponytail, and she wore a denim romper. "No, just their cell phones. They want photos for Instagram and such."

"They love it here," my father said, giving me a significant brown-eyed glance over his glasses. "And you do, too."

"I do," I admitted. "And you can visit anytime. Derek said so."

"Yes, he spoke to us this morning. He and Connie went into town for breakfast. What a cute couple they make," my mother said.

"And where is Gen?" I asked.

My parents exchanged a secret look that I saw through. "She's taking a bike ride with Paul," my mother said.

"Ah. Well, I guess we're all accounted for." I turned to Zana. "Are those cinnamon rolls?"

MY PARENTS PAID a visit to the chapel before they left; they wanted to say a prayer for Garrett. I sat in a back pew and looked at the bright stained glass, wondering if he had looked up at the saints before he had closed his eyes.

I felt guilty somehow: guilty that I had found him too late, that none of us had seen through Bethany's facade, that we hadn't found a way to protect Garrett from a run-in with his past, as Derek had protected Connie.

As we left, my father put an arm around me. "It's very sad," he said. "But it's a beautiful and peaceful place to die."

THE "CASTLE MAN" who had given my brothers a forest tour was not Derek, Tim, or Paul, it turned out. It was John

Dashiell, looking like a boy himself as they emerged from the forest and he laughed and joked with the twins. Jay and Luke both held giant sticks, a pastime they had pursued at age three and apparently enjoyed still. What was it about men and sticks?

I watched John Dashiell, carelessly handsome in the casual attire that spoke of a day off—jeans and a Beatles T-shirt, his hair ruffled into attractive disarray by the slight wind. Butterflies roamed around my stomach, but a seed of resentment was growing in my heart. I hadn't seen him in almost two weeks. I had thought he would be here constantly. I had thought we had an understanding. . . .

They reached the back patio, where I sat having coffee with my parents, Derek, and Connie (Paul and Gen were still absent). Dashiell smiled at me, and I smiled back. "I don't think we've been introduced," said my sharp-eyed mother.

"Mom and Dad, this is Detective John Dashiell. He was the one investigating the castle murder. Dash, this is my mother, Melanie Blake, and my father, Brendan Blake."

"Good job, son," my father said. "We'll sleep better knowing that the danger is over and that our daughter is safe."

Dash shook his hand. "I would never let anything happen to your daughter," he said solemnly.

My mother's eyes widened slightly; she looked from Dash to me. "Well—can we count on you checking in here once in a while to make sure all is well?"

Dash met her eyes with that sober gaze of his, and she blushed. "You can absolutely count on that," he said. "It was nice meeting you. I see Derek is beckoning me, like an actual king."

We laughed, and Dash moved toward Derek and Connie, where Derek pulled him into an animated conversation.

My mother looked at me. "You held out on us," she said. "That policeman likes you." She studied my face, which I imagined was blushing just as much as hers had done, and narrowed her eyes. "And you like him. You said you were like a bunch of brothers and sisters."

"In the castle," I said. "He doesn't live in the castle."

"Semantics," my father said. "You have a boyfriend, and we expect an invitation soon so that we can get to know him."

"You're a little premature. We have liked each other only from afar. That might be all it is."

My mother donned her wise expression. "That's not all it is," she said, and she reached out for one of Zana's delicious cookies.

TWO HOURS LATER my family was lined up near my parents' car, and we were saying our goodbyes. Gen was there, too, because she was going to follow my parents and brothers home and spend some time with them. Paul was trying not to look bereft.

"You must come back soon," Derek said to the group. "It's been a delight to have you here. Just what we all needed."

My parents were effusive in their thanks, and the twins left some strong hints with Derek that they should come and stay for a week or so before the summer was over. Then they bundled into my dad's Chevy, taking some last snapshots on their phones, and I waved after the departing cars, my eyes spiked with surprising tears.

I turned to see John Dashiell leaning on the east wall of the castle, his arms folded in front of him, his expression patient as a Buddha's.

He waved, and I walked toward him, furtively wiping my eyes. "Hard to say goodbye?" he said.

"Yeah, sort of. You should have come over. They're very interested in you."

"I didn't want to intrude anymore on family time. But I did want to hang around and show you the creek, if someone hasn't beaten me to it."

I shaded my eyes with my hand so that I could study his face. "I thought you had forgotten. It's been a while."

His brown hair was still mussed by the breeze, and his hazel eyes looked gold in the sun. "I'm sorry. I did text you, though. And I came to the first cocktail party mystery."

He had done that, and requested "Unforgettable" as he slipped a tip into my jar and whispered compliments in my ear, his mouth close to my skin. He had sent texts, little tantalizing ones, that had kept me interested. And now he had met my family, made my brothers laugh, and lingered on castle grounds to show me the creek, a promise he had made in June.

"Do I need anything? Are these shoes okay?"

"They're fine. You look great." He held out his hand, and I took it. We walked toward the western woods, where an alluring path beckoned.

"I've seen this path before. I always meant to follow it."

"It's worth following," he said, leading me into the cool shadow of the trees. He let go of my hand when the path narrowed, and I followed him along dirt soft with moss and fragrant pine needles. "There—can you hear it?"

A distant sound—a rushing, gurgling sound—reached my ears. He quickened his pace, and I jogged behind him, eager to see the brook I'd first heard of from Connie. Suddenly we were there: the vista opened up before us. The creek was not some tiny trickle in the forest; it was a significant body of water rushing past to some eternal destination. It was too wide for us to jump to the other side, but someone had built a rustic bridge over it, and we climbed on the wooden structure and looked down at the clear flowing water. Varicolored rocks were visible on the sandy creek bottom, and I spied the quick, colorful glimmers of darting fish. "It's beautiful. It even smells good," I said, breathing in. "I could stay here all day."

He put a hand on my forearm. "Listen. You hear that sound?"

I tried to focus in, past the sound of the water. "What am I listening for?"

He grinned. "Frogs. Plopping in from the creek bank. Oh, there's another one."

I listened again, and this time I heard a small *bloosh*. "That sounds fun! Oh, to be a happy frog on a summer day."

He turned me gently toward him, his hands on my elbows. "I wouldn't want to be anybody but me right now looking at you."

"Why?"

"I'll tell you why"—his face was inches closer—"in a minute."

His mouth came down on mine, soft, warm, exciting. The brook made its music while I shared my first kiss with John Dashiell, the gardener-detective–trail guide. I slid my arms up over his shoulders, luxuriating in the moment.

Eventually he pulled away and took a deep breath. "That was—"

"Exciting," I said.

"Yeah. It was." His hazel eyes studied mine. "Nora."

"Dash."

He laughed and reached out for a lock of my hair. "You know what image I can't get out of my head? When you came rushing into the sunroom, holding a basket of kittens, your hair in your eyes."

I stared at him, my mouth open slightly.

He studied my face for a while as if searching for secrets. "I would like to date you, Nora."

"I would like you to date me, too."

"But I mean—exclusively. You live with a lot of hand-some men."

"I have no interest in them. I have a *significant* interest in you." I held up a pointer finger. "However . . ."

His eyes narrowed. "Ah, there's a catch."

"I am not a high-maintenance girlfriend, as a rule. But I do kind of expect a guy to be around, Dash. You know, to prove he's not a figment of my imagination."

He nodded, his expression chagrined. "I get that. I'm sorry I've been AWOL. Things got busy—"

"But you'll always be busy, I'm guessing. You would have to make time for me."

"I can do that. I will do that. I *want* to do that."

I smoothed the collar of his shirt. "Remember the day we talked, back when you were a gardener?"

"Yeah." He smiled.

"I liked you right away. I really wanted you to come into the woods with me and kiss me. That was my fantasy."

"I had a fantasy, too. I wanted to run my hands through your long black hair." He sifted through my hair, weighing it in his hands. "It's even silkier than I imagined."

"Well, dreams sometimes come true," I said as his mouth lowered once again to mine.

The birds sang, the frogs plopped, and the brook bur-bled while I embraced John Dashiell on a little drawbridge outside an unlikely castle on a day in late July. Eventually he pushed my hair behind my shoulders and said, "I guess we should get back."

"Mmm," I said lazily.

"Maybe we can hang out in your room. I'd like to say hi to the cats."

"Really?" I brightened. "Do you like them?"

"Who doesn't like kittens?" he said.

We left the bridge hand in hand and returned to the path.

*   *   *

THAT NIGHT I ran to my car to retrieve a book on tape that I had promised to lend Connie. I could see Derek's profile in the doorway, watching over me as I traversed the dimly lit parking lot. I paused for a moment to look up. The stars glittered above our castle, clustered together like spilled diamonds, and the moon shone bright.

A cool breeze blew, and I heard the distant rustling of the trees.

My gaze moved to the castle, a dark hulking shape against the navy blue sky. I had not wanted to come to this place. Derek had persuaded me, and the castle itself had done the rest. Its allure remained, despite the tragedy and terror.

An owl hooted deep in the forest behind me—a thrilling night sound, full of mystery.

I walked toward the main entrance. Behind that door, everything waited: my job, my friends, my kittens, a piano, a probable text from a handsome detective.

The road that wound away from here would eventually take me to the city, where other possibilities could be found. Right now, though, in the fragrant night, alive with the sounds of nature, I heard a message from the universe to me.

I walked up the steps, the door swung wide, and Derek ushered me inside, putting an affectionate arm around me.

He shut and locked the massive door, and I was in for the night, safe behind the walls of Castle Dark.

Acknowledgments

With heartfelt thanks to Kim Lionetti; Michelle Vega; Gigi Pandian; Ferne Knauss; Jenn McKinlay; Katie Granholm; Ann O'Neill Foster; Kara McBride; Linda Henson; Sue Tindall; Jeff Buckley; Graham Buckley; Ian Buckley; my dog, Digby (who looks an awful lot like Hamlet); and my own three cats, who are muses for me as the Brontës are for Nora.

About the Author

Veronica Bond is a pseudonym for a bestselling mystery writer who lives in Chicago with her family and a menagerie of animals. She teaches high school English, and she loves reading and writing mysteries.

Ready to find
your next great read?

Let us help.

Visit prh.com/nextread